Caleb's Portion

by Lucius Tical

 FriesenPress

Suite 300 - 990 Fort St
Victoria, BC, V8V 3K2
Canada

www.friesenpress.com

Copyright © 2020 by Lucius Tical
First Edition — 2020

All images are and remain the exclusive property of the Author

All rights reserved.

No part of this publication may be reproduced in any form, or by any means, electronic or mechanical, including photocopying, recording, or any information browsing, storage, or retrieval system, without permission in writing from FriesenPress.

ISBN
978-1-5255-8403-9 (Hardcover)
978-1-5255-8404-6 (Paperback)
978-1-5255-8405-3 (eBook)

1. FICTION, BIOGRAPHICAL

Distributed to the trade by The Ingram Book Company

Caleb's Portion

A JOURNEY BACK TO ANCESTRAL
TIME AND FORWARD INTO ETERNITY

Narrated by Alter Ego Lucius Tical

To Maarten & Jennie
   Van Driel
 dear friends and
 brother and sister in Christ.

   Caleb aka

Dedications

This book is dedicated
to my beloved Tirzah, my family, my loved ones,
and all who share in and will experience
the blessed hope of eternity

Acknowledgements

I have never considered myself a man of letters, but I have always been amazed by those wordsmiths who are able to make the English language resonate. My sisters and daughters would say that I have a smattering of knowledge on many subjects which do not stand up to rigorous scrutiny. Be that as it may, I would hereby like to acknowledge all those of my family who have been wonderful studies of the human character. Their criticisms and encouragements are deeply appreciated. I am also indebted to former English teachers who praised me far above my abilities, and undoubtedly flattered me.

There have been many bends in my road and compromises made. The straight paths include my love for my awesome Saviour and my lifelong devotion to my wife, Tirzah.

Caleb

Contents

CHAPTER I: Primogeniture   1

CHAPTER II: The Growing Years   33

CHAPTER III: On the Farm—The Bucolic Years   71

CHAPTER IV: High School   95

CHAPTER V: Neophyte Lumberjack   119

CHAPTER VI: The Gene Pool Asserts Itself   143

CHAPTER VII: Dreams Do Come True   171

CHAPTER VIII: Trying to Heap Up Worldly Riches   199

CHAPTER IX: Caleb's Theory of Nearly Everything   227

CHAPTER X: Caleb's Portion—Found   251

Foreword

The Lord had said to Abram, "Go from your country, your people and your father's household to the land I will show you. (Genesis 12:1)

I want them out of my head and onto the pages. I, Lucius, have observed as Caleb longed in his youth to follow the silver thread back in time. We are one person but comprise different parts. Caleb is the doer, and I weigh, analyze, and caution. We have agreed that I shall narrate. Over the years, our imaginations formed what our parents did not know and what we could not unravel. Slowly our ancestors formed in our consciousness by a lifetime of wonderings and experiences. They have been clamouring in our early morning reveries and nighttime awakenings to give them a voice. Part of this book allows the more insistent ones to speak through me.

"I am making everything new!" (Revelation 21:5) resonated within Caleb when the wild geese called. When the decay of all that man makes confronts us, we know we have no lasting portion here. Even the mighty pyramid Cheops is in a sad state and need of repair. Though the mighty energy furnaces of the universe should one day wink out, You, our God, will always be there!

***

Foreword

Large scale movements of humans and animals are not always explainable by logic. Instinct travels throughout groups like an electric current and sweeps its millions, lemming-like, along with it. How else to explain why Caleb's parents would pull up roots and leave their prosperous, millennial, ancestral home to seek their fortune in unknown lands? They joined the millions, from all parts of Europe, who had survived the Great Wars of the twentieth century and were determined to make a new beginning.

So it was with Caleb's parents, and in this book our purpose is to pass on the human drama of change, decay, and renewal. Man may plan, but God determines. Many memories, imagined and real, as well as the stories with which we grew up, play a part. This book contains the chronicle of one family's origins and exodus story, as narrated by my alter ego, Lucius, who sees through the eyes of myself, Caleb Nachtegal. Many of the characters are fictional composites of the many people I have known and how I have imagined them to be. It is also the story of my life as it developed in a new land. Each immigrant's story was unique. Many common threads were shared however and will resonate in the hearts and minds of those who were part of a great movement.

There will be those who ask, "What's so unique about your story, Caleb?" I have but one reply: "I have a portion that is only for me, and as I become more aware of what it is, I also want to share it." Please be aware that the timeline shifts between past and present. We will do our best to connect the threads.

Lucius/Caleb

CHAPTER I
Primogeniture

You, O God, have always known me.

Slowly he emerged from his daily mini-death and lay rigidly still so that beauty would not be wakened. She desperately needed the sleep that came so easily to him. As he stroked into the pool of his consciousness, he asked the oft-repeated question: "Why me, Lord? You took so many away who were close and gave me such a large, undeserved portion."

The importance of the dream events was still fresh in Caleb's mind, but the pertinent details eluded him until he turned the full power of his concentration onto remembering exactly what had happened. Age, with its accompanying decline, and the relentless tug of gravity could not be denied. The quick, knowing glances that he intercepted between his children reminded him of what he and his siblings had done when their parents started to decline. It was the way of all life, and he was comfortable with knowing that. If his book was ever to be written, it had better be done while his seventy-five-year-old brain allowed the files to still be accessible. Caleb belonged to a large family group and had participated in the post-Second-World-War migration from the Netherlands. This is his story as he heard, lived, and imagined it. I, Lucius, as always, shall narrate. The silver skein rolled back the images to a time long ago ...

***

The Roman

The wind-driven fury of sleet bit into any part of the Roman's face not protected by his leather and brass helmet. Lupernicus, firstborn pride of his father, cursed his commanding officer, who had ordered him to take the heavily armed galley *Isis* from the Classis Britannica fleet and display the Roman Eagle standard up and down the coast of the lowlands. He wondered what had ever possessed the great Julius Caesar, who hundreds of years earlier had added these fog wreathed forsaken lands to the Empire. The last Emperor of Western Rome was determined to control, enlarge, and preserve the lands previously added to the Empire.

Large swatches of reed-covered swamplands were interspersed with sand dunes and hummocks of peat soil. The lightly-dressed slaves who manned the oars continued to row under the duress of the unsheathed short swords in the hands of the eighty Legionnaires who comprised the Centuria fighting force. A midship brazier, heated by smouldering peat, warmed the gruel that kept the rowers alive. Flapping protective canvass covers partially protected the food as well as the skeletal men.

Lupernicus was keenly aware of the limitations of the fixed sail as he steered around the many obstacles. Everyone aboard knew that their lives depended on the exertions of the condemned rowers. Crouched under the gunwales, they maintained body heat only by plying the long, heavy wooden oars. Lupernicus slapped his hands across his chest to keep warm and shifted his memory back to the cozy Roman settlement at Nijmegen and the two pregnant Flemish lasses, Sisje and Stijn, who had eagerly accepted his Roman trinkets and worshipped his Roman gods. A loud yell from the legionary in the bow startled him out of his reverie, and he directed his gaze to the flames and smoke coming from the reed-thatched roofs of a small group of wattled mud huts clustered in the centre of crude, low, encircling dykes. Lupernicus noted the size of the Viking galley that had pulled up on the clay bank and gave the order to prepare his men for battle. No one noticed the two additional Viking boats hidden behind hummocks until they suddenly appeared and cut off any escape route.

The fighting was fierce, bloody, and short. No one asked for or received quarter or mercy. As Lupernicus hacked at the swarm of bearded savages, his own savage past flashed through his mind. The senselessness of all the battles and killings he had engaged in was revealed with a frightening clarity. Mighty Rome straddled the known world, but it was helpless to prevent his present peril. He appealed to his gods to preserve the life of his wife and five children living in Spain, as well as the lives of the children growing in the wombs of his Flemish concubines—yet to be born. Two Viking boats were rammed by the iron prow of the Roman boat. The Romans knew it was kill or be killed. The Vikings soon overwhelmed the Romans by sheer force of numbers. After the slaughter, the Romans and their slaves were stripped of all clothes, arms, and valuables. Then they were unceremoniously dumped into the murky waters that they had so feared. The smoke from the village blended with the smoke from the burning galley.

Roman Galley

Generation after generation the tall, blond, long-haired raiders came in their low, fast longboats and attacked and pillaged the coastal settlements of the lowlands. The Norsemen left their wives and children behind, whom they often never saw again. When they were resisted, the Vikings burned and killed with a cold cruelty that was feared by all the inhabitants of the lowland settlements.

***

Rorik's hand clasped the cold brass handle of the large, spiked, steel ball. Before he was fully awake, he swung his arm in a protective arch around his head. "What's the matter, Alfred?" he yelled to his bodyguard. "Why do you allow strangers to approach me without warning? I will settle with you after I have settled with them."

The three strangers were all dressed in ankle-length robes and bore no external weapons. They wore a carved wooden cross on the front of their tunics and carried scrolls in their hands. They greeted the assembled Vikings with a respectful but unafraid demeanour. Rorik proceeded with a rough body search and was startled to discover that a woman was among the strangers. After he was satisfied that no weapons were concealed, he proceeded to yell for a translator.

Rorik was a giant even among the large Vikings, and when he saw that his strutting and yelling had little effect, he gestured to the visitors to sit down. It was fortunate that the mid-day carousing had not yet started and that Rorik was able to comprehend some of what the translator was slowly explaining.

"Are these mewling weaklings saying that the great Thor is a false god?" he bellowed. "I will quarter and dice them and show them the power of my gods."

Divine intervention used the power of the gospel and the beauty of the unafraid woman's face to stop the descent of the killing blows. The Flemish girl, Katje, with Lupernicus's Roman blood in her veins, had found her peace and security in the Christian faith that gave women an equal place in their male-dominated world as well as in the world to come. Two months later, the murdering and looting ended and the entire Viking raiding party was baptized into the name of the Triune God—under the stern gaze of Rorik, their newly married leader.

***

The Viking Crusader

Could it really be true? John, son of Epie the baker, wondered. *Would God part the waters as He did for the ancient Israelites?* In the year of our Lord 1212, John joined thousands of young people in their quest to liberate Palestine from the infidel Muslims. Over and over, the fanatical Nicholas struck the waters of the blue Mediterranean and intoned, "In the name of Jesus Christ, I command you to part and let us go through."

"Perhaps, Nicholas," advised John, "you need to listen to the advice of the Pope and admit that you were wrong."

"Never! Never will I admit that the vision and the voice were not real," screamed the emaciated leader, his eyes burning and spittle drooling from his emerging beard. "God has spoken to me, and even the Pope cannot convince me that God makes mistakes."

With a heavy heart and sickness of soul, John turned away with the realization that humans are infinitely capable of self-deception.

Before he was ready to depart on the long journey back home, John stayed at the home of kindly Italian farmers, where his strength and skills were put to good use in exchange for food and lodging. It was a glorious Tuscan morning when John, equipped with sturdy sandals and a stout stick, resumed his homeward journey.

The majestic grandeur of the Southern Alps formed the barrier that forced John to take the westward road toward his home in the lowlands. Often he was joined by fellow travellers, but this evening he settled down alone beside a glacier-fed brook. After invoking God's blessing, he enjoyed a simple meal of homemade cheese with rye bread. Usually the cross on his tunic caused the pious peasants he met on his way to open the doors to their homes and larders. However, lonely long distances or hard faced stares would require him to deplete his meagre supplies.

Tucked under his rough sheepskin blanket, he was about to fall asleep when a series of high, piercing screams coming from nearby jerked him upright. Grabbing his walking stick, he carefully advanced to the adjoining glade, where he saw three young ruffians harassing a wild-looking, unkempt peasant girl who had been collecting firewood. John had taken a vow of purity and non-violence at the beginning of the crusade, so he walked with open arms into the glade and gently asked the girl's persecutors to stop. A barrage of unintelligible, but obviously profane, utterances erupted from the mouths of the youths, who immediately launched an attack against him. After absorbing three stinging blows, John's Viking heritage asserted itself and his sturdy walking stick was soon belabouring the backs and legs of the surprised and retreating bullies. When they were gone, John abruptly sat down, sickened by the murderous impulses that had coursed through his entire being. For the first time in his life, he was confronted with a part of his character that had lain dormant until now.

After his killing rage had subsided, John turned his attention to the terrified, trembling girl. "Please hold still," he soothingly told her as he cleansed and bandaged her wounds. His smattering of Italian words were enough to let her know that he would not harm her.

After a warming fire and some nourishing soup, the girl thanked him for rescuing her. "My name is Tonia, and I owe you my life," she blurted out between large slurps of broth. "I'm an orphan living with distant relatives who hate and abuse me. Those vermin you chased away, have often threatened to kill me if they could ever catch me, and today they almost succeeded."

"Tomorrow I will bring you safely back to your home and speak to your foster parents about their Christian duty," John asserted, not understanding all that the girl had told him. With many hand gestures and fractured phrases of Italian, mixed with his Low German dialect, he made his purpose known to the girl.

Early the next morning after a simple meal, Tonia faced John and spoke simply: "Do not send me away; let me stay and I will never leave you. You are the only kindness I have ever known. No one will ever miss me here. Please let me come with you."

John's heart melted as he looked into the clear blue eyes of this girl who had suffered so much. "If you come with me, you must remember to not touch or hold me, since I have pledged to be pure to the end of my journey. If God allows us a safe journey home, then I will ask my parents if I may marry you," promised John.

On their slow journey west, they met other groups of boys and girls who had been fortunate enough to be among the few survivors of the ill-fated children's crusade. Many of these urchins stayed with families during the long trek back to their homes, and so it happened that John and Tonia were also invited to stay with an elderly and childless farming couple, who treated them with uncommon kindness. They soon learned to communicate with each other in the spoken and unspoken language of affection. Under the care of a loving surrogate mother, Tonia bloomed into a lovely, desirable girl. Her love for John could not be hidden, and she contrived to be near him as much as possible. John struggled with increasingly strong desires, and Tonia did nothing to help him overcome them. Nature trumped pledges and it was not long before the farm wife realized that Tonia was pregnant. They were a couple with strict morals and had been led to believe that the attractive boarders were brother and sister.

"We need to ask you to leave our farm," the old farmer said with a heavy voice. "God is only pleased when children are born in holy wedlock, and it would be shameful for us to continue to have you here."

The next morning, John and Tonia gathered their meagre belongings and continued to the west. They had pushed on into the centre of present-day Germany when Tonia stopped and gasped, "The baby is coming, John! Please help me. I'm so scared."

Terrified and sweating profusely, John stumbled to his knees. "I have sinned, Father, grievously and often, and I promise to do the most rigorous penance if only you will spare Tonia and the baby."

They had miscalculated the baby's arrival and were pushing onward to arrive at John's home before the autumn rains.

"Push, Tonia, push with all your might. If only we could have made it to the next town, I could have found a midwife. What do I know about delivering babies?"

Tonia's screams were agony to John's loving heart, and then suddenly it was over. After cutting the cord, he wrapped the squalling infant in a blanket and placed the little girl in her mother's arms. Relief flooded his whole being. Holding Tonia and their baby close, John offered up a prayer of thanksgiving. He began to gently clean Tonia and the baby and had just finished when a bright red pool of blood flooded over the ground.

"No! Please, God, no," he begged, but before he could speak again, the light faded out of her beautiful blue eyes, and she was gone.

Recrimination and self-blame washed over him as he reached for his hunting knife. "I did not honour any of the pledges I made to You," he cried in anguish to the heavens. "I am cursed and of no use to anyone."

"No, John, put away the knife and do not harm yourself," commanded the strong inner voice. "The baby needs you, and I have much work for you to do."

By the time John had scooped out a shallow grave, the body was cold and stiff. Gently he folded Tonia's hands over her breast. He then protected the body from scavengers by placing rocks over the corpse before he back-filled the hole with the pungent topsoil. Gathering the crying infant in a carrying cloth, he again took up the westward road.

***

"Yes, son, we have a nursemaid for your baby," grunted the stocky horse dealer. "It's going to cost you, though. Have you got money?"

"Not a cent," replied John, "but I appeal to your Christian charity to support a child of the crusades in his need."

"Every urchin that comes to my door uses that gimmick," snorted the dealer as he sized up John with squinting eyes. "No-siree, my fine lad, you look like you can handle a day's work.

Work two months for me, and my Katrine will nurse your baby as well as her own. Have we got a deal?"

John gladly accepted, and after two months, he agreed to work two more. It was his burning desire to provide the best possible care and love he could for his beautiful, gurgling, chubby baby.

***

"Where did you find her?" was the terse response of John's mother when she saw the baby he carried. It had been four long years of wandering before John finally arrived back at his ancestral home. "Your father died of the fever two years ago, and I have remarried. My new husband will not want a crying baby around the house!" Even the sight of beautiful one-year-old Maria stirred no immediate maternal instincts in a heart grown cold and calloused by brutal circumstance.

"Realize, Mother, that I am the firstborn of my father's children," warned John. "I stand first in line for the inheritance of this farm, regardless of what your new husband says. This girl is my child, and her mother is dead. Please find it in your heart to be a mother to her."

John's stepfather quailed before the blond giant who confronted him with a face as impassive as a slab of granite. Maria softened the hearts of all who saw her, even the heart of her oma, who soon could not be parted from her.

***

The French Connection:
Surviving the 1350 AD Black Death

"Will you not leave me even one, oh my God?" prayed Chloe as she watched the carpenter nail down the lid of the rude plank coffin. Sixteen-year-old Caleb was the last one to die of the seven children she had given birth to. Her husband had been the first one to be taken by the plague that was devastating all of Europe. Now it was only she and the youngest girl who were left. Sixteen people were still alive in the Normandy village where a hundred had lived such a short time ago. Sturdy fisher-folk and farmers were not exempt from the "Scourge of God," as many called the plague, spread by the large rats abounding in the region.

"I am asking you to marry me so that life may go on in this village," Martin Bedard rudely proposed to Chloe shortly after the death of Caleb.

"I will marry you, Martin Bedard!" Chloe was surprised to hear herself respond this way. "I have five child-bearing years left, and you must promise me that if we should receive a boy, he will be called Caleb."

Three more robust sons were born to Chloe, and like their parents, they were impervious to the plague. The first to be born was named Caleb, according to the promise. Generations passed as the Caleb Bedard line continued.

***

The Killing Fields

First light was etching the horizon in the French village when the insistent knocking started.

"Open up!" yelled Caleb Bedard over and over. "If you value your life, wake up."

"Just hold your horses, will you," yelled back Katherine Bedard to her married son. "Why on earth are you waking me at this beastly hour?"

The year was 1572 AD, and the dog days of August were ripening the crops for harvest. Recently widowed for the second time and still caring for two sons at home, Kate, as people called her, was a busy mother and grandma.

"It's the news from Paris, Mother. It's terrible," blurted out Caleb. "The king has ordered that all the Huguenot Protestant leaders are to be killed. You know how fervently Pa preached against the Roman Catholic teachings while he was alive, and now we'll become targets when the Romanist mobs and soldiers reach our village. I estimate that we have two days to flee to the Lowlands and escape the killings. There are safe Protestant havens there that the Spaniards and French don't control."

Over and over the impossibility of the situation played out in Kate's mind. For generations the Bedards had lived in this Normandy village, and now, in order to save her children, she needed to leave it all behind. "Your father's books, my black oak furniture, our cozy house nestled in the rolling fields ... how can I leave it, son?" she cried. *"If only you hadn't gotten involved in all the religious and political arguments, Paul,"* she silently accused her dead husband. *"I completely agreed with you that our salvation rested in the one sacrifice of Jesus Christ alone, but did you have to proclaim that so boldly to the papists?"* She realized that it was all too late for recriminations, and now she would do her utmost, for the survival of her family. Resolutely, she began to pack the bare necessities.

***

Eager hands helped the bedraggled French refugees climb out of the leaking coracle that had brought them from the mainland to the island of Goringa. Thousands of French Huguenots had fled from France to other parts of Europe to escape the killing frenzy of Romanist mobs ignited by the St. Bartholomew's Day massacre in Paris. The Reformers urgently alerted all their adherents to aid and assist the Huguenot refugees. Lodging, warm clothes, fish, and large helpings of pea soup were supplied to the famished Bedards, and slowly they began to integrate into island life. Many generations passed before the first marriages between the Nordic/Germanic island stock and the Huguenots took place. Fishing and farming were the chief occupations on the islands, and the Bedards set to work with a willingness. For three hundred and fifty years, no Bedard moved away from Goringa.

***

The Spanish Bloodline

Pablo was sickened with the whole business. He was a soldier, not a butcher of civilians. In 1650, the entire Netherlands village, under Spanish control, had been herded into the public square, and a priest holding the host stood beside the Inquisitor. "Swear that these elements of the Mass are holy, or bear the consequences," yelled the black-cowled, menacing Spaniard.

The brutal conquest of the Lowlands by the Spanish general, the Duke of Alva, was designed to crush the Reformation and establish the supremacy of Rome as the "one true church." Those heretics who refused to bow and swear before the priest holding his crucifix were run through with the long narrow swords of the Spanish soldiers, and leaders were tied to a large stake and burned. The court martial of Pablo for refusing to carry out the despicable murders was to be held the next day, and there was no doubt as to the outcome. Pablo had been a solid Romanist believer, but what he was experiencing now convinced him that this was not from God.

The grunts of the garroted Spanish sentries as they died were followed by the sudden rip of the prison wall. The steel chain, pulled by the sturdy, gelded Belgian horses pulled the wall apart. The Reformers, who had freed him took Pablo to the outer islands of the Lowlands.

***

"What I really miss most of all is my tobacco," Pablo confided to the stolid flower grower, with the unpronounceable name, in whose house he was being hidden. "Once you get used to a good smoke, you cannot do without it anymore."

"All you really need is faith in God and a good woman," rejoined the farmer. "We'll study the Bible together, and when the Spanish are gone, you'll marry my daughter, Trina. Trina isn't a looker, but she has a heart of gold and can work like a mule."

It took some time before the pride of the slim and elegant Spaniard allowed him to accept the old man's proposal, but it was Trina's sweet disposition that won the day. They married and received one daughter, whom they named Maartje. Pablo, when alone, always called her Maria.

***

Generations passed, and after the turn of the twentieth century, a sturdy peasant woman named Maartje Hulshof gave birth to the largest baby ever recorded in the ancestral village. Fourteen pounds at birth qualified Diego for the following praise: "Well I never!" exclaimed the birthing nurse. "The Queen would be proud to have received such a baby!"

Diego Hulshof was not your average Dutchman. Deep-set eyes and a large Roman nose accentuated the purpose and seriousness of his nature. His friends would tease him with nicknames. "Good morning, Hidalgo; Hey, conquistador," would greet him as he walked with a forward stoop. Meningitis had nearly killed him during his army service and had left an indelible imprint. For many generations, the Hulshofs had been flower growers. Diego's passion for tulips and dahlias was only surpassed by his passion for a girl named Rita.

Seven healthy children were born to Diego and Rita, but none of the seven showed the Spanish heritage so evident in their father.

In her fortieth year, Rita gave birth to her final baby. They called her Maartje, and she was the image bearer of a long previous Maartje. She was a lovely baby and became a beautiful girl who was very aware of her nose.

***

The Tribes Unite

The French dragoon pointed to Marinus son of Peter with his cavalry sword and barked, "Arret!" The long line of Dutch peasants stopped and at the next command slowly advanced toward the desk of Jean Montier. If the peasants spoke French, they quickly proceeded on their way home, but most of the dour men present required the services of an interpreter. At the beginning of the nineteenth century, Napoleon had decreed that a census of all his subjects in the Netherlands be undertaken and that every family head be given a surname. Jean had compiled a long list of surnames, and all the peasant males who were called by their first name and identified by adding their father's first name would forthwith now be known by their given name and a unique surname.

Marinus stared at the hated French invaders who had polluted his beloved island with their revolutionary cant and ungodly and blasphemous attitudes. He shook his head in the negative when he was asked, "*Parlez-vous francais?*" The interpreter snapped, "Stand up straight, man, and explain why it is that all your ancestors, for four generations, were named either Peter or Jan, but you are called Marinus?" The question was occasioned by the many false names provided by people who resented the intrusion into their customary traditions.

"Marinus! I was called Marinus instead of Jan because my mother's father, Marinus, had no sons. My parents hoped for, and did indeed receive, the inheritance from my maternal grandparents in trust for myself. My firstborn son, however, is again called

Peter." The loud guffawing that his explanation engendered only served to deepen the hate that Marinus felt, and when Jean noticed the searing look in the peasant's eyes, he snapped his fingers and two more mounted dragoons guarded the tent with the flapping tri-colour flag of the French Republic.

***

"You should have seen the French *popinjays*, Betje!" roared Marinus to his wife. "They looked like barnyard roosters prancing around with dung stuck under their boots."

"I did see them, husband," Betje replied. "I thought they looked magnificent in their uniforms, and I have never seen finer horses. By the way, Marinus, what is our name now to be?"

"**Nachtegal**, Betje. Can you believe it? Which one of our neighbours will ever call us Marinus and Betje Nachtegal?"

"Nightingale! Marinus! What a beautiful name," murmured Betje as her memory recalled the song to which her father used to rock her to sleep:

> *Galloping, galloping, come the magnificent steeds.*
> *Blue coats swirling, bouncing in their saddles.*
> *The French cavalry glory in the sight they make.*
> *Galloping, galloping, come the magnificent steeds.*
> *Baby don't cry — hear the Nightingales sing for you.*

***

"He's a fine sturdy boy, my son," the very old lady hoarsely gasped. Betje lay on her deathbed, but was still able to appreciate her grandson. "Let's go home, Pa," Jantje whispered in a frightened voice. "I don't like that lady!"

"Hush, boy! Come and give Oma a kiss," urged his father.

Obediently, Jantje kissed the parchment cheek and whispered, "Goodbye, Oma. I think that you soon will die." Slowly and plaintively the old lady's quavering voice sang the "French Cavalry" lullaby song. The French words rose and then faded away into exhaustion.

***

Peter Nachtegal, son of Jan Nachtegal, grew up as an only child in the middle of the nineteenth century, and he did not benefit from the over indulgent attention of his parents. He grew to become a handsome man with sly, shifty eyes, and soon Berendina, the town gossip, gave him the nickname that stuck with him all his life. "He is a "*krom houtje*" (crooked stick), she declared, and Peter did his best to prove her right. Petty theft, poaching, and hard drinking turned him into a thoroughly disreputable character.

"Nonsense, officer, it's all a pack of lies," Jan protested to the constable who presented him and Sophie with a long list of crimes committed by their son. Their protests were stilled, however, when the neighbour's pregnant daughter, Coby, filed a paternity charge against Pete, which he admitted to. He was given the choice to marry the girl or join the army and ship out to Indonesia. Crooked Peter opted to join the colonial army.

Initially, Indonesia proved to be exactly to Pete's liking. Like the French Foreign Legion, the Dutch colonial army was a haven for those who had a past they wished to evade. Pete waded into all the available vices like a pig into a wallow and managed to do very little actual fighting. The chaplain attached to his infantry unit often spoke to Peter with the warning, "Realize, Peter, that there is a terrible price to pay for what you're doing. You are a baptized covenant child of God, and He will not be mocked."

Peter replied with a sneer on his handsome features. "Go back to your books, kill-joy. This is an island paradise, and I intend to enjoy it."

The enjoyment stopped when the doctor delivered his diagnosis to a very sick Peter Nachtegal. "You have sustained severe damage to your heart and liver due to parasites," he began. "You have also been infected with syphilis, which I'm not able to cure. I recommend that you immediately be discharged from the army and sent back home."

No one in Pete's hometown recognized the broken, yellow-skinned man who stepped down from the tram. Sophie cried for days as she compared the son who had left with the wreck who had returned.

***

The gentle knock at the Nachtegal's front door was answered by Sophie, who started in surprise as she recognized Coby. She was holding a sturdy five-year-old boy by the hand. She had been sent away by her parents to live with relatives and had just arrived back from her prolonged absence. "May I see Peter?" she asked in a soft voice. Sophie clasped her in her arms and hugged her grandson. Then the tears flowed freely.

"Please be forewarned, my darling girl," warned Sophie. "He may not even reply to you. He barely acts civil to us, his parents."

Holding her boy's hand Coby slowly approached the sallow gaunt man on the bed. "Here is your son Peter. He needs a father and I need a husband."

"Are you saying that you want me to be your husband after all I've done to you?" exclaimed Peter with a hoarse voice. "Do you realize that you'll be nursing a man who has less than a year to live?"

"I do," Coby asserted. She proceeded to present young Jan to his father but he showed little interest..

After the marriage, Peter lived for three more years under Coby's loving nursing but showed little regard for her devotion and love.

It was Berendina who voiced his epitaph after the burial: "That Peter Nachtegal was a crooked one right to the end!" she opined with a triumphal look that clearly said, "I was right from the very start."

Sturdy, phlegmatic generations followed, and in 1899 the mold was broken when a boy was born who became a mystic, philosopher, poet, and dreamer: Peter, first born son of Jan Nachtegal. Breaker of traditions.

***

1945

A heavy fog blanketed the island, and many coal stoves were lit, which added to the close atmosphere. "It's a boy, Kate, and all is well." Katharine heard the voice of her husband from far away. "Let's call him Caleb. Your father will like that." The birth of her seventh child took place in her own bedroom, and before she gave way to the sleep of exhaustion, her vision was filled by the broad and solid silhouette of her husband, and she remembered his promises. "You, Kate, will be a queen." Peter Nachtegal rejoiced that after the birth of five daughters, God had seen fit to provide him with a second son. As the tension drained from between his shoulders, his mind drifted to a time not so long ago. A time when it had all started.

***

Peter Nachtegal

At six in the morning, the pale winter sun smudged the dirty-grey horizon formed by the dikes. Peter did as generations of his forbearers had done, those who had inhabited the little island wrested from the hungry seas. The swish of his scythe cutting through the coarse reed grasses formed the backdrop to the plans he was formulating. Were those preceding ancestors watching him, and would they approve? Ankle-deep in the mud generated by the incessant rains, he stolidly accepted the severe conditions that would have felled a lesser man. He could handle the back-breaking labour, but he also knew that the reed he was cutting was destined to be placed on the roofs of rich people's summer cottages. No socialist jealousies perturbed him, however, but he eagerly sought for a way to improve his financial lot. *I'm still single at twenty-eight years old*, he thought. *But before I marry, I first need to stop labouring for others and start working for myself. I don't have enough money to buy land, so I'll have to try to rent it with borrowed money. Perhaps Pa will give me a loan.* He knelt on a soggy hummock and prayed that God would help him make his dreams come true and provide a suitable wife.

***

Katherine Bedard

She felt the strike of the large potato between her shoulder blades, and the sudden hurt and pain made her scream. Katherine Bedard turned toward her father with a rage in her eyes that spoke of what she dared not say.

"That will teach you to lag behind, girl. Keep up, or else it will be worse next time," warned Caleb Bedard. The small, wiry, transplanted Huguenot forked out the fine yellow-fleshed potatoes with a furious energy that Kate was unable to keep up with. At home it was more of the same: a constant demand, by her mother, to do more.

Why are they both so hard and mean to me? she thought, self-focused and unaware of the bitter struggle for survival her parents had experienced. Beautiful, dark-haired, and born with an impetuous nature, Kate dared to dream. The dream that came most often included scenes from a magazine display that showcased finely-dressed ladies living in beautiful homes. They also included all the curiosities of a lively, intelligent mind that had been stifled. They did not include (at least not at first) a ruggedly handsome boy from the neighbouring village who stared at her whenever church functions allowed their paths to cross.

***

The young man from the volunteer fire brigade stood in the Bedard kitchen, cap in hand. Kate saw him turn to her as she came down the stairs, and she supposed that he had come to continue his courting attempts. But then she saw his tear-streaked face.

"It's-s-s-s-s your brother, Kate," he stuttered. "He has drowned swimming in the canal."

The keening wailing of her mother lasted an eternity, and Caleb Bedard was never the same again. It was Caleb Jr. who on a hot, dusty afternoon stripped off his heavy work shirt, climbed onto the stone parapet, and unaware of the rogue gene in his genetic code, dove into the canal. It wasn't the first time he had gone for a dip, but observers testified that Caleb went under and never surfaced. Five minutes later, they pulled him from the water, but it was too late.

Kate had shared a deep filial bond with the slim, handsome boy who would not have been out of place strolling along the Champs-Élysées in Paris. They were kindred spirits, and he was Kate's only confidant. "Why, God, oh why did You take him and have him leave me?" she mourned in her desolation.

Being the youngest in a family of seven children meant that Kate bore the brunt of caring for parents, who were becoming old and querulous. Her father had lost his life savings in an ill-advised venture involving shares in a cookie factory. "Never again will I sign my name to anything," he would rant whenever he was asked to sign any document. This caused Kate to be removed from school at age thirteen. The recollection of the disappointment at being denied the chance of learning with her friends still stung. She recalled the attentions of callow youths whose only desire was to perpetuate the drudgery she so disliked. Marriage did not rate highly, but the thought of spinsterdom truly alarmed her. "Just remember, girl," her mother warned, "boys do not look at girls anymore when they're past twenty."

At age twenty-two, Kate started to return the looks that shy Peter Nachtegal sent her way.

***

A Very Important Romance

From the dawning of his memory, Peter Nachtegal dearly loved his mother, Greta. She in turn doted upon her eldest son, born in the late fall of 1899 AD. Peter's authoritarian father allowed one opinion to prevail in the household: his own. One result of his stubbornness was that he allowed none of his children to attend school. The government had decided that all school-going children needed to be vaccinated, and Jan Nachtegal was not going to allow any government to tell him what to do! As a result, all the children rejoiced—except for Peter, who was looking forward to the wonder of learning. Greta Nachtegal, a former teacher, took her young son aside and promised him that she would teach him all that she was able. She kept her promise and left a legacy of priceless worth with her son. Peter was no scholarly, anemic child, but he loved books and eagerly soaked up all that he could learn about theology, politics, and world history. In conjunction with his studies, he also developed a robust physique and became a sought-after worker by the local farmers.

When will they ever learn that they can't get away with it? Peter thought as he cornered his three youngest brothers in the blind alley. After administering a sound flogging and hearing three "I am sorry" refrains, Peter took his brothers back to their father, where they again received more corporal punishment. Peter had no desire to be his father's policeman, but when the younger siblings were rude to their mother and refused to be taught the basics of reading and writing, it was too much for him, and he acted.

***

The minister continued to drone on about the miserable state of mankind as Peter squirmed in the church pew. Generations of Nachtegals had attended the old brick church at the end of Main Street, but Peter was drawn to the preaching in the new church at the other end of town. The gospel he heard there was faithful to what he read in his Bible. He had gone there without his father's permission, and for the first time heard, and became impassioned about, what it meant to live a new life in the Spirit of Jesus Christ.

"No, Peter, you cannot do this to me!" screamed his father. "The church you want to join teaches heresies; why, they even allow the men and women to sit together during the services."

"I'm sorry, Father," Peter rejoined, "but I must go where the true gospel is preached."

It took many years for the rift between father and son to partially heal, and Peter became a pariah to the members of the old church, where tradition was stronger than gospel. He joined the Young People's Bible study group in his new congregation and soon was voted to lead the group's activities. He showed little interest in girls, and when he passed his thirtieth birthday, many thought him to be a confirmed bachelor.

He awoke to his maleness while arranging group discussions with the young people from the village of Bosveldt. It was there that Peter saw her. She was beautiful, and Peter's eyes told her so. After one year she consented to bike-riding dates, and after that she said yes when Peter proposed. Peter was bedazzled, and he promised her that one day he would make her a queen.

Love and Marriage Go Together Like a Horse and Carriage

Promises are hard to keep, and throughout her married life, Kate remembered when they were broken and often reminded her husband that he had broken them. It was a rocky road right from the start when both families showed vehement opposition to the marriage. Kate's dad and brothers had been landowners and told her to get rid of a renting sharecropper who would keep her dirt-poor all her life. Peter's family warned him about his girl's uppity ways. His father took him aside and said, "Son, be realistic. You're ten years older than Kate, and with those flashing eyes, she'll be nothing but grief to you. Do you want other men looking at your wife?" It was all water off a duck's back to the couple. They were in love, and it was a passion that at times threatened to consume them.

Peter was determined to make Kate proud of him, and that was where the marriage troubles started. He rented a large home for his Kate and then worked long, arduous days in order to pay the rent. Kate was not a woman to be neglected or left at home, so she joined Peter working in the fields until well-advanced into her first pregnancy. She refused to listen when her husband commanded her to stay home. All Peter's friends, brothers, and brothers-in-law sniggered behind his back about his headstrong wife. Both shared a pride that refused to compromise, and while love was strong, so was resentment. "One day I too will be a landowner," Peter promised himself. "Kate will never do field work again, and her brothers will rue their gibes."

When will men acknowledge that women are their equals, and often their betters when it comes to intelligence? Kate thought as she vigorously applied her hoe to the ever-emerging weeds. *I'll make Peter acknowledge that I'm an equal partner in this marriage and that I won't be bossed around or talked down to.* She felt the stirring of her baby, dropped her hoe, and sat down for a brief rest.

The old man shook his head as he surveyed his young, slender, but very pregnant daughter-in-law hoeing sugar beets. "When a heifer is narrow in the flanks, it's always trouble when the first calf is born," he remarked sagely to his son, Peter. He let fly a stream of tobacco juice and jerked his thumb toward Kate. She heard the deprecating remark and turned away so that he would not see the anger that flashed from her eyes. Every discussion with her father-in-law ended in bitter arguing, and Kate constantly stirred up her husband to stand up to the "tyrant," as she called him.

Kate delivered ten healthy children into the world, in her own bedroom with the aid of a midwife, within the space of twenty years. She would later say that it was not the having that was hard, but the caring and nurturing.

"What a blessing it is to be able to breastfeed," Kate told her disapproving sister after the third baby was born. "That's my only opportunity to see my toes for a while. Just you see! I'm going to give Peter a piece of my mind."

"It would be better for your bank balance if you could be raising a few more pigs," huffed Kate's oldest sister. "Tell that Peter of yours to use his brains, and tell him I said so!"

"It's okay, Katie," Peter told his angry young wife later. "Just imagine what a fine life you'll have when our children are grown. Think of all the other members of our families who only have one or two children. Where will they be in their old age? Totally dependent on others, Katie, that's where they'll be. You, on the other hand, will be waited on hand and foot, just like a queen."

Kate couldn't stay angry for any length of time with her husband, because she realized that she needed him as much as he needed her. Both were capable of doing prodigious amounts of work, and both were ambitious.

"One day, Katie, just you wait and see ... you will be a queen," Peter promised as he watched her brushing her thick, shiny, waist-length hair. After a hard day of work and planning, it was one of Peter's greatest pleasures to just sit and enjoy the sight of his wife brushing her hair.

Sometimes when she was angry with him, Kate would threaten, "I think I'll have my hair cut short, because it's so heavy and long."

That threat usually never failed to upset and anger Peter, but now he simply smiled and softly said, "Someday I'll take you away to a land bright and fair, a land of freedom with room to spare."

***

War

Holland had declared neutrality during the First World War, and the Kaiser's Germany had respected that declaration. The Nazi regime of the Second World War, however, broke the neutrality proclamation and occupied Holland in seven days. Declaring the Dutch to be Aryan brothers, the Germans became offended when instead of welcoming cheers, they were greeted with hostility and armed resistance. After some bombing and strafing strikes on the island of Goringa, the first German soldiers landed, and the years of terror began. Able-bodied men were rounded up and sent to labour camps. Smugglers, resistance fighters, and those who sheltered Jews were rounded up and shot in the village squares. If any Germans were killed in or around a village by the Underground, the police would round up a quota of men and summarily execute them by firing squad. All the Jews and gypsies, except those hidden by sympathetic islanders, disappeared.

"What exactly do you think you are doing?" demanded the Wehrmacht corporal, fixing his bayonet and pointing his rifle at Peter Nachtegal's mid-section. "Snell! Speak! Or I will put a bullet in your gut."

Peter's nerveless fingers dropped the saw he was using to cut down the wooden poles erected by the Germans. They had dug them behind the dykes with connecting cables in order to snag Allied gliders from hopping over the dikes.

"Please don't shoot. Let me explain," stalled Peter as he noticed his oldest son, Jan, hiding in the drainage canal. "I have a family of six hungry children, and we have no fuel in order to cook our food."

The corporal carefully looked around him and then lowered his gun. "Snell! Get out of here as fast as you can, and don't ever let me catch you here again. I also had to leave my wife and children in Austria, and I miss them terribly." There were, however, many islanders who unfortunately were apprehended by soldiers who showed no mercy, and they died.

"Wonderful! Real dark chocolate and real coffee," exclaimed Kate as the friendly Canadian paratrooper liberally emptied his backpack.

"Your children are so thin, ma'am," he exclaimed as the whole family crowded around him. "Wait until the trucks arrive and then you can start to fatten those skinny kids."

The entire village was celebrating "De Bevrijding" (freedom) when suddenly the cheers died. A platoon of German soldiers, on their way back to Germany, entered the village square and in lock-step marched down Main Street without a glance at the Canadian soldier. The war was over, but the memory of the terror caused many to run for cover as the platoon marched by, loudly singing "*Mein Vaterland*" ("My Fatherland").

Some days after the euphoria of liberation was fading radical elements in the village began to incite mob justice.

"No, I will not join you in your revengeful endeavour," remonstrated Peter to those of his family who had invited him to join them for "payback" time. "I can understand how you feel about those who have betrayed many to their deaths, but we cannot descend to their level. Let the justice system deal with them."

They stalked away yelling insulting and hurtful remarks toward the whole family. Those who had been Nazi sympathizers were identified and dragged into the village square. There were many families in which at least one or two members were known sympathizers to the Nazi occupiers. Peter and Kate hated the mob justice that prevailed in all its ugly display: beatings, burning of homes, and shaving the heads and exposing the breasts of girls and women who had consorted with the Germans. The events caused a division between the Nachtegals and the rest of the village. They were always considered to be different after not taking part in the mob justice that was meted out.

Farming Is in the Genetic Makeup

"Beautiful crops, son," said Peter's father with a hint of surprised compliment in his voice. "I never thought you could make a go of paying the rent on ten hectares of land and then make a living from it. But I was wrong. Your theology is all mixed up, and you shamed your parents when you left our church, but I will acknowledge that you are a fine farmer and a good provider for your family." He ended with a terse remark as he prepared to depart: "Any two of your children are welcome to come for Saturday morning breakfast with Opa and Oma. They will be treated to fresh boiled eggs and fresh oranges."

The admission was sweet music to Peter's ears, and he simply replied, "Thanks, Pa." He had never heard his father admit to being wrong before, nor had he received much praise during all the years that he contributed to his father's income. The one hundred year lease on the rented ten hectares of land almost provided a feeling of ownership until the yearly rent needed to be paid. It was always a chorus of competing demands between Peter's growing family and the amount to be set aside for the rent. Peter grabbed a lump of soil in his hands and prayed: "Please, Lord, someday let me have my own farm."

The grey, heavy clay soil of the island was brutal to work with, but the crops it produced were astounding. Thousands of fine silt layers had been deposited before the encircling dykes had shut out the ocean tides. Horse drovers and their horse teams were hired to do the plowing and bring in the harvest.

"I'm going to go to hell, Peter Nachtegal," stormed Joop the drover as a continual trace of drool glistened on his jaw. "The swearing that I have done today can never be forgiven, and it's all because of your rotten muddy field!" His horses were ankle deep in the clay slop, and the wagon wheels were buried up to the axles in the ooze. Yelling men cracking bull-hide whips would hitch on extra teams of horses and extricate the heavily-laden wagons from the mud onto the gravel roads. The gentle Belgian draft horses were sorely used and abused. When their wind was broken or their legs refused to support the terrible strains, they were sold and butchered for human and pet consumption. The yelling continued as demands for more payment were, at first, refused and then renegotiated.

The five years after the war were economically good years for the Nachtegal family, but Peter was still restless, and the children often complained about being teased and bullied. They were made to feel that they were outsiders at the local schools. When Kate delivered a third son, born in the image of his father, Peter felt that he needed breathing room for his large family. He kept his thoughts concealed and bided his time. Grand dreams of Australia, South Africa, Brazil, and Canada filled his head. *I'll wait until the little ones are older and stronger*, he thought. *Then I'll tell Kate that I can really make our dreams come true.*

Not Appreciated

I wonder why my Peter is never nominated to be an elder at church, puzzled Kate. *Could it be that there is still resentment against him because of his refusal to join the village mob after the war?* Kate was a picture of health and beauty after the delivery of a robust boy, her ninth child. She put on her coat and grabbed her purse as her eyes filled with the glow that presaged trouble for someone. She looked with scorn at her husband when he refused to come with her and make an issue of the matter. The council meeting of the church was surprised and offended when Kate stormed into the all-male bastion, demanding answers. She could discern no faces in the swirling clouds of cigar smoke but made sure that all could hear her. "My husband is a God-fearing man, and you should be ashamed that you've never nominated him to be an elder. Be ashamed of yourselves."

"We will certainly look into the matter, Mrs. Nachtegal," placated the chairman. "We'll get back to you as soon as possible."

Kate was not surprised when no answer was ever forthcoming. Soon the Nachtegals were worshipping in the new liberated churches. Kate and Peter's brothers and sisters seldom came to visit them. The unnerving presence of her many, noisy children, as well as Kate's persistent refusal to be awed by their material possessions, soon caused their visits to dwindle away. She was always concerned for their spiritual well-being, even though her busy life was occupied with the care of her children. The rift between Kate and her parents was also never fully healed, even though she often visited them. Life had broken them, and the ability to communicate was lost.

"What kind of a man are you anyway, Peter Nachtegal!" stormed Kate with anger and tears vying for dominance. "You have twice the brains of those men who were nominated for town council, but you just allow yourself to be bypassed and put down."

Peter smiled and let his wife's anger cool without remonstrance. *I have other fish to fry, my Kate, but I'm not ready to tell you just yet,* thought Peter as he oiled and sharpened the field implements he worked with every day. By nature phlegmatic and stolid, it took a lot to arouse Peter's anger, but every so often Kate would cross the boundary. On this occasion, however, Peter merely smiled, kissed his Kate, climbed onto his transport bicycle, and pedaled off to work.

It was in the fields that Peter was happiest. What a glory it was when God provided a warm, sunny day and he could feel the rich grey clay between his hands. Potatoes, sugar beets, carrots, and violets were the chief crops that he grew, and they all prospered under his skilled hands. Getting up often from his kneeling position while weeding, he would at regular intervals just look at the growing, gleaming, healthy crops and soak in the enjoyment that only a true farmer can experience. A sudden cry quickly brought him to where he had left two-year-old Caleb. The youngster had wandered away on unsteady legs and fallen into a dry drainage ditch. Peter laughingly grabbed him by the back of his breeches and firmly placed him between two stacks of jute bags. He took bunches of dry straw and made a small cooking fire to make tea. After he had sharpened his hand tools, he gathered Caleb in his arms and enjoyed a ten-minute cat-nap. All his children would benefit equally from any possessions, and so would end the ages-old tradition of lineage authority that passed assets to the eldest son. Peter knew that he was the last heir in a long succession of first-born sons.

CHAPTER II
The Growing Years

THE MOLDING
Carefully mold while the clay is wet,
After it dries, it will be set.

Alienated Lives

Louie was woken once again. Previously, a pack rat had scampered over his face, and now once more his abused senses became conscious of a disturbance. He was irritated by the insistent knocking on the rough wooden door of his filthy, tar paper shack. Clothes and bottles lay scattered on the floor, attesting to the Friday night drinking bout. Crippled by a logging accident after the Second World War, the French Canadian had moved to Sears determined to drink himself into oblivion.

"Go away! Scram! Beat it!" were the words thirteen-year-old Caleb Nachtegal heard as he pushed open the door. It took some time for his eyes to adjust to the dim light and make out the bearded old man lying on the cot. The fetid air was heavy with alcohol and pack rat odour.

"Can you help me?" Caleb asked. When no reply was forthcoming, he repeated in a louder, frightened voice, "My car is stuck, and I need a horse or machine to pull it out of the snow!"

Louie horked loudly, stood up in his Stanfield long johns with the rear flap unbuttoned, and hoarsely croaked, "Speak up! Whaddya want?" After numerous repetitions, Caleb finally got through to the alcohol- addled brain. "You look like a French boy with your skinny face," Louie muttered. "What's your name?"

Louie finally got his horses harnessed and hitched to the 1956 Ford station wagon, buried in the snow bank. A terse "Giddup" came from his mouth, and the two Clydesdales eased into their logging harnesses and easily pulled the car back on the road. He refused the twenty-dollar bill that was offered and then gave Caleb a lecture on "stupid young punks' driving habits" and led his horses back to the barn.

Caleb never saw Louie again, but he also never forgot him. Broken lives littered with regret and recriminations abounded in the lonely shacks that dotted the northern woods around the town of Sears where he grew up. Mostly men, they came from all areas of Europe and China. and each one had a tale of woe to tell to a curious young lad who was willing to take the time to listen. "Nobody had the right to do to me what they did!" was the common theme woven into each story. A severing of all ties was so easy to accomplish, and so hard to restore. *Never*, Caleb swore to himself, *will I let my life come to such a sorry pass*. The famous American, Howard Hughes, with all his billions, was very similar to what Louie had come to. How Caleb appreciated the courage of his father and mother to come to a new wonderful land. Their hard work and discipline, connected to God's commands, brought about a life that was filled with purpose.

***

Awakening

The spring of 1945 was, by Caleb's father's account, beautiful, weather-wise. The war was over. The hated Nazis were chased out of Holland by the heroic Canadian forces. Caleb's mother brought him kicking and squalling into the world. Her first words to her husband were, "A boy, Peter! Without a mark!" Caleb's older sister did the village rounds and proudly announced to all who were interested, and those not, that she had a new brother, a peace baby. His early childhood memories were wrapped in a halcyon haze of loving family and an incredible aptitude to get into trouble. Scooter accidents, falling into ditches, and causing embarrassing moments for his parents were all in a day's work. Many adults today speak about the horrific circumstances of a loveless upbringing, but for Caleb, only good memories remained of those early days. He soon became aware of the inner, observing voice that often cautioned him. When his sisters caught him talking to himself, he would reply that he was speaking to Lucius.

Economic and Morality Lessons

The small confectionary shop on the dyke in Caleb's hometown was a never-ending place of marvel to his five-year-old senses. Endless rows of glass bottles filled with delectable candies provided him with imaginary taste treats. It was there that his first lesson in the mechanics of credit and honesty took place. His mom often took him along when she shopped there, and he soon noticed that all she had to do was ask the proprietor, and he would give her the item.

"It's true!" Caleb assured his three best friends. "All I have to do is tell old Teunis that my mom would like whatever we'd like and he'll give it to us."

"Naw, Caleb, you need to give money in order to get anything in that store," retorted Hans, his six-year-old friend. "My mom always gives paper and coins to old Teunis when she gets tobacco, coffee, and licorice."

"I'll show you then," Caleb replied. "Come with me and tell me what you'd like to have."

Teunis looked over the top of his reading spectacles as all four urchins trooped into the small store. "Yes-s-s-s, Caleb, where is your mother today?" he stuttered with a scowling face directed toward the four boys with their dirty corduroy knickers.

"She's busy, Mr. Teunis," Caleb airily lied, "but she asked me to get her some ice cream, sausages, and four small bags of Turkish delight candies," he assured him with his best smile in place.

"You're sure your mother asked you to get these items, Caleb? She's never ordered Turkish delight before," he queried.

In spite of the guilt that was starting to redden his cheeks, Caleb persisted in his lies, and soon four rascals were on their way to an abandoned barn on the edge of town to enjoy their treats. After all was eaten, four satiated boys with sore stomachs returned to their homes just in time for dinner.

"Eat your supper, boy!" Pa warned that evening as Caleb sat on the black oak kitchen bench feeling very full and queasy.

"I can't. Pa. I'm not feeling well," he replied as the mixture of ice cream, candy, and sausage roiled in his stomach.

"Caleb, your aunt Mirjam told me that she saw you and your friends coming out of the confectionary this afternoon," said his mom. "What were you doing there?"

The sudden eruption of his ill-gotten goods over Mom's clean kitchen floor and the disgusted yells of his sisters were the prelude to a confession of guilt and repentance. A sound spanking followed by a lecture on the evils of stealing and lying were deeply imprinted on his young mind and never forgotten.

"It's not only hardworking people that you've wronged," Pa lectured Caleb as he sobbed, grinding his fist into his tear-smeared face in a futile attempt to staunch the flood of tears. "Above all, you sin against God when you take anything without paying for it."

Family and Beach Time

Caleb's cousin Jan became his kindergarten teacher after he turned five, and she was beautiful in his eyes. His sisters were mostly dark and tall, but Jan was blonde and matronly. She had a constant smile on her cherubic face and blatantly spoiled him. She was one of seven girls in her family, and her only brother had died at a young age from contracting scarlet fever. She would always hug Caleb at the end of class and give him a licorice candy. When his older sister Anna was mean to him, he would tell her to appreciate him the way Jan did. "A spoiled brat, that's what he is," Anna told their parents, "but don't worry, I'll toughen him up." True to her word, she seized every opportunity to do so, while assuring Caleb it was all for his good.

The west side of Goringa Island, facing the North Sea, showcased beautiful, white sandy beaches bordered by sand dunes. On very special hot days during summer, the Nachtegals would go on a family outing and spend the whole day swimming and exploring. During one of those sun-drenched days, Caleb managed to evade the watchful eyes of his parents and siblings and soon was out of eyesight of everyone, except his sister Trina. Knowing his propensity for trouble, she tagged behind him and observed his sudden precipitous tumble into a submerged concrete bunker left by the German occupation forces. Ten feet under water, Caleb rolled onto his back and saw the blue sky and sun gleaming unobtainable far above. He gulped the first swallow of water and then saw Trina's marvellous arm and hand slowly descending toward him. Many years later when he visited the Vatican's Sistine Chapel and saw the fresco "The Creation of Adam" by Michelangelo, it reminded him of that saving hand.

***

Away to a New Land

After the black war years were over, restless currents swept over the European nations, and a tiny eddy blew into Peter Nachtegal's hometown on a small island in the North Sea. It infected fifty-year-old Peter with wanderlust and a desire to buy his own land. Just like the call to the biblical Abraham to leave his land, so Peter felt that God was calling him to a new place and a new beginning. For three hundred years no Nachtegal had left the island permanently, but that was about to change. Pictures of happy farmers standing in golden Canadian wheat fields intoxicated him. "This is our opportunity, Kate, the chance we've so long waited for," he cajoled his apprehensive wife. "We're both healthy and strong, and we can forge a new and better life in a free Canada. Think of our children, Kate. What future is there for them here? We're living in a socialistic, bureaucratic nightmare. It's now or never, and I say it is now."

"But our families, Peter! If we go at our age, we'll never see our parents and families again," cried Kate. "I still have a new nursing baby to care for. Many people who are your age are planning retirement, and you propose a whole new life. You forget that you're already fifty years old."

The next day Pete informed his wife and large family that they were going to Canada. "Lethbridge, Alberta has cheap land for sale and a lot of it. One-hundred-and-sixty-acre homesteads can be had for a pittance. I've written to a farmer there who has agreed to sponsor us."

At six years old, Caleb didn't notice the look of terror on his mom's face, nor did he notice the cries of dismay from some of his siblings. Life was a great adventure, and Jan, his oldest brother, was his hero and capable of handling whatever would come.

"Have you taken leave of your senses?" boomed Opa Nachtegal as he confronted his eldest son. "You have a good life here, and now you're cruelly taking my grandchildren away, and I shall never see them again." He stabbed his forefinger toward his temple and stalked out of the house in a rage.

A long parade of clucking, disapproving relatives tried to dissuade Peter, but it was all to no avail. "Our relatives are no-vision-stuck-in-a-rut poor people, Kate," Pa opined as he carefully smoked a rare Ritmeester cigar. "They're not even interested in what happens on the mainland of Holland, let alone the rest of the world. If only they would take the time to read and open their minds to new ideas and opportunities." Kate remembered again why she had married this man. With all his faults and shortcomings, he was a dreamer, a poet, and a doer.

There were many months of preparation required before the emigration papers and exit visas were approved. Doctors and nurses inspected and poked everywhere as they examined the twelve Nachtegals for serious defects. The last trauma were the inoculations to prevent smallpox. Caleb put up serious resistance to being treated, since he'd had ample time to observe what was coming. The stern grip of his pa on his arm ensured that the sharpened nib in the nurse's hand was able to etch two small X's on his skinny upper right arm. The presiding doctor then poured a small amount of liquid from a dark blue bottle onto the bleeding marks. A smart rap on his behind brought his anguished bellowing to a quick halt, but his soft whimpering continued for some time after. His mom comforted him as best she could and kept murmuring, "No, Caleb, no, they're not hurting you on purpose."

"Yes they are," he insisted. "Just wait and see what will happen to my arm." Those words proved to be prophetic.

The howling laughter of many aunts and uncles who had gathered to see the Nachtegals off was precipitated by one question: "Tell us again, Caleb, all the English words that you know." They would ask him with anticipation written all over their broad Germanic or narrow French faces.

"Vacuum cleaner, please, bugger, no money in my pocket, taxi," he replied with a deadpan face, not realizing why his hard-learned English words provoked such merriment. It was finally Uncle Martin who, between attacks of near hysteria, explained to him that he was never to say "bugger" in Canada.

"Why not, Uncle Martin?" Caleb asked. "My best friend, Hans, told me that no one in Canada would dare to pick a fight with me if I used that word."

"Just the opposite, Caleb," he admonished. "You'll be severely beaten by anyone you call by that word."

Tearful hugs and slobbering kisses were received and grudgingly given by Caleb when prompted by a pinch from his Pa. Caleb did, however, manage to elude one particular scary aunt who insisted that she needed to hold her darling Caleb. She had never showed any affection before, so he felt no need to start now. One quick dart of his Pa's arm and he was deposited into her ample lap. What happened during the next five minutes did insult to his six-year-old dignity and was only assuaged by the view of all his siblings receiving the same treatment.

Over the Ocean and over the Sea,
Going Where Canada Is Waiting for Me

The former troop carrier, *Volendam*, plunged into the troughs of the North Atlantic's large storm waves. How the prow managed to lift up each time was a miracle to six-year-old eyes. Icy spray filled the air, and unending towering waves smashed into the ship and rattled every rivet in the hull. The ship shuddered convulsively each time the propeller lifted out of the water. She was old and rust seeped out from every weld joint. How could any man-made thing endure such a pounding? The Nachtegals were a praying family, and many earnest prayers ascended from terrified souls during the crossing. None of them had ever ventured onto open ocean waters before, and they were frightened during the first days at sea. All the deckhands assured Caleb that the weather would soon clear and it would be a grand voyage. They lied. None of the Nachtegals ever saw the sun during the entire crossing, and Caleb's nightmares were filled with slowly rotating bodies descending in the cold water, with small bubbles escaping from gaping mouths. Most of the people on board became seasick, and meals in the mess halls were sparsely attended.

The sound of the harsh loudspeakers announcing the serving of the third of four dinner sessions drew little interest from the seasick, suffering passengers. However, the serving of an unlimited food supply was reacted to immediately by Caleb and the few passengers who were not seasick. Pea soup followed by mashed potatoes smothered in gravy was topped up by hot custard pudding for dessert. Cries of "Stop it!" were yelled at him when he would describe, to his sick siblings, the delicious meal he had just enjoyed.

Caleb became adroit at dodging vomit sprays from the upper deck areas as he explored the boat. The nights were firmly imbedded in his consciousness, primarily because of the smell. Males older than six were segregated in their own sleeping quarters, and those who were not sick slept on top of the three-tier bunks. Caleb hung on as best as he could to the steel stanchions as the ship wallowed in the heavy seas, but when he fell asleep, his grip slackened and down he would go. "Mama, Mama!" he cried, but soon angry shouts from disturbed older men silenced him. His pa fashioned a large sheet into a twisted rope and used it to lash him to the bed. The drowning people in his nightmares were becoming smaller and smaller. The swaying ceiling lights flickered on the yellow scum that swirled over the floor with each roll of the ship. The comfort in experiencing misery is that it can't last forever, and it did not. The old scow berthed in Quebec harbour, and when Caleb found his land legs again, all was right with the world.

Never-Ending Land from Shining Sea to Shining Sea

Clickety-clack, clickety-clack, it went on monotonously as the wheels of the iron monster, belching a steady stream of black smoke, devoured the land. The Nachtegals marvelled as rivers, lakes, forests, and endless prairies were outlined in the dirty, soot-blackened, steel window frames of the Canadian Pacific Railroad's passenger coach. Fine black soot penetrated into everything. His Pa's eyes shone with the realization that this new, huge land would surely provide him with the farm of his dreams. At every whistle-stop, Peter Nachtegal and Kate would ask directions to the nearest store to buy food for the children. They would all rush to the station washrooms so that their faces could be washed white again. It was, at times, a close call, because the train waited for neither man nor beast past the allotted time. Peanut butter and jam sandwiches quickly lost their appeal, and it became difficult to be thankful as they bowed their heads in a prayer of blessing. Games of tag and hide-and-seek did not make the Nachtegal children popular with the train conductors, or with the passengers in the crowded aisles. They quickly learned how to adapt to crowded conditions and to dodge the feet and fists that surreptitiously came their way. They all encountered the native Canadian people, whom everyone called "Indians," for the first time when they stopped in Winnipeg.

After six days the train rolled into the Lethbridge depot, and the whole family was eager to see their new home. Three men chewing on unlit cigars greeted Peter, and all could see that the discussion was not good. The sponsors told Peter that an early frost had frozen the crops in the ground and that there was no work for him or for his son, Jan. Hands were moving rapidly and voices were becoming louder, but the upshot was that the Nachtegals could not stay. "Go to British Columbia, Nachtegal," advised the largest of the trio, stroking a stained handlebar moustache. "There's work in the lumber industry in the northern town of Clayton, and Dutch immigrants have established a church there where you can worship."

Peter and Kate, with their brood of ten children ranging in age from one to twenty, were shunted onto a spur line belonging to the Grand Trunk Railway that connected with the Canadian Pacific Railway in Calgary. Kate and her older daughters wept apprehensively as night enveloped the heated sleeper car. Overhead plywood bunks were dropped and cantilevered away from the walls. They provided a hard, smelly bed.

The next morning, they entered the foothills of the Rocky Mountains and a world that was amazing. No Nachtegal had ever viewed the reality of mountains before. "It's a visually beautiful country, Kate," Peter said in a worried voice, "but how are we to farm on those vertical slopes?" As they travelled northwest to Jasper, they saw mountains that no flatlander had ever imagined. This surely had to be the abode of God. The farther west they travelled, the colder it became, and the more worried and nervous Kate became. On October 13, 1951, the train platform in Clayton, British Columbia was covered with two feet of snow, and the people standing there looked like the Eskimos that the Nachtegals had seen in picture books. As the doors opened, a cold blast of wind blew through their light Dutch clothes.

Cheery, red-faced men stood on the platform expelling geysers of steam from their mouths and noses. Daughter Nina laughingly remarked, "Look, everyone, they look like fire-breathing dragons!"

They greeted the Nachtegals with booming hellos and hard hugs after the family left the train—all except one. Kate refused to get off. Her face was rigid with anger and fright as she cried out, "Is this what you promised me, Peter, to live in this cold, forsaken land? Please! Please! Let us go back!" This outburst was followed by a storm of tears and recriminations. Sensitivities and niceties, however, were in short supply, and Peter, having already taken baby Phoebe in her carrying basket, managed to cajole and half drag Kate off the train. What she experienced in the years that followed convinced her for a long time to come that she should never have left that train.

No Flatlander Paradise

The settlers in Clayton were rugged pioneers. Some of them had already lived there since the 1920s. They proudly brought the Nachtegals to a four hundred square foot, rough lumber, tar paper cabin and dumped a hindquarter of moose meat on the crudely built table. The family was regaled with stories about how fortunate they were in comparison to the first settlers who'd come before them.

The whole family grew to hate that tough, gamey, stringy, dry moose meat. Peter had the worst of it, since his teeth were in poor shape. Often after a hard chewing session on moose meat, he would suffer from a toothache. It was then that Caleb's love and appreciation for his parents deepened. With their backs against the wall, they showed their true mettle. They asked surrounding families to temporarily house the older children. Peter landed a job forty miles away in Sears, working for the railroad. Kate turned that awful cabin into a warm, cozy home, and Caleb spent all his spare time, before and after school, getting firewood from the planer mill.

Sister Lila pleaded with her dad to also let others take a turn to go into the well and chop out the ice for the family drinking water. During cold weather, twice a day, she would be lowered into the well with a rope around her waist and a sharp axe in her hand. Lila was strong, agile, and small, so her plea fell on deaf ears. Caleb was deathly afraid that someday he would have to go into the well to chop a hole in the ice, but thankfully that never happened. It did, however, crop up in his repertoire of nightmares.

Dark Angel

"Dear Lord, don't let me die. I'm too young," was Caleb's reaction to the burning fever that consumed his body. He awoke in the middle of the night, and his smallpox-inoculated upper arm was twice its normal size. What had been small crosses were now distended, purple lesions. All over his body, red patches of skin were erupting into boils, and pell-mell he ran into his parents' room with howls of fear. There was no hospital in Clayton, so a church member who owned a pickup truck was awakened and asked to perform ambulance duty. It seemed a never-ending trip over the snow-covered road to the town of Sears, where he was brought into the emergency ward of the local Roman Catholic hospital.

Seven long days passed with never-ending shots, pokes, and terrible tasting fluids, which the nun-nurses ensured ended up in his stomach. He had never been away from home before, and the nights were filled with fear and loneliness. "Eva! Eva!" he would yell in the middle of the night, hoping that the only nurses' aid who spoke Dutch would hear him. She was the only person who worked in the hospital who could understand him and answer his questions. When she was absent, the nuns would make it abundantly clear that he should stop his howling. Flowing black robes around the white faces of the nuns were the precursor to hard slaps on Caleb's skinny frame. His oldest sister, Tess, and his Pa also visited him once during the day. When they left, Caleb followed them to the front door, climbed up into the window frame, and watched until they disappeared from sight.

When the doctor announced, "I think he can go home now; his fever has gone down," Caleb attempted to jump up and kiss him, but the nuns held him down. He saw the same pickup that had brought him to the hospital chug up the hill to bring him home from the hospital. Before it arrived, he had climbed up into the front hall window trusses to get a better view through the large front windows. The nurses' aides needed a step ladder to get him down again. When Caleb saw his Pa walking toward the hospital, the halls rang with his war whoops. It appeared that he had suffered a full-blown case of cowpox. The vaccine that was used to stop smallpox was derived from cowpox virus, and a certain number of people who were inoculated contracted this disease.

***

Survival

In December it got really cold. The mercury plummeted to -40° F. Brother Jan did not receive his wages, because the sawmill operator he worked for went broke. It often happened that father Peter walked the thirty-six miles from Sears, starting at two o'clock on Saturday afternoon, to come home at two o'clock on Sunday morning. The rubber gumboots he wore had never been designed for long distance walking. Each passing car that ignored him left a strong feeling of "They don't care."

"What have you done, Peter Nachtegal?" was a constant refrain replaying in his brain as a silver moon glittered on the icy hill before him. Snowdrift Hill was the highest point between Sears and Clayton, and cars kept passing him in a swirl of icy snow, ignoring the outstretched thumb of the ice-covered man. Five miles of steep road lay in front of him, and many men would have done it once but never again. Peter wiped the hoarfrost from his balaclava and trudged on as he had many times before. Three wolves trailed a hundred yards behind, waiting for a stumble or sign of weakness. Peter felt the handle of the sharp sickle he carried in his backpack, took it out, and faced the pack. The wolves sank back on their haunches and let their tongues loll out. It seemed that their grinning faces taunted him with, "We will get you yet."

"You mangy curs," Peter yelled, "c'mon and get a taste of steel!"

Blessed with an iron constitution, he was never sick and seldom tired. He trudged the last fifteen miles until he saw the cabin porch light and knew that his Kate was waiting for him with warm food and loving hands. *I must do this*, Peter thought determinedly. *My ten children need the money I earn until they can fend for themselves. Two more paycheques and I'll have enough money so that we can move to Sears, and this cursed walk will no longer be necessary.* He was determined to care for his family and keep the promises he had made to his Kate.

On Sunday, the family all gathered together and attended church. The rotund, short preacher reared back on the balls of his feet and literally danced as he encouraged the small congregation. "It does not depend on you to accept Jesus as your Saviour," he instructed. "God is at work in you to will and accept him." Young Caleb and his younger siblings did not understand the implications of the Calvinist versus Arminian controversy at the time, but they would later on. A roaring, cast iron, pot-bellied stove provided the heat in the meeting hall, which was made from shiplap lumber that allowed the wind to whistle through the cracks. Good fellowship, biblical preaching, the sharing of coarse but wholesome food, and the knowledge that God cared for them always made for a fine day.

***

Schooling and Finding Friends

They were after him again. A pack of wild dogs would wait until Caleb left the cabin to go to school or collect firewood. He had to get over six sets of railroad tracks to the safety of the travelled road before they could catch him. One day he was too slow. Surrounded by the pack and fearing the worst, he was surprised when a small girl wearing red gumboots grabbed a stick and waded into the pack, beating snarling jaws left and right. He was astounded to see that a small show of aggression was sufficient to send the entire pack yelping away with their tails between their legs.

"Don't be afraid of them," she advised Caleb. "Show 'em who's boss. Here, use my stick."

The lesson was well learned. Thereafter, Caleb always left the cabin with a stout piece of spruce wood in his hand. Pine or balsam sticks would quickly break, but a fine piece of spruce lumber was a fearsome weapon. The snarling pack circled him one more time, and Caleb landed a few solid thumps with his weapon. This convinced the pack that there were easier pickings elsewhere.

Then there was the herd of semi-wild horses that would stampede through the town at all odd hours. Farmers and loggers allowed their idle horses to forage for food, and these large, dangerous animals would band together and follow the food scent. The thunder of galloping horses through the rutted main street of Clayton would rouse the deepest sleepers in the early morning hours. The Nachtegals all felt that after the neat and orderly living conditions of Holland, they had now truly ended up in the Wild West.

"How can I ever teach so many kids who don't understand me?" wailed the red haired, female teacher as Caleb tried for the third time to understand and answer her questions. She was expected to teach six grades in one room and was required to shovel coal or place wood into the pot-bellied, cast iron stove. Caleb decided to move his desk and quickly slipped into a seat beside a boy he had seen in church. Fred had a working knowledge of English and Dutch and a helpful, caring attitude. He offered to help the teacher with feeding the stove and received a warm smile and thank you for his help. With his help, Caleb was able to understand what was asked and quickly learned to respond to requests. The feelings of being lost and alone were assuaged by the "milk of human kindness." After two months, the teacher, Miss Leach, said yes to the first marriage proposal she received, and the class had to break in a brand new, scared, green, victim again.

***

The Trents: Real Pioneers

On weekends, Fred Trent would invite Caleb to come over to Lakelse Station, where his family lived. The Trents farmed two hundred acres of rich, river-bottom land, and Caleb's visits to their home was the stuff of dreams come true. A bumpy dirt road skirting around steep cliffs provided difficult and dangerous access to the homestead. Their rusty old Dodge pickup twisted and creaked as it negotiated large potholes and steep inclines. Four Trent brothers had driver's licenses, and they all competed for the fastest time to arrive at the farmhouse. After the last hairpin turn, the view would open up to a panorama of flat fields bordered by a sparkling river. It was a beautiful place. Fred, with his parents and his six older brothers and four sisters, lived like true pioneers. One of the brothers had accidently burned down the main farm home, and they now lived in tents and a makeshift cabin. All ten children had wavy dark or blond hair, and the girls looked like princesses to Caleb's youthful eyes. The boys, on the other hand, looked like wild pirates and acted as such. They immediately started asking him questions about his sisters.

"Do your sisters like boys?" Clete, the oldest, asked in a demanding voice.

"Uh, sure ... I guess so," Caleb stammered.

"Would you like to fire my rifle?" interjected Cal, placing his .300 Winchester into Caleb's hands.

"Lay off him, Cal!" Fred yelled. "The kick of that gun can hurt him, and I'm going to tell Dad on you."

Cal slapped Caleb on the back and laughed. "Just kidding, kid, and remember to say hi from me to your oldest sister. Tell her that I think she's pretty." A scuffle then broke out between Clete and Cal about who had first calling rights on the older Nachtegal sisters.

A sudden yell from Clete alerted the three oldest boys to the sight of deer grazing in the hay pasture. "There's free, fresh meat there, boys," he yelled. "Let's go get it!"

Stuffing their pockets with ammunition, three of Fred's older brothers grabbed rifles and moved through the covering woods toward their quarry. Suddenly, the deer heads shot up and instantly a volley of shots rang out. Two of the larger bucks in the herd jumped straight up in the air and then collapsed. The oldest Trent girl, Cally, grabbed a leather apron with skinning knives stuck into its pockets and then jumped into the dusty, red Dodge pickup. With dirt spinning from the rear tires, she drove out to bleed, gut, and collect the carcasses. "That's work for the girls," Clete told Caleb with a sly grin. "We men do the killing, and the ladies do the butchering."

That evening, Caleb joined the Trent family in a meal rich in venison but lacking in vegetables. Before the meal started, Mr. Trent opened with a long prayer, and then he said, "Go ahead, Caleb. We always ask our guests to pray with us before we start."

As he stuttered his way through the prayer, Caleb could hear the muttering of the Trent boys, who were upset that the venison was getting cold. They were all strange and wonderful people to him, and he always eagerly accepted Fred's invitation to come and visit. Fred was so different from his brothers that Caleb often thought he must be adopted.

When he would return home, his Mom would ask, "Well, Caleb, how was it at the Trents' today?"

He would reply, "Compared to them, we're pretty boring, Mom." Then Caleb would regale her with all the adventures he had experienced. He would end his tales with the following recommendation: "I think brother Jan should court and marry the oldest Trent girl, but don't let our girls date the Trent boys, except for Fred." It was inevitable that the Trent boys would court the older Nachtegal girls, but of the seven boys, none would ever marry any of the seven Nachtegal girls. Likewise, none of the three Nachtegal boys ever married any of the Trent girls.

Caleb's Pa always stated that the Trents were a special breed apart. *"Ze passen niet,"* ("They don't fit"). He would tease his daughters by singing, "The Trent boys are handsome and fine but will never marry a daughter of mine."

***

Clayton Is a Pity, but Sears is a city (Clancy's Palace)

"Kate, I've managed to rent a large home in Sears, close to my work," Caleb's Pa proudly announced to his Mom. "It's a palace, and you'll love it." Clancy's Palace, as it was called, was a large, unpainted, rambling home. It had a verandah all around and indoor plumbing. The Nachtegals moved there in the spring of 1952, and after the cabin, it certainly was a palace! Unfortunately, the roof leaked, the basement flooded, and Clancy kept hiking the rent.

"Hi, Peter! Howzit going?" was always Clancey's opening gambit when he met Peter, and then he would whine about the wear and tear to his house caused by "all those snot-nosed kids." Caleb and his younger siblings used to try to get close to him just to catch a delicious whiff of the whiskey, tobacco, and aftershave lotion that Clancy liberally applied. "Get those @#& kids away from me!" he would swear at Peter. "Whatever possessed you to get a passel of money suckers like that?" This was invariably followed by a demand for ten dollars more to be added to next month's rent.

Peter hated trouble and would agree, but Kate finally had enough. She first confronted Clancy with her fractured English. "If I ever hear you cursing, or swearing, or using ugly language around my children again, I will complain to the police." Then, without a word to anyone, she went to the local lawyer and returned with a rental agreement that stipulated how rent increases and tenant complaints would be handled. Clancy fumed and threatened to evict the family but ended by signing the agreement. All the children were proud of their Mom because of her indomitable spirit and keen sense of justice.

The question, "What was in the forbidden room?" piqued the curiosity of Caleb and his sisters. Clancy had one locked room in the house, which he warned them all not to enter. He might as well have waved a red flag in front of a bull. One Phillips screwdriver was all it took to gain entrance into a room of wonder: all the fine furniture of Clancy's departed wife or significant other, party clothes, and above all, a record player with a stack of long-playing records by RCA Victor. Country Western star Wilf Carter yodeling and singing "In the Blue Canadian Rockies" trilled throughout the house. Doris Day, Patsy Cline, and Slim Whitman all contributed to the learning of English, as well as a whole new genre of music.

Clancy had claimed to be a bachelor, but he'd lied. It was evident in the forbidden room that somewhere in the past there had been a lady in his life. No bachelor would ever have collected all the feminine articles stashed in the treasure room. The neighbours gossiped that he had beat her and she had run away. The dreaded cry, "Clancy's coming!" would necessitate a frantic scramble to replace the forbidden items in their proper places and to bolt the door. Inevitably a time came when Clancy did find out that his renters had been in the room, and after an eviction notice was served, the Nachtegals had to vacate the house. He also threatened to sue Peter over the extra toilet that had been framed in and placed in the basement. This time, however, he went too far and beat a hasty retreat when he saw the anger in Peter's eyes and the huge clenched fists. With four family members contributing income, it was now possible to purchase their own home, and that was what Peter did.

***

School of Hard Knocks

The summer of 1952 was dry and hot, with endless play and adventure for Caleb and his younger siblings. "Caleb," his new friend, Cleever, asked, "can you get a box of matches?"

"Certainly," he retorted, "be back in a sec." He knew exactly where his mom hid them and was soon back with a full box of Eddy's Sure-Lite Matches. Cleever demonstrated how to light a small patch of grass and then extinguish the flames with wet jute gunny bags. The patches of fire became larger and larger, and then a sudden gust of wind carried the fire into the adjoining pine forest. The pine trees exploded with a roar and crackle that terrified everyone!

Cleever and his brother took off like shots, only stopping to yell, "It's all your fault, Caleb! You were supposed to put the fire out!"

Three Nachtegals all ran home as fast as they could, and young sister Mirjam and Caleb crawled under their Mom and Pa's bed. They could hear the wail of the arriving fire trucks and the yelling of the fire fighters from their hideaway.

Before long, an RCMP constable knocked at the door and told Peter that the neighbours had seen his children start the blaze. "We have it on good authority that there are children in this house who were at the scene, and we want to speak to them," commanded the constable called "Big Jim."

Peter's long arm snaked under the bed, and with each retraction, a crying, terrified child was pulled out. A stern lecture by the constable, a sound spanking from their Pa, and a week of removed privileges had the desired effect. A budding career of becoming an arsonist was nipped in the bud.

In September, Caleb went back to school and was again placed in grade one. Walking home in a daydream of new impressions, he was confronted by an older student. The sudden shock and pain of a fist driving into his mid-section dropped Caleb whimpering onto the gravel road beside the school. Another nightmare was coming true. He managed to gasp out, "Why did you do that?" Two hard kicks followed in response. Butch Neban was feared in Sears Elementary by all the students and most teachers, and somehow, unfortunately, Caleb had attracted his attention. "Dutchies are DP's (displaced persons), and if you ever wear those knickerbockers to school again, I'll tear them off," he calmly told Caleb, and then he walked away without a backward glance.

That evening, Caleb told his parents that he wanted them to buy him a pair of blue jeans to wear to school. "There's no money to buy jeans, Caleb," they responded. "Besides, you have four pairs of perfectly good corduroy pants to wear, given to us by your doting aunties. Blue jeans wear out quickly, but corduroy lasts forever." After he adamantly claimed four days of being sick, his mom gave in and presented him with a new pair of blue jeans.

Butch looked Caleb over on his first day back at school and announced for all to hear, "He's okay now." Butch never spoke to Caleb or bothered him again. Sears Elementary was a large school, and it was there that Caleb first encountered bullying, racism, and close contacts with native school children.

"Caleb, come to the front of the class at once!" yelled his grade one teacher, Mrs. Dinty. He was still not comprehending all that was spoken to him, and when the long, leather rawhide strap came out, he had no idea what it was for. He was surprised that such a decrepit old lady could provide such hard smacks on each hand. The pain was excruciating, and he was now aware why his classmates spoke in hushed tones about "the strap." The punishment was given in order to teach him that Dutch kids needed to be put in their place. It was the first time Caleb had seen an adult with hate-filled eyes directed toward him. Mrs. Dinty later rued that unfair punishment, because when Caleb's Mom saw his swollen hands that night, her eyes shot blue fire and she marched straight into the principal's office the next day.

With her broken English and the hand gestures that hearkened back to her French heritage, Kate clearly conveyed her outrage over Caleb's strapping. "No! No! Mrs. Nachtegal, we do not hate Dutch immigrants," placated principle Herman. "Rest assured that I take this very seriously and will investigate," he promised. It was the latest incident in a long list occasioned by Mrs. Dinty's alcoholism, which caused her permanent removal from the grade one classroom.

Mrs. Stenson, Caleb's grade three teacher, liked him. Caleb liked school and was eager to learn all that he could. The school day started with the Lord's Prayer and then the class sang "O Canada." The day ended with the singing of "God save our gracious Queen." Caleb loved to sing and did so with gusto. No one in the class could match his volume when it was time to sing the anthems.

"Does anyone know another name for the bubonic plague?" Mrs. Stenson would ask the class during Social Studies, with a warning look at Caleb to be quiet. He had a nasty habit of yelling out the answer without being asked. He would cringe, however, when no one knew the answer, because then with a smile, turning to him, she would say, "Does 'my boy' know the answer?" This habit of hers did not endear Caleb to his classmates and often entailed more fisticuffs after school.

Caleb did not physically retaliate during his first years at school, but one day his Mom took him aside. "Son, I know that you've been taught that Christians shouldn't retaliate when they're abused, because retaliation begets more violence, but what is happening to you is different. When people bully other people, they need to be stopped. You often come home with dirty, torn clothes, and I want it to stop. Remember how I had to stop Mr. Clancy when he tried to intimidate us? You're tall and strong, so fight back if they pick on you." He wondered about the theological correctness of his Mom's reasoning, but Caleb did obey her.

The next time Billy Regan tripped him in the hall, Caleb turned with a cocked fist and let him have it. It took the rest of the school year for the bullies to get used to the fact that he was no longer a punching bag, but they did get it. Fighting usually occurred at recess times, or if it became serious, after school. Caleb's most effective fighting strategy was a closed fist feint to the right and then a tripping motion to his left. He then applied a nelson armlock on his opponent's neck, or at times on a bossy sister, and that hold could not be broken. There was no playground supervision, and teachers seldom interfered. Fighting would often start as a result of the games that were played. If any boy won too many marbles, gathered too many hockey cards, or paid too much attention to a popular girl, jealousies were aroused. It would start with pushing and shoving and then escalate to name-calling. If no one backed down, the fist blows would start, followed by wrestling holds that sought to choke the opponent. The magic words, "I give up," would almost always end the altercation, and the games would go on. It became a regular part of school life, but Caleb never forgot the terror and fright of the first episodes.

Hockey and Other Fine Games

"Hey perfessor!" was followed by a friendly poke between Caleb's shoulder blades from Ned Arnold. "Can you please tell me how to spell 'the'?" Ned was having his usual difficulty with the short story assignment, and Caleb usually ended up writing it for him. "I really appreciate your help, and to show you that you're an okay guy for a Dutchie, I'd like to give you my second best pair of skates, plus I'll teach you some cool wrestling tricks." Ned was a great example of how talents are distributed to people. Somewhat light in the brains department, he certainly was the best skater Caleb had ever seen. To see him and Beverly Lane skating together to the music of "Sail Along Silvery Moon" was a pure delight. "C'mon Caleb!" he insisted, "You can't live in Sears and not play hockey!"

That evening, Caleb asked his mom and pa if he could practice two evenings a week on the Sears junior hockey team.

"There's no money for any equipment," Pa stated, "but if you can get it for free, then it's okay with me."

Rolled up Simpsons-Sears catalogues served as shin pads, and with three thick sweaters and Ned's skates, he was ready to play hockey.

"Those aren't ankles, Caleb," joshed Ned, "those are sticks."

Caleb was painfully aware of his skinny calves and thin ankles, and it soon became apparent that his skating skills were less than stellar. Ned tried his very best to help him, but Coach Laveck took him aside after the third practice and convinced Caleb that hockey was just not in his future.

Placing his arm around Caleb's skinny shoulders, he remarked, "Basketball, boy. Yesiree, that's the game for you. Skinny and tall is good for basketball."

Years later, a scout from the National Hockey League observed Ned playing hockey and remarked, "Gimme twelve pairs of legs like the ones on that boy, and I could win the Stanley Cup." Ned was sent to a farm team to play but was released when he proved to be incapable of learning the most basic plays.

"No more pencils, no more books, no more teachers' dirty looks," was the ditty that ended each school year and then it was glorious summer holidays. Sears was the perfect place to be an adventuresome nine-year- old. Outfitted with bikes, surgical rubber slingshots, fishing poles, and sharp hatchets, Caleb and his friend Nelus sallied forth like David Livingstone in the darkest jungles of Africa. Forests, streams, and lakes were everywhere around Sears, ready for exploration.

"Who are you planning to marry when we finish building this log cabin?" inquired Nelus. "Every cabin needs a girl to keep it neat and tidy!" he exclaimed. "I intend to remain a bachelor, but I've seen you looking at my sister."

"Carly? Nah. It will have to be Cheryl-Lou," Caleb replied. "She told me she likes me. And by the way, why does it have to be me that gets married? You're older than I am."

Often they would go on hunting expeditions to shoot red squirrels, which were considered to be pests. They became deadly slingshot hunters and would get a twenty-five cent (two bits) bounty for every squirrel tail they delivered. When a dollar was earned, they would be off to the pool hall, where four packs of hockey cards, with bubble gum in each pack, cost one dollar. Caleb collected the entire roster of the six-team National Hockey League, except for Jersey Number 7, Ted Lindsay, who played left wing for the Detroit Red Wings. Only two of Ted's cards were to be found in all of Sears, and no amount of bribing or cajoling by Caleb could convince the owners to part with Ted.

Long, hot summer days meant that underage children often went to the lakes to try their hand at swimming. The lonely lakes were mostly unsupervised, and very few elementary students had swimming lessons or could swim adequately. Trial and error was the method, and furious dog-paddling was the stroke of choice. Every summer there were drownings, and though Caleb and his friends had close calls, tragedy was for a time averted.

"Caleb, can we hitch a ride on your bike to Dude Lake?" asked his sister and her friend Carly, who was Nelus's sister.

She was blonde and pretty and Caleb liked her. "Sure," he replied. "Mirjam, you go on the handlebars, and Carly can sit on the cross-bar in front of me." The trip to Dude Lake was about two miles with steep hills on the way, and it took all his energy to get there. An afternoon of fun and swimming ended and the threesome began the bike ride back home.

In the middle of the steepest descent, both girls started yelling and laughing, "Faster Caleb, faster, pedal your heart out!" His legs became a blur of motion, and at top speed the entire bike disintegrated. Both girls pitched headfirst onto the gravel road, and Caleb fell right on top of them. Mirjam's and Carly's legs were raw hamburger from ankle to thigh, and their screams of pain continued unabated on the long walk back home. Caleb escaped, physically unscathed, but in sympathy cried as loudly as the girls. It took a long time for the girls to heal from that accident, and the scars always remained. Caleb never triple rode again on the new bike that he earned after doing a year of chores.

Horrors and Adventures

It was not yet time to get up, but his upstairs bedroom was filled with eerie, flickering light. Caleb looked out of the dormer window and saw that the low tar-paper shack beside their house was engulfed in flames. Gouts of water from the fire truck smashed into the Nachtegals' house to prevent it from igniting. Screaming children and adults with their clothes on fire ran out, or were being carried out of the burning shack. Five of the eight First Nations people who were crowded into the shack perished in the flames that night. Thin sheet metal heaters called "air-tights" were popular with many people who lived in poorly insulated homes. They provided instantaneous heat and burned easily obtainable waste wood. Often when left unattended, the air-tights and the overhead pipes would become red hot and ignite the surrounding wood framing.

"Will they all go to heaven?" Caleb and his sisters, Mirjam and Anna, asked their parents after the ambulances had taken the charred bodies away.

"We don't know where people go when they die, my children," Pa gently explained. "They're in God's hands, and He is fair and righteous."

On at least two occasions, it was only by Kate's fearful vigilance that fire in the Nachtegals' own home was prevented. The first occurrence happened when the carpenter who had finished the renovations to the living room had not left sufficient clearance between the stove pipe and the Donna-Conna finishing panels. It was one of those desperately cold January evenings when Peter had loaded the living room stove with sufficient wood to prevent the family, and the plumbing, from freezing during the night.

Kate's terrified screaming jolted everyone awake. "Peter! Peter! Children! Wake up and get out of the house! The house is on fire!" Peter stood bare chested in his underwear and completely ignored Kate's good advice. His huge calloused hands ripped the smoldering panels and wood framing from around the red-hot pipe, and he threw them outside into the snow. Kate threw a bag of salt into the stove to douse the flames and then buckets of water finished the job. It was a joy and a comfort to their children to see how their parents could work as a team when disaster threatened them, but it was during the aftermath that the accusations flew. "How many times have I told you not to put so much wood in the stove at night?" Kate upbraided her husband. "Why did you hire such a lousy carpenter who did such sloppy work?" she continued.

Peter rolled his eyes and placated his Kate by acknowledging, "It was your vigilance that God used this evening to save our lives, Kate." As he sank down on his knees, he humbly prayed, "Let us give thanks to God."

The next occurrence was caused by a pan of soup overheating and burning while Kate was attending to a child's emergency. It was not as serious as the first fire, but any fire could turn the poorly-designed house into a lethal fireball in a matter of minutes. The insulation used in the construction of most Sears homes was dried wood shavings from the local planer mill. One spark was all that was needed to start a deadly conflagration.

***

Hey-Ho off to Work We Go

"What's the matter, you skinny little bugger?" yelled the red-faced, overweight trucker. "Your dad told me you could work like a man, and that's why you were hired. Now hurry up and get those planks up here."

Caleb had been eager to make some extra cash during the summer holidays, and his pa got him a job as a swamper with Deely Trucking. The boss told him that all he needed to do was assist the driver to load his truck with rough cut lumber produced by the local small, portable sawmills. When they arrived at the first sawmill, they found that the beam supporting the stacked load had broken and all the lumber lay scattered in the mud. The driver told Caleb to pick the planks out of the mud and hand them up to him. He stood five feet above Caleb on the truck deck with a wood pick in his hand. Ten planks wide and twenty-two layers high comprised a full load, with each plank weighing fifty pounds or more. Somehow Caleb finished, after six hours of back-breaking labour. Over and over he would pick each plank up at one end, out of the mud, and then drag it onto the end of the truck deck, where the driver kept yelling, "Higher kid! Raise them higher." His huge gut prevented him from reaching down with his pick. Caleb dimly recalled the driver berating him on the long trip back to town through the fog of exhaustion.

"Whad-dya want, kid?" the boss said as Caleb stood in front of his desk.

"You said I'd be paid ten dollars cash for every load we delivered. You also said that all I needed to do was help the driver, not lift the entire bloody load out of the mud by myself," Caleb boldly asserted. "Furthermore, I think I deserve at least fifteen dollars for the work I did."

"Nervy brat," he spat as he rounded his desk and cuffed Caleb on his head. "Get lost and don't let me see you here again."

For the next three days Caleb arrived promptly at 3:30 p.m. to collect his pay, and every time he was told to beat it. On the fourth day, he told his Mom and she went with him, with murder in her eyes. She entered the owner's office without knocking, looked at him and then pointed to Caleb without a word being said.

"You owe me fifteen bucks!" Caleb shouted. He was given his fifteen dollars.

After that learning experience, he worked part-time during summer holidays for his older brother, who had purchased a portable sawmill. The sawmill was twenty miles out of town, located on a steep mountainside. This meant that the crew stayed in a rough cabin during the work week. Caleb had his first experience cooking and doing dishes for the lumberjacks. He loved being with his brother and worked his heart out for him. There was also time to explore the woods and hunt rabbits. When the weather was hot, he'd lay on top of the sawdust pile and dream.

"Wake up, Caleb, wake up! Dreamers become poor, and doers grow rich," brother Jan would tease. "Get down to the cabin and whip up a meal of instant potatoes and pork-n-beans."

Reluctantly, Caleb would emerge from his wonder world where Lucius held sway. He imagined himself driving toward the basketball hoop on his way to score the winning basket in the Sears championship game. After supper, Jan would take out his mouth organ and play a medley of songs from the Second World War. "Tipperary," "Lily Marlene," and many doleful songs about dying and mourning loved ones who had died in battle filled the long evenings. Caleb was fascinated by the guns that hung on the cabin walls. A British made .303 Lee Enfield rifle was the largest and most powerful weapon that brother Jan possessed. The first time he was allowed to fire the .303, it kicked him so hard that he toppled backwards on his duff.

"What should I do with this box of old dirty bullets that are filled with rat turds?" he asked Jan, who was engrossed in reading a romantic novel.

"Whatever," he replied, "don't bother me now."

"Should I throw them in the air-tight stove?" Caleb asked again.

"Sure, sure," Jan mumbled without taking his eyes off the page.

Caleb opened the lid and threw the bullets into the fire. The twenty or so .22 long rifle cartridges went off like the Fourth of July fireworks. Fortunately, no one in the cabin was hit by the flying lead, but the stove looked like perforated cheese.

"Son-of-a-&%$#," yelled Jan. "You stupid idiot! What possessed you to do a dumb thing like that!"

"I-I-I asked you and you said I could," Caleb blubbered, trying to dodge the cuffs and kicks Jan aimed at him.

When Kate heard about the incident she was mortified. "It will be a miracle if that boy ever reaches the age of twenty-one," she moaned.

Camp Robbers

Caleb snatched at the white and grey whiskey jack and missed as it swooped into the cabin, opened its beak, and picked up his cheap Timex watch off the table. It then flew out the door to the top of the tallest jack pine tree beside the cabin. Olaf, the tree faller, called them camp robbers, and it was an apt description. The bird's camouflage colouring made them hard to spot, and any shiny object or scraps of food were quickly snatched and placed in their nests high up in the trees.

It was the stealing of his change money beside the camp cot that finally galvanized Caleb into action. Olaf's advice was to trap a number of the birds and cage them to scare away the others. "Yes! Yes! C'mon," Caleb whispered to himself as the cagey bird inched toward the shiny tinsel he had placed under the empty dynamite box. One end of the heavy wooden box was propped up with a stick that was attached to the string in his hand. Curiosity won the day, and he soon had six raucous, noisy whiskey jacks penned in a steel mesh cage. Capturing the birds solved the problem of further robberies, but he still needed to get his treasures out of the nest. Instantly, the solution came to him: his brother's gun. He took the .22 repeater from the wall mount, and with a box full of shells, he started to whittle away at the branch holding the largest nest. He used up five dollars' worth of shells to retrieve two dollars of possessions.

"You need to count the cost, Caleb." Brother Jan remonstrated. "You thought of a solution but failed to reckon the price. You could accomplish the same goal by taking several strips of lumber and screwing them together to make a long pole. When the pole is long enough to reach the nest, then you can poke it to the ground." He proceeded to put his instruction into practice, and soon all the nests were brought down. A treasure trove of spoons, coins, jewellery, and sundry objects were retrieved and returned to their rightful owners. Jan's solution to the problem was smarter than Caleb's, but using the gun was more fun.

***

Morality Learning Situations

After the second week of grade four, Caleb was summarily ordered to the front office. "Why did you steal Jonas's guitar?" were the first words he heard from Mrs. Newlands, the new Sears Elementary School principal.

"Wh-a-a-a-at do you mean?" he stuttered. "I never saw or took anybody's guitar."

"Jonas and two other students saw you remove the guitar with its case while they were serving detentions. They identified you by the eagle crest on the back of your coat," she snapped. Caleb's heart sank as he remembered that he had lent his coat to Freddy during recess.

Freddy Star's mother was dead and his father was one of the many town drunks that hung around the beer parlours on Main Street. Freddy had a generous nature but never viewed property rights in the same way that most of his classmates did. He also fiercely defended his dad if anyone put the old man down.

Caleb refused to speak and was strapped for the second time in his life. This time he was also spanked at home, because his parents were informed and required to pay for the stolen guitar. One week later, he was again called to the office, and there were Freddy and his father standing beside the principal. The stolen guitar was also present. Freddy didn't apologize for stealing the guitar, but he said he was sorry for the trouble he had caused his friend. Freddy never finished grade four, and soon after he moved with his father to another Native reserve. Caleb never saw him again. When Caleb graduated from grade six (the last year of elementary school), not one of the Native children, who Caleb had started grade one with, were in public school anymore. Bright, laughing children suddenly became adults who missed the carefree teenage years and then disappeared from school for good. *What will happen to me when I grow up?* Caleb wondered. *Will God guide and teach me, or shall I have to find my own way?* Ambition stirred within him, and a surge of desire to make something of himself pervaded his whole being.

***

Fear gripped the entire town of Sears during the polio epidemic of 1955. Bernard Jolson was the only son of a successful Sears businessman. He was also Caleb's friend and had a quiet courage that everyone who knew him admired. When his classmates played "dare," Bernie always dared. When Caleb asked where Bernie was one day, the teacher informed the class that Bernie's absence from school was caused by a nasty flu. Bernie died three weeks after contracting polio. Those who didn't die were often crippled by this dreaded killer.

What a blessed day it was when Dr. Jonas Salk discovered the polio vaccine, which has wiped this disease from most of the world. It seemed that every winter, legions of people spent many weeks in misery with illnesses like measles, flu, colds, pinkeye, earaches, boils, warts, and other bodily ailments. Many parents refused to allow vaccinations, even when they were freely available. Fear, ignorance, and misguided religious views contributed to unnecessary illness and death. Kate was a wonderful nurse for her family during illness episodes and possessed healing hands. "You are my boy," she softly whispered with her dry, warm hands on Caleb's feverish forehead as he endured his annual flu. "You are a Bedard, in looks and nature, just as surely as your older and younger brothers are Nachtegals, in the image of your pa." As he grew older and stronger, the frequent illnesses of youth disappeared, but his Mom's love and support were always there.

***

Ying and Yang nearly ripped the leashes out of Caleb's hands with a pull of wild exuberance. His principal in grade six, Mrs. Newlands, was also his teacher. She allowed Caleb to exercise her two boxer dogs during school hours and would ask him to make her bank deposits at the same time. During Christmas Advent, she allowed him to take his toboggan and hatchet and find a bushy spruce tree growing in the surrounding woods. Then the whole school would take part in putting the ornaments on the tree. They had a special bond after the "stealing" incident of grade four, and she was always looking for ways to express her trust in him. She had no children of her own but made her pupils her surrogate children. She was an excellent, original teacher with a great sense of humour. She never talked about God, nor did she attend church, but Caleb always thought that she was a believer. Her husband was dour and anti-social so they were called the "odd couple." People gossiped about how such a smart lady could marry such a dull man.

Worship Call

Sunday was "going to church day." Caleb's parents attended two worship services every Sunday in the Reformed Church of Sears. When they first moved to Sears, Peter and Kate's intention was to join an existing church. Since they were Protestants, Peter looked for a congregation that was faithful to the teachings of the Bible and the principles of the Great Reformation. He determined to attend church services in the Sears Pentecostal Assembly, since the sign in front of the church said that this assembly was a "Bible-Believing Church." Shortly after the service had started, people became excited. "Hallelujahs" were shouted from all sides, and people stood up with outstretched arms, moaning. Peter and Kate's sense of decorum was offended. This certainly was not the worship style that they were used to. It was during the passionate altar call that Peter became very worried. Some of his daughters were so mesmerized by the minister's preaching that they stood up in order to walk to the front, heeding the altar call. Their parents quickly pulled them back and then hastily exited the assembly.

"In a faithful Christian church everything is done with decency and in good order," explained Pa when the family arrived back home. "We go to church to hear God's message, not to make a spectacle of ourselves." Soon after, with the help of the Reformed church in Clayton, a new Reformed church in Sears was instituted. The worship services on Sunday were full of awe and respect for the greatness of God. Emotion was encouraged but tempered with biblical knowledge. Caleb had always known that God was there, but it took some time for him to realize that He was also really there for him in a personal way.

***

The eerie silence jolted Caleb awake. He slowly opened his eyes from a deep sleep and realized that everyone in church, including the minister, was looking at him. He had fallen from the front church bench and continued sleeping, curled up on the wooden floor. Being a borderline narcoleptic often got him into trouble in church, as well as in school. His father, who was an elder, walked across the church and chunked him firmly back on the bench, with a promise in his eyes that more discipline would be coming later. And it did.

Caleb also practised his mimicking skills in church. Facial tics, gaits of various members, the singing styles especially of some of the older members, as well as the preaching orations used by visiting ministers were all fair game. Occasionally he would be admonished by those who realized what he was doing, but it was often accompanied by a small smile. Caleb had always been a people-watcher and often needed to repress himself when he saw a humorous character. He later was amazed and delighted to see the same proclivities surfacing in his children and grandchildren.

Amidst all the distractions, he often still listened carefully to the sermons of the preachers. After supper was over on Sundays, he would pepper his Pa and Mom with endless "why" questions. I, Lucius, reminded him that God was real, but he wanted to know why things were the way they were. Sometimes he found that life was not fair. "Where do I come from? Why am I here? Where am I going?" were percolating in his mind at an early age.

"That's enough, Caleb, you have exhausted my answers," his Pa would expostulate, ending the "why" session for another Sunday.

Kate would smile and say, "Never lose your wonder and curiosity, son, about why we're living on this beautiful planet."

Economics 101

Money was always a problem during those first years in Canada. There was never enough of it. Kate liked to spend, and Peter was determined to save for the day when he could buy the farm of his dreams. Banks were not to be trusted, so he hit upon the idea of hiding a stash of money in an empty soup tin, which he then hid in the woodshed. Caleb quickly noticed his pa's interest in the shed, which heretofore had been his domain. The tin was soon discovered, and Caleb triumphantly presented it to his Mom. When Peter came home that evening, he was astounded to see that all the children had new shoes and coats! "Did the church deacons come this morning, Kate?" he asked.

"The most amazing thing happened, Peter," Kate gushed. "Caleb has found a substantial amount of money, and when I found out that the neighbours hadn't lost it, I went on a much-needed shopping trip."

"Where did you find that money, Caleb?' Peter asked his son with an ominous tone. Caleb was quietly edging toward the door when his Pa's long muscular arm snaked out. It was a great day for his mom and siblings, but not so good for him.

Pa continued his saving practices, but now the Royal Bank of Canada was the recipient of his funds. After seven years of hard work, and with the contributions of the older working children, Peter, at age fifty-seven, bought 160 acres of hilly, rocky, and partially wooded land. "Look at that view, wife and children!" he enthused as his family stood on top of the steep hill where the old log house was standing. "Every morning when we awake, the valley, river, lakes, and mountain glaciers will remind us of God's greatness."

"It is truly beautiful, Pete!" Kate replied. "Unfortunately, you can't eat beauty. May I ask how you propose to make a living here?"

"Details, Kate, just details," Peter replied, his enthusiasm not dimmed a whit. "This is ours, truly ours, and we'll turn it into a fine home." The older children were opposed to moving from their comfortable home in town to a rocky outpost with no indoor plumbing. "Stop your opposition, Kate," Peter sternly admonished. "All my life I've yearned to own my own farm. I've leased, rented, and worked for others, and now God has given me a chance to have my own farm."

"You may call that a farm," Kate interjected, "but I can't see how you can ever provide a living for your family on that rock pile. Listen to me, Peter. I will support you, but I do not approve of this venture." Pete smiled to himself, knowing that he had won the contest of wills this time.

Only the four youngest children made the move with their parents, since the older siblings were either married or working and rented their own places in town.

Amazingly, everyone's predictions proved to come true. The farm never was able to provide an adequate living, which would have enabled Pa to quit his day job. It did, however, prove to be a wonderful place to live. Kate always called the ten farm years the most satisfying and happy years of her life.

CHAPTER III

On the Farm—The Bucolic Years

Survival of the Fittest

In 1958, Peter Nachtegal bought a quarter section of hilly, rocky land eight miles northwest of Sears. The view was fantastic, but this farm would never provide a viable living for his family. Kate was initially opposed, but when the move was done, she gave all of her considerable talents to making the old farmhouse home. No running water and no indoor toilet made for a rustic existence. Whatever could be improved by paint and scrubbing was soon done, and the partially insulated attic provided sleeping quarters for three girls and two boys.

Two horses, three hundred chickens, and twenty beef cows rounded out the inventory of farm animals. Eighty acres of fertile but steep slopes provided the arable land for growing hay, grain crops, vegetables, and potatoes. "I think we can make a good living here, Caleb," his Pa reassured him as he chewed on a Timothy hay blade while holding a pail containing his last egg collection.

"I can't see it, Pa," Caleb replied, "but you're the farmer, and I hope you know what you're doing. Just in case, though, Pa, I'd hold on to your day job if I were you."

Peter smiled knowingly with a look he reserved for junior intellects and replied, "When you're mature you can pick out a fine strong farm girl, Caleb. Marry her and then we can purchase the neighbour's farm together, and you can make a good living."

Caleb smiled back at his Pa but didn't reveal that his plans were moving in a different direction.

***

Brothers

Older brother Jan's red Mercury pickup stood idling by the wood pile as Caleb piled into the passenger seat. Jan always asked Caleb to come along on Saturday afternoons to watch sporting events in Sears and to enjoy ice cream and cinnamon bun treats. Mr. Wing baked the best cinnamon buns that Caleb had ever tasted, and they were always superb. Soft and white, with just the right amount of icing, he would buy a dozen and they would all be gone by the end of Saturday.

"Sorry, Caleb," Jan curtly blurted, "you can't come along with me today."

"Why not, Jan? You always let me come along before," Caleb demanded to know.

"I know, Caleb, but now I have a girlfriend, and you'd be in the way. Please understand that it just will not do," he concluded with finality.

"You mean to say that you'd prefer to be with some silly girl rather than enjoy the great time we always have?" Caleb spat out with the hurt of rejection. "Pa is right about you. He told me that you put yourself ahead of your family and can't be depended upon," Caleb vindictively yelled, with tears spurting from his eyes.

Soon after, having communed with his inner Lucius, he apologized to Jan for his mean remarks and learned another valuable life lesson. The bond between a man and woman who are in love is the strongest human tie that exists.

***

The sweat ran in rivulets down Caleb's face as younger brother Brock and he picked rocks after the August harvest was done. "How did we ever land up on this rotten place?" his exasperated younger brother gasped. "In town we had it made, Caleb, and then Pa had to go and ruin it all."

"Shut up and keep picking, kid," Caleb replied. "The sooner we finish this field, the sooner we can go to the lake for a dip."

Brock glared and then quickly chucked a rock at Caleb. He retaliated by putting him into the nelson headlock until he promised to behave. They loved each other as brothers but were very different in appearance and temperament. Caleb was four years older than Brock but had great difficulty besting him in frequently occurring wrestling matches. At ten years of age, Brock was already showing promise of inheriting the powerful build of his Pa, and he enjoyed wrestling with all comers at Sears Elementary School.

Short summers and frosty autumns were soon followed by the long Sears winters. The old farmhouse that the Nachtegals lived in was not built to withstand the harsh temperatures. Caleb awoke in the middle of a bitterly cold January night to the sound of clicking teeth.

"Caleb, wake up," chattered Brock. "I'm so cold, I think I'm going to die."

The outside -35°F temperature was not much colder than inside the uninsulated part of the attic where Brock and Caleb slept. The stars were plainly visible between the large cracks in the cedar shingles.

"Give me a hand dragging the mattress from that unused bed over our blankets," Caleb told Brock as he rubbed his blue hands and feet. They pulled on all their clothes and then hugged each other to build up some heat. As they started to thaw out, the problem of full bladders, stimulated by the cold, became unbearable. The girls had filled the large white chamber pot and it had frozen solid. There was no way that they would be able to reach the outhouse in time, and they had no intention of trying. Both then proceeded to pry open the one small window and then they let 'er fly.

The next morning at breakfast, Pa remarked, "It was the strangest thing last night, Kate. It was cold and there wasn't a cloud in the sky, but I could have sworn that I heard rain falling outside."

Hayseed

Graduating to junior high school and moving to the farm had a great impact on Caleb as he entered the teenage years. He had always liked girls, having grown up with seven mostly-doting sisters, but it was in grade seven that he started to really like them. Elvis Presley haircuts, engineer boots with chains, and black leather jackets were a must-have in order to be cool. Impressing the girls was the intent, but milking cows at 6:00 a.m. and then trying to get the offensive smell off his hands was definitely not cool.

Pa was making increasing demands of Caleb, who often reacted by erupting into a frenzied, screaming rage. "Why do I always have to do everything around here?" he would arrogantly yell as he manoeuvred away from Pa's fist.

"We made a deal, boy, and I'm holding you to it!" Pa yelled back. "Stand still so I can teach you not to yell at your parents."

A few hard cuffs followed, but Caleb had become expert in learning how to move away and minimize the impact. A period of sullen silence and resentment usually lasted for the rest of the day, and then the matter was forgotten. Well, arrogance was about to take a fall.

Into the Fire

Peter Nachtegal had a peculiar way of drawing out the "a" in Caleb whenever he had something to say that required him to do a chore. "Ca---leb, come here, I have something important to tell you! Sit down, son, and listen carefully so that I don't have to repeat myself. I'm capable of growing crops and raising chickens, and I also need to hold down a full-time job to make ends meet. You, son, have a talent that I never possessed; you are a natural with machinery. Your three-month summer vacation is coming, and you'll handle the field work using the machinery. You'll also take care of the livestock. Your older brother needs to work at the sawmill and is planning to marry, so we can expect no help from him. Tell me son, can you handle that?"

"Sure, Pa, no problem. Leave it to me!" Caleb responded with all the chutzpa of thirteen years.

"That's settled then, and I hereby appoint you Number One Farmhand, with your younger brother and sister under your authority," he finalized.

Caleb could barely wait to exercise his new authority. "Bro ---ck," he soon yelled, followed by "Pho ---- ebe," which soon provoked a full- scale rebellion.

"Go fly a kite," was Brock's response, followed by more not-nice words. Fiery Phoebe launched a full-scale frontal attack with raking fingernails that precipitated a strategic retreat.

"Caleb," his Pa instructed, "use the carrot and stick approach with your sibs, and don't come running to me when they don't listen."

It took a whole summer of cajoling, threatening, and the occasional physical altercation, but by compromising they did manage to get a lot of work done.

On the Farm—The Bucolic Years

"Child abuse, Peter, that's what it is!" scolded Kate when Peter told her that Caleb would be handling the machinery. "That boy is barely dry behind his ears, and he's not ready to work with those dangerous animals. One kick from that wild Nelly horse and he'd be dead."

"How many times must I tell you to keep your nose out of my business," Peter railed back. "I will decide if Caleb is ready or not to do the work." Caleb walked away from the heated argument, confident that he could do the work, yet also realizing that Pa had no idea what that work entailed.

Every time Caleb experienced a machinery break-down, his Pa would become very excited. "How is it possible, Caleb?" he would yell with exasperation. "Ten minutes ago it was working perfectly, and now you say it's not working! I never break down, so how can a strong steel machine quit just like that?"

At first he tried to explain the problem, but he soon gave up and just endured the endless "whys." He somehow understood that a man who was never sick or fatigued could not understand weakness in others or in machinery.

"Whoa, Nelly, whoa, girl," Caleb cajoled when the large brown mare rolled her eyes and flattened her ears. Gas powered Tractors he could handle okay, but he had not realized that his pulling power would be two large, half-wild horses. Stan, the former farm owner, promised Peter that he would fully train Caleb to work with the horses.

"Don't you worry none, Peter," he reassured him, barely missing his shoe with a stream of tobacco juice. "When I'm done with the lad, he'll be a top-notch horse drover. He looked at Peter with his sly, conniving face and made Caleb realize how easily his Pa could be hoodwinked. "Relax, kid," he sneered when Peter was out of earshot. "Feed them peppermints, boy, when they perform well," he advised Caleb, "and lay on the whip if they become lazy". Having spoken those words of pathetic advice, followed by another stream of brown tobacco juice out of the corner of his mouth, which narrowly missed Caleb, he jumped in his rattletrap Dodge pickup and sped away. They never saw him again.

It took Caleb three hours to harness Nelly and Tommy for the first time. Nelly snaked her head in a vicious arc to try and bite him, and Tommy aimed a kick his way. That only angered Caleb, and when he brought out the corded leather whip, the horses quickly settled down. The two chestnut brown horses made a beautifully matched team and were a sight to behold. He soon discovered that horses had temper tantrums just like people. When they behaved, he treated them like royalty, but they soon learned to fear him when they did not listen. He would never be a horse whisperer.

Mowing the hayfields was the first order of business, and after Caleb hitched the horses to the mower, he jumped on the steel seat, snapped the reins, and off they went. There were no problems in the first field. The grass was sparse and the slope was gentle. The mower blade whirred in its holder, driven by the rotation of the steel, notched mower wheel. A green cascade of grass fell behind the blade, and Caleb was waving to his watching siblings while standing on the steel hubs of the mower with the manner of a conquering Roman general. Peter turned to Kate with a gleam of triumph. "Admit it now, Kate, that boy can do it. I told you so."

The second field was steep and had a thick growth of grass. Tommy balked at climbing the hill, and Caleb's philosophy of being kind to animals was put to the test. Peppermints did not work, but the whip did, and away they went. The first circuit was not yet completed when suddenly the pitman arm, connecting the wheel to the blade, snapped. After that was repaired, the cast iron gearbox broke into shards during the next circuit.

Before the second field was mowed, he was onto the third horse mower and using the first two for parts. Fortunately, they were cheap to buy, since most farmers were switching to tractor-powered mowers. Caleb became adept at doing the repairs quickly, since any long delay would bring his Pa trotting out to see what was wrong.

"I don't want Caleb mowing on that steep hill and driving those wild horses!" Kate upbraided Peter, with her blue eyes flashing danger. She was heaping mounds of cauliflower and yellow potatoes beside the bear meat on Caleb's plate, and a large pan of vanilla flan was simmering on the cast iron cooking stove. "He's only thirteen," she continued, "and would be unable to stop the horses if they were ever spooked."

Pa carefully staked out a large section of the food he had mashed together, and the children all watched in wonder as he manoeuvred his fork under it and transferred it into his mouth. After some time of contemplative chewing, since most of his molars were decayed, he replied, "Keep quiet, Kate. I started full-time work at ten years old, and Caleb is almost full grown. I will decide, not you, what happens on this farm."

"He is my boy," Kate replied angrily, with tears breaking out, "and I am holding you responsible if anything happens to him."

Increasingly, Caleb noticed that he was becoming a pawn in the disagreements between his parents, and it troubled him when he was asked to side with one or the other.

Calamity

After four days of mowing, Caleb was growing in ability and confidence.

He was also becoming careless and did not check the condition of the horses' harnesses as well as he should have. "Easy, girls, easy!" he yelled as the mower was descending a steep hill. Nelly and Tommy resisted the push of the mower by settling back in their harnesses. The front collar of the harness was attached to the steel ring of the mower double-tree, and all the resistance and stress centred at that point. The leather straps on Tommy's collar broke, and the mower blade skewed around and cut into his rear legs. The screams of the wounded horse were frightening and terrifying. They would echo in his nightmares for months after the accident. Tommy collapsed on to the double-tree, and Nelly panicked and circled the field at full gallop two more times, with the wildly careening mower just missing her by inches. Caleb bumped along the ground behind the mower, tangled in the leather reins that were attached to his waist. "Please, Lord, don't let me die," was the recurring refrain in his brain. It was only after Nelly, covered in lather, was totally exhausted and finally stopped that he managed to break free. Bruised and bleeding, Caleb removed the encircling reins and ran for help.

Kate had hired a carpenter who was installing cabinets in the farm home. After many incoherent attempts, Caleb finally explained what had happened. The carpenter then gathered his cutting tools and they went back to the stricken animals to cut them free. Tommy had to be put down after large doses of penicillin and sulfa drugs failed to halt the infection in his deep wounds. After the loud bark of the Lee Enfield army rifle faded away, all Caleb's sisters broke out into a long crying jag. His father put his hand on Caleb's shoulder after he had put the rifle back on its holding pegs. "It wasn't your fault, son," he comforted. "You handled it like a man." It felt good to have his Pa praise him, but Caleb knew that he had not been careful. Tommy was dead, and he had narrowly escaped serious injury because he had failed to put safety first. He should have carefully checked the harness bindings. A long prayer followed after the evening dinner in which his Pa detailed a long list of dreadful scenarios that could have happened had God not prevented it.

The illustrated Bible, which Peter often read from, had dramatic drawings of horses pulling ancient Pharaoh's chariot. The charcoal and pen drawings of the fiery steeds pulling Elijah the Hebrew prophet into Heaven were fascinating to Caleb and elicited many questions, which always ended with his Pa's exasperated,

"Enough!" Since the dawn of time, man and horses have been together. During times of war, exploration, recreation, and building, these magnificent animals have served mankind and been their companions. Caleb's hopes of becoming a competent horse master were never realized during the ten years that he worked with them. He did not have the patient temperament that a horse handler required.

"You can see it in their eyes, boy," explained Tony, their neighbouring farmer. "When they trust you, they look at you like a woman who loves you."

"What a bunch of blather," snorted his Mom when he told her what Tony had said. "Horses are beasts and have instinct, but do not possess emotions as we do." There were many times, however, that Caleb noticed very human-like emotions in the large, lustrous eyes of the horses that he worked with. The soft nuzzling of large lips on his arms as he forked hay into their bins and the pleasant nickering, which sounded when they were combed and tickled between their ears, were very pleasing and created a bond between horse and human.

Hoodwinked

"Is not responsible, Peter, to lef a young boy to vork wif half-wild horses and vorn-out harness," admonished their Norwegian neighbour, echoing the words of Caleb's mother. "If him vork wif me for a vile so I teach him the vorking safe." After three days of back-breaking labour digging a well, during which he did not learn anything, Caleb told old Lundgren that he was not coming back.

"Vots de matter, boy?" he rasped with his heavy Norwegian accent. "Ven I vas your age, I cud dig twelf huren straight wif no lunch."

When Kate heard that her boy had been digging a horizontal water tunnel fifty feet underground, without cribbing and using dynamite for blasting, she lost it completely. The Nachtegals could hear her yelling at old Lundgren half a mile away. Old Lundgren confided to Peter much later that what Kate had told him was unrepeatable, and the manner in which she did it confirmed his desire to always remain a bachelor. He had been married once upon a time but never spoke about his wife. Peter also found out that he had a daughter.

One fine summer morning as the Nachtegal children walked to the school bus, a handsome, middle aged women with two small girls greeted them. "Hi, kids, I'm Mr. Lundgren's daughter, and I hope we'll get to know you." She smiled at Caleb with a cheery wave and invited all the children to come over sometime and have juice and candies. "Please tell your daddy that he can come too."

Kate soon told her husband to stay away. "That women is divorced and on the prowl," she caustically remarked.

"Oh, come on, Kate" Pa laughed. "You're too old to be jealous."

Comic Relief

Sunday! Beautiful, glorious Sunday! Sleeping in past 7:00 a.m. and a whole day to go to church, visit with friends, and check out the girls. That was the promise of each breaking Sunday. On the farm, however, there were always those emergencies.

"Stop the car right now, Caleb," his Pa commanded as he was about to pull onto the county road.

"What's the problem now, Pa?" Caleb screeched as he slammed the brakes on the yellow Ford station wagon, which he had been driving without a license for years.

"The cows are in the oat field again!" his Pa yelled as he jumped out of the car and tore through the waist-high grain field in his black Sunday suit. "C'mon, everyone, we need to herd them back to the pasture."

"Nice going, Pete!" yelled Kate as the children, in their Sunday finery, all stood bedraggled and wet after the last ornery cow had been penned. "It's a wonder that you're still an elder after missing so many morning worship services. Why don't you build proper fences so those stupid beasts stay in their proper place?"

Peter squashed the anger that flared for a moment in his eyes, and then Phoebe giggled and broke the tension. "Can we take a family picture, Mom? You all look very funny with cow shit streaked all over your Sunday clothes." The whole family roared with laughter, and they enjoyed one of those special times that can never be repeated.

***

"You can do it, Pa," Caleb cajoled. "I'll teach you how to harness the horse and then hitch her to the water sleigh. When I'm in school and Mom runs out of water, you need to be able to bring a fresh water barrel up from the well."

"Your mother is a strong woman son," Pa remonstrated. "She can easily walk to the well and get a pail or two by herself when she runs low." The withering look in Caleb's eyes caused his Pa to mutter, "Okay, I will do my best to try it." After two successful runs, Pa proudly announced, "Caleb is busy with field work, so I'll now provide the household with water.

"Are you sure you can handle that wild beast, Peter?" Kate asked. "We don't need any more accidents around here."

All went well until one fine winter day guests had assembled at the farmhouse. They had parked their cars on the crest of the hill and were enjoying the scenery when Peter arrived with the water sleigh. He slipped and fell on an icy patch and his startled yell caused Nelly, the pulling horse, to bolt. The horrified guests watched as the heavy sleigh side-swiped their shiny cars and sloshed water on the cold metal. Pandemonium reigned, and everyone started yelling in accusatory tones.

"It's all your fault, Caleb," Pa accused him some time after the incident. "That accident cost me a lot of money and made me look very bad in front of our guests. From now on you will be responsible for hauling the water barrel."

"Sorry, Pa," Caleb commiserated, "but did you see the look on the faces of those uppity people? It was priceless!" He quickly dodged the cuff he knew was coming. He stayed out of his Pa's reach for a few days.

Learning the Ropes

Dutchman are often stubborn, and Caleb ran true to type. "We need a tractor, Pa," he insisted. "With a tractor, I can turn this farm into a productive venture."

"Shut up, Caleb," replied his Pa. "I have no more money to buy a tractor."

"What? No more hidden tins of money, Pa?" Caleb teased, remaining a safe distance away. "Surely you can borrow from the bank to buy that sweet, bright red, W-4 McCormack tractor from Bonny's Used Farm Equipment?" He never found out how his Pa financed it, but two weeks later a delivery flat deck truck dumped that same tractor on the yard.

That was a happy day for Caleb, and that tractor and he made a great team. It was not all smooth sailing, of course, but if he forgot about roll-overs, frozen radiators, and other sundry mishaps, then he was left with good memories. Caleb was finally able to enjoy the odd hour of leisure time due to the greater efficiency of the tractor.

The McCormack reaper, built in the previous century and covered with chicken shit, sat in the tool shed with its steel wheel buried six inches into the ground. It had not been used for at least twenty-five years. "Do you think you can get it working, Caleb?" his Pa asked, looking anxiously at him. He knew that if they could not get the reaper to cut and bind the grain, they would have to rent a mobile combine at a considerable expense. The canvas sails on the reaper had many holes, and the gears on the twine tying mechanism were rusted solid.

"Sure, Pa, I can get 'er going," he assured him. "I'll need penetrating oil, two large Stilson wrenches, and a lot of gear grease." Caleb removed the horse hitching mechanism and fabricated a hitch for the tractor. With Caleb driving the tractor and his pa sitting on the steel reaper seat, they harvested and stooked the entire grain crop for that year. It was on the last circuit that the large steel drive wheel broke into four pieces. Caleb carefully lowered the transport wheels and pushed the reaper back into its former resting place. To the best of his knowledge, it is still there today.

Fred Bass was one of the ugliest men Caleb had ever seen. His face gave no indication about his nature, since he was invariably pleasant and easy to get along with.

"Where shall I put 'er?" he asked Caleb, referring to the old decrepit John Deere threshing machine that he pulled behind his pickup.

"Right here, Mr. Bass," he replied, pointing to a level spot beside the old log pole barn. It was always a mystery to him how Fred could keep the old John Deere threshing machine operational. It was rusty and filthy, and all the drive belts had been spliced and patched in many places. The steel hoppers had patches upon rusted patches.

Fred squinted at Caleb in the bright August sun and rolled the huge cud of chewing tobacco to the alternate pouch that had been formed in each cheek. "Yassiree! She's an oldie but a goodie," he would fondly exclaim, wiping a blob of grease from the flywheel and wiping it onto his coverall, which was slick from many such wipes. Mrs. Bass had never put Fred's coveralls into a washing machine, and Caleb was sure that they would have stood up straight and proud even when Fred's ample body was absent. After Fred had looped the drive belt around the drive wheel of the tractor, the old machine would come to life with a banging and screeching that precluded any further speech. Peter and his son forked the grain bundles into the open maw of the thresher.

Mangled straw and empty husks blew out of the rear end of the machine. A steady stream of golden wheat, oats, or barley would flow into a large hopper. According to Fred, his machine produced the cleanest grain and had the least spillage of any machine in the entire valley. Peter always believed him.

Wheeler Dealer

When autumn arrived, Peter would cull the beef cow herd and ship the fattened steers and heifers to market. "Miserable bunch of critters you got here Nachtegal," was the remark that opened the negotiations of cross-eyed Henry Kahl, the local cattle dealer. "Prices are terrible lately, so I can't afford to offer you much for them; even so, I'll have a hard time just getting the money back that I'm willing to pay you." It was always the same song and dance with Henry, and Peter was no match for him.

"Let me negotiate with him, Pa," Caleb would plead, but to no avail. Henry literally stole those animals every fall.

"You must understand, son, that Henry also needs to make a living," his Pa would explain.

"Yes Pa," Caleb answered sarcastically, "Henry has two children and lives in a fine modern home; he is really suffering!"

The low price of the final sale of cows made by his pa was bad enough, but when Henry still had not paid for them after three months Caleb and his Mom both saw red. Peter refused to go and bother Henry to collect his own money, so Caleb's Mom asked him to collect. She promised him a collection bonus if he succeeded. Every second day, promptly at 5:30 p.m., he would knock on Henry's door and get the runaround. Caleb finally ducked under Henry's blocking arm and told his wife that they were unable to buy groceries because of her husband's late payment for the cows. The Kahls were prominent leaders in their church, so this threat to their respectability was too much. Caleb also asked, and received, a 5 per cent late payment charge on the amount of the invoice. His

Mom gave him a great big hug when he gave her the cheque. She immediately went to the bank to cash it before Henry could relent and put a stop-payment on his freshly minted cheque.

"Can I ask you a personal question, Pa?" Caleb asked after the Kahl fiasco. "Why is it that you, who are the strongest and toughest person I know, are afraid to go after shirks and cheaters. You also buy junk from almost every salesman that stops by our farm."

The lightning strike from the feared right-arm started but then stopped in mid-stroke as his Pa looked at him with a strange look. "That's how I was brought up, Caleb, to respect my betters and to not make trouble. I also need to control my temper and not let it get the better of me," he explained. "Remember, son, that Christians do not retaliate when they're wronged. God will repay the wrongdoers." It was good for Caleb to notice that his Pa treated him with a new respect after the Kahl incident. Peter also seldom tried, in the future, to resort to using physical discipline on his son.

Lessons in Politics and Intrigues

Angry voices from the living room disturbed Caleb's sleep, and he noticed that his sisters, Anna and Mirjam, were already kneeling by the open heat register that allowed some heat from downstairs to enter the upstairs area. "Move over, girls," he teased them, "let me in on what they're saying down there." Acrid smoke from the five cigars clenched in five stubbled jaws stung their eyes as they strained to hear every word of the confrontation.

It was the sixth man, Mr. Steen, who was not smoking but yelling, who was at the center of the drama. "Time and again I've been passed over to become chairman of the council, and I've had it with your politicking, Nachtegal!" he yelled at Caleb's Pa. "I may not be able to bribe council members with cigars, but I know that I'm fully capable of providing leadership and being a good chairman."

"I don't think we should be listening to this discussion," Caleb whispered to Mirjam, "Pa will skin us alive if he catches us eavesdropping." The voices dropped to an indistinguishable drone as the young people moved away from the register, but it was very apparent to them that the dignified elders who marched to the front of the church on Sundays were having a serious dogfight.

Not long thereafter, the elders arrived for another meeting at Nachtegals' farmhouse, and a loud snarling noise erupted from the family's usually friendly dog, Sparky. He grabbed the pants of elder Steen in his teeth and nearly knocked him down. Steen pulled away with a frightened look and ran to his car. A strange smile played around Peter's mouth and he later remarked, "That Sparky is a smart dog; he recognizes character, or a lack thereof, when he smells it."

Peter, to Kate's delight, was often chairman of the church council before the church had its own pastor, and he later also became chairman of the Christian School Board.

Dreamer

Crows were cawing safely out of range of Caleb's Cooey .22 repeater rifle as he lay on his back in the tall grass of the south forty acres. The hay had been raked and now he lay daydreaming in the hot August sun, safely hidden from his Pa's view. Lucius took over as his imagination leapt far beyond the little valley town to wonderful scenes found in the picture magazines of *Life* and the dog-eared copies of *National Geographic Magazine.*

His pretty grade seven teacher had told him, "Caleb, you can be anything you want to be," and he believed it. Explorer, scientist, preacher, singer, athlete, or movie star—there were so many choices. Which one should he pick?

Then the small, quiet voice would come. "Caleb, it's not all about you. I am here. I have claimed you, and you must serve Me."

"How, Lord? How do I go about it?" he would yearn, but there was no answer—only a stillness soon interrupted by the crows. There were so many things to contemplate, and he was unable to focus on any one thing for long. Then his thoughts would shift to the only person who he knew would completely understand him. She floated, unobtainable and fantastic before him, but he believed that someday he would find her. His friend Fred already had a steady girl and was talking about a house and marriage, but Caleb was certain that such a relationship with a girl was far ahead in the future for him.

The present receded, and his mind's eye saw the tiny blue planet floating in the periphery of the galaxy. Where was his place on this speck called earth, among the billions of stars in the universe and the billions of humans that swarmed the earth's surface? Caleb wondered, *how did I get here? Am I real or just an illusion?* What was he to make of all the information that streamed into his brain? He had become an omnivorous reader, and Bible readings competed for space with the science fiction books by Isaac Asimov and Larry Niven. He was excited by adventure stories of the great explorers and the wonderful tales of derring-do on the great oceans of the world. Short forays into the works of Shakespeare and the philosophers stirred his imagination.

Fiction works from the local library often contained passages dealing with human sexuality, which often left him feeling confused and excited. His parents' limited knowledge of the English language prevented them from censoring his reading materials, so it was only the elderly librarian who, looking over the rim of her reading glasses at him, would caution, "Sonny, I do not think your selection is appropriate for your age; perhaps you'd consider what I deem to be appropriate."

Science lessons at school taught an entirely different view about the origins of humanity than he had been taught at home and in church. His world view was being formed and his mind grappled with issues that were bewildering.

On Sundays the voice of the preacher intoned, "In six days God made the heavens and the earth, and all that is in them." During Thursday's science class, teacher Fitch insisted that "Only the Theory of Evolution scientifically explains how life came to exist over a period of millions of years on earth. Religious myths and the stories in Genesis are grounded in superstition and fear of the unknown. Only science can rationally explain our existence." One constant, however, emerged and remained: if he was real and possible, then it followed that God could also be real and possible. Science had made tremendous progress possible in using existing resources to change the environment and health care, but it could provide no satisfactory answer to the question, "Who am I?" If God had the power to make the stars and galaxies, then anything and everything was possible for him. The choice was between believing humans, who could not even correctly record or interpret yesterday's news, versus trusting a deity who proclaimed without ambivalence, "I am the truth and always will be." With increasing certainty, Caleb grew to know that Jesus Christ was his Creator God and Saviour.

In Charge ... Sort Of

"Caleb!" his Pa yelled from close range, "how will we ever get the hay in the barn if you lay mooning around all day? Get to work—and I mean right now! Your daydreams about pretty girls will get you into a peck of trouble."

The reverie was broken and he scrambled to his feet. "Yes, Pa, I've finished the raking, and before nightfall I'll have the windrows of hay in the barn." He loved his Pa, but his determination to keep him working every available minute would often bring out the rebel in him. "I am not a slave! I have rights! You never appreciate me!" Caleb screeched as his breaking voice changed into high falsetto. "Other kids my age don't have to work nearly as hard as I do! Give me a break." A blur of motion followed by a hard cuff was usually the end of these outbreaks, but as he became older and stronger, corporal punishments stopped. Caleb's nature repelled all attempts to exercise authority over him, and he found that he shared this trait with most other people.

"You're not my boss, and I will not listen to you!" retorted Brock, Caleb's younger brother. "It's too hot to work, and I'm going fishing."

"Fishing! My foot you are," Caleb yelled. "Pa wants the hay in the barn before nightfall, and you're going to help me." Brock lunged at him and bowled him over, but Caleb soon had him in a nelson headlock. "Promise to listen!" he yelled as he squeezed harder, bending Brock's head forward.

"Never!" he gasped, but the "nevers" became weaker as Caleb increased the pressure, until he finally gasped, "I give up!" It seemed that only physical coercion could bring about Brock's compliance, but Caleb knew that there must be a better way. Youngest sister Phoebe was half Brock's size but made up for her lack of size with spirited compliance. With both his sibs in tow, he proceeded to load the hay on the wagon and offload it into the barn.

It was during the last trip to the barn with the loaded wagon of hay that it happened. Caleb turned the corner too hard and too sharp, and the wagon flipped over. Phoebe was sitting on top of the load and was buried in the cascading mounds of hay. Instantly, Brock and Caleb were pulling and digging into the hay pile, but they could not find her. The realization that their baby sister was suffocating under the huge pile of hay terrified them.

"I see the hay moving," yelled Brock, and sure enough, before long, Phoebe emerged sputtering and coughing. What a relief! They danced and hugged each other with joy. In the space of five minutes they had experienced abject terror followed by ecstatic joy. Phoebe's close brush with death brought about a closer bond with God and a deeper awareness of their own mortality. After supper, their father offered up a prayer of thanksgiving followed up by a stern lecture on safety, and then they reloaded the wagon and finished the job.

New Interesting Neighbours

"Come in!" yelled Kate from the Nachtegals' dinner table. The rattling of the battered old screen door announced that a guest was there.

Monica Goslin, short and well-developed, pushed her way past work boots and coveralls and boldly asked, "How are the Nachtegals today?"

"We're doing just fine," Kate replied with an icy reserve in her voice that remained unnoticed by Monica. "What can we do for you?"

Monica and her parents had just moved into the old Miller farmhouse up the road. Her dad was not a farmer and had rented the old house because the rent was cheap. Monica was making frequent appearances at the Nachtegals' farm, and Caleb's Mom's blue eyes had a look that he knew and feared. Monica's tight sweaters and bold attitude did not please his mother, who correctly divined that Monica was not there to play with the Nachtegal girls. She had tried to sit beside Caleb on the school bus, but he had plainly told her the seat was reserved. It was not that he had no interest in Monica, but it was not cool for his friends to see him sitting beside a girl. "I noticed that Caleb has a new motorcycle," she announced. "I'd sure like to have a ride if he has the time." She was oblivious to the gasps of surprise from the Nachtegal sisters.

"Caleb is busy with his chores," Kate replied. "He has no time to go bike riding with bold girls."

"Well then if Caleb is busy, maybe Brock has time to take me," Monica responded. Brock was able to ride the small Honda bike that Caleb had recently acquired, and he gallantly offered to take Monica for a spin. She jumped behind him and pressed her well-endowed front into his back. When Caleb questioned him later how it had gone, he turned red and told him to mind his own business. Monica's interest soon gravitated to easier conquests, and soon her visits dwindled until they did not see her again. Many years later, they heard that she had become a newspaper reporter.

***

Bending the Rules

Peter was never able to master the intricacies of driving the 1956 yellow Ford station wagon. Kate became the only licensed driver for three of the nine years years that they lived on the farm before Caleb obtained his license. She was terrified to drive in the winter however, when ice and snow covered the roads. She had previously lost control on a black ice patch and had ended up in the ditch. She refused to ever drive in winter conditions again. Peter had an ingenious solution, which took no account of the fact that the law required a person to be sixteen years old before a driving license could be obtained. He reasoned that safety came first, and necessity required that they drive on public roads. "Caleb is a good driver," Peter told Kate. "He drives up the steep mountain roads. Just let him drive when there's ice or snow on the roads."

"Don't be ridiculous, Peter!" Kate snapped. "He's only thirteen years old and will be severely fined if he's caught driving."

"Let's ask Caleb if he can do it," Peter interjected. "What about it, boy? Can you drive the car to town if need be?"

"No problem, Pa. It's a cinch to drive the Ford," Caleb replied, and indeed he had already driven his Pa to town on numerous occasions, whenever his Mom was not around. During the next three years, until he obtained his license, Caleb drove the car and never had an accident or was stopped by a policeman. He never carried a "good luck charm" either, like his Roman Catholic buddies did. At age fourteen he drove all the way to Surrey, B.C., in order for his parents to attend their fourth daughter's wedding. His parents' attitude regarding the observance of laws that governed traffic and permits seemed to be echoed by many in the immigrant community. While there was no bending regarding the moral laws regarding stealing, property rights, or sexual permissiveness, they often winked at obtaining fishing or hunting permits. They had been promised freedom in Canada, and that included ignoring government meddling in what they considered to be their own rights.

The law also prohibited First Nations reserve people from selling their salmon harvest for commercial gain, but the people in Caleb's neighborhood would arrive *en masse* to purchase the sixty-pound Tyee salmon from the loaded trucks arriving from the reserves. This ambivalent attitude extended to Caleb driving without a license as well. If need conflicted with bureaucracy, need would win out. Peter had a general law governing such events, which was, "When nature opposes the law, nature generally wins." This also extended to Caleb's favourite pursuits of hunting and fishing.

One major exception to this rule was in the arena of morality. "Absolutely no sex until after marriage!" his Pa would thunder. "Do not shame your parents and your God." When there was opportunity to fish or hunt, Caleb did, and the forests around their farm supplied the family with grouse, wild hares, and other game delicacies for the supper table. As for the latter, opportunities in Sears for a rube from the farm to be alone with a pretty girl were very few.

Hard Knocks

"Sit down, son, we need to talk to you about a very serious matter," was his parent's introduction to what he knew would affect his life. "Your father needs to have a hernia operation," started his Mom. "The doctors say he'll need to give up his job for the next year and only do light work. We'll be without income, and your younger siblings still need to be supported."

His Pa then added, "I know how much you like going to school, son, but I'm asking you to go to work after you complete the ninth grade."

Crash! Went Caleb's world. "How can I give up all the studies and school events I enjoy so much," he sputtered. "Is there no other way for me to continue my schooling?" All the expectations of a bright future dimmed as the economic reality of being poor sank in. Tears of self-pity rolled down his face.

"It's not all about you, Caleb," Lucius reminded him. The words sounded in his soul, and suddenly, the dark mood lifted. He would, and could, do a man's job and help provide for his family.

Mirjam woke to the noise of loud voices and the crying of her Mom. As she squirmed deeper under the blankets, she wondered why Caleb always made such a big deal out of everything. At twelve years old, she already showed the promise of the beauty she would inherit from her mother. "What was all the fuss about early this morning?" she asked Caleb later. "I thought that boys your age didn't cry anymore, and I heard you crying. I also heard you talking to a person you called Lucius. Who is he? Tell me or I will tickle you until you do. Come on, Caleb, who is Lucius Tickle?"

"I have to quit school and go to work," he blurted out. "Pa can't support the family for the next year, and we have a choice between accepting charity or me going to work. We've decided that I'll start working in July. Who knows when, if ever, I can go back to school?" he told her.

Mirjam hugged him closely and said, "I know that you can do whatever you want, Caleb. God will support you, and I think you're a wonderful brother. I may not be as much of a help to you, like Phoebe is, but I'll always share all my life's happenings with you, and ask you to promise me that you will do the same." The closeness that Mirjam shared with her older brother continued up to the time that she was married.

So began a chapter in his life that continued for the next seven years, as farm and logging work competed for his time, and most every day and night ended with a thankful rolling into bed and a time of deep and uninterrupted sleep.

CHAPTER IV
High School

Sailing between the Obstacles

Grades seven, eight, and nine comprised junior high school in Sears, and at age thirteen Caleb entered a whole new world. Grade sevens were called "gummers" or "newbies" by the senior classes and were subjected to hazing and ridicule. "C'mere kid," were the first words Caleb heard, on his first day at high school during morning recess. Roy Cassidy was a squat, mean looking grade eleven student who seldom took his hands out of his jean pockets. He wore a black leather jacket with the word "Condemned" stitched on the back, and he clanked down the school halls in chain-draped engineer boots. The two satellite cronies with him had the amazing ability to instantly change their facial expressions. When they looked at Roy, their faces looked scared and fawning. When they spotted a potential victim, they quickly aped their leader's scowls. Sneering and hostile expressions competed with a vacuous emptiness that was intended to intimidate.

Subjected to tri-hostility, Caleb chose wisdom over valour. "Yes, Roy, what do you want from me?" he meekly responded when Roy greeted him.

[1] "*Two bits* kid, two bits every Monday, every week," he informed Caleb in a flat monotone.

"I don't have two bits," Caleb responded, "and why should I have to give money to you?" he foolishly retorted. A hard punch to his stomach followed by a couple of hard slaps caused him to bite off any more response.

"Remember, kid, just two bits every Monday morning," warned Roy as he slapped him hard again by way of reminder. "Just two bits means that you'll be under my protection, and I'll look after you! Got that? Good!" If looks could kill, Roy and his goons would surely not have survived the daggers Caleb aimed at their backs.

Two days after the shakedown attempt, two RCMP policemen arrived at school and interviewed the entire grade seven class. When it was Caleb's turn, he told them exactly what had happened. The following week, Roy and his henchmen were no longer at school. The home room teacher later informed the class that all three boys had been expelled and sent to a reform school. When they returned to school during the next school year, they caused no more trouble.

Finding His Groove

The positive experiences of going to high school, however, far outweighed the negative experiences. Caleb loved the social interactions, academic work, and extracurricular activities. Chief among these was his involvement with the offered sports programs. He enjoyed playing baseball, basketball, dodgeball, and being part of the junior boxing team.

Len Cordes was sports coach at Sears High School, and Caleb would go through fire to please him. "Boxing! Caleb, with those long arms of yours, you're a natural to be a winning member of the boxing club," he enthused.

"Sure, Coach, if you think I can be good at it, then I'll do it. My friends call me 'skinny,' but they know I'm tough," Caleb responded.

Every Monday afternoon he practised in the gym with fifteen other gladiators, and at the end of the school year they all took part in noon hour exhibitions to determine the junior championships. The first two weeks went very well for Caleb, and after seven straight wins, his coach told him that he was a shoo-in for the title. His long reach and work-toughened muscles gave him a big advantage. His confidence grew with every win.

The title fight took place on a Wednesday lunch break, and Brad Firmin and Caleb shook hands before the bell rang. Brad was a quiet, Irish boy with red hair and a stocky build. He had moved to Sears recently with his father and had just joined the boxing club. During the first round, they jabbed at each other and circled warily, testing each other's defensive tactics. In the second round, Caleb feinted with his left and then came around with the right hand, which never landed. When he regained consciousness, he looked up to see two worried faces looking down at him. Brad and Coach Cordes got him up on shaky legs and helped him to a seat. Soon after winning the junior boxing crown, Brad and his dad moved away again. Caleb, however, never regained his enthusiasm for the sport and decided to focus on basketball instead.

[1]*Quarter; 25cents*

***

Puberty

Marked physical changes began to happen to his body, and one of the most troubling was the swelling and pain occurring in his chest nipples. One Saturday morning, Caleb ran into his parent's bedroom and wailed, "Mom, Pa, am I a girl or what? Why are my nipples becoming so large?"

He was incensed when they laughed at him but quickly cooled off when they explained what the onset of puberty meant. "You're becoming a man, son," his mom softly explained, "Be prepared for many more changes that will happen soon. Don't worry about your nipples; they'll soon go back to normal."

There were many nights when the rapidly lengthening bones in his legs pulled at the slower growing tendons, and the pain prevented sleeping. His sisters made fun of his breaking voice, and soon all of his clothes no longer fit. Instead of sport victories and heroic acts of bravery, his dreams now often included fair maidens who needed rescuing and other attentions.

Caleb's Pa decided it was time to start his sex education, so he took him down to the corral where the bull was mating with the Hereford cows. "Remember, Caleb," he instructed, "we are not animals, but there are similarities between what you're seeing and what humans do when they mate. Love, commitment, and marriage are the necessary requirements before God allows a man and woman who are in love to come together as one."

Caleb squirmed with embarrassment and felt relieved when the lesson was over and his Pa told him to get back to his chores. Caleb's older sisters teased him during what they called "Caleb's becoming a man time." Mirjam, however, remained his closest confident in the family. They shared all their dreams, hopes, and fears together, and he learned to ask her advice on everything to do with girls. She often teased him by asking what Lucius Tickle had to say.

When he would tell her about some of his dreams about girls, she would laugh, shake her head, and say, "Girls are different, Caleb. My friends and I dream about romance, getting married, meeting a gentle, strong man, and having babies ... but not how to get babies." Mirjam taught him how repulsive it is to nice girls when boys or men use crude and suggestive language or display open lust in their attitudes. She taught him that girls should never be regarded as objects. He not only asked her advice on everything to do with girls, but on most other topics as well. When he compared the locker room boys' talk to what he heard from Mirjam, then it was plain just how ignorant most boys are about girls when they are growing up. Caleb realized what a blessing it had been for him to grow up with sisters whom he respected and loved.

Missing the High Road

What was he to do about Patsy? Patsy was the plainest and most unhappy girl in grade seven. Everyone except Caleb and the two effeminate boys in the class called her "flea-bag." She smelled bad, had holes in her clothes, and looked at Caleb with eyes of misery. Many of his classmates tormented her, and even though he refused to join in the torment, he did not help her either. He excused himself with the reminder that Patsy often behaved so horribly that it was no wonder no one liked her. All the dreams of nobility and greatness that he nurtured crashed when she looked at him. He knew the example of Jesus Christ and His love for the downtrodden of society, but he could not find the courage to reach out to Patsy and try to help her. The opinions of his classmates mattered more than doing what was right. He knew that he needed to find the courage to stand up to the bullies who always unerringly found the weak to pick on. Sister Mirjam, however, did speak with her and found out that she was a foster child who lived with an abusive family. One day her seat was empty, and they learned that she had run away from her foster home. Patsy never came back, so she joined the guilt pantheon in Caleb's memory banks of those whom he should have helped more.

It was also in junior high that he became aware that some of his male friends preferred boys to girls. They, along with Patsy, became outcasts and were the object of taunts and teasing. They were, however, the sons of prominent families in Sears and were able to retaliate. Scuffles and bullying, which occurred mainly in the communal showers after gym classes, were effectively squelched by the coach and other male teachers. Homosexuality was a *verboten* topic, at home, at school, and in church. Caleb had several good discussions with both boys, but it was a bridge too far. How any boy would prefer to look at other boys when girls were around could not be fathomed by his mind. Already at a young age, his mind had resonated to his Pa reading from the Song of Solomon in the Bible. The glowing descriptions of courtship and love between a man and a woman were forever imprinted on his mind.

You Are What You Communicate

During all three grades of junior high, English was Caleb's favourite academic subject, and his grades showed it. Fran Grayson, his English teacher, looked over the top of her reading spectacles and shook her head. "Stop that boxing business at once, Caleb!" she remonstrated. "Your brains are far too precious to be slapped around." He was still sporting a large blue lump on his jaw where Brad Firmin's fist had put an end to his boxing career. He was the only boy in grade seven who enjoyed writing essays and who always finished the grammar exercises. His sisters, while they attended school with him, also showed great ability in their English studies. New ideas, religious and political debate flowed freely around the Nachtegal dinner table, and on Sundays the house would be filled with visitors who contributed to the discussions. Kate was a born entertainer and loved to be part of every discussion, even while busy with a myriad of household tasks. That was the fertile seed-bed out of which all the Nachtegals sought to improve their communication skills.

"I want you to write a ten-page essay about 'Origins,'" Mrs. Grayson, his English Literature teacher ordered, breaking into his reverie. "Write about the ideas that Charles Darwin has put forward about how life started on this planet." He knew that Mrs. Grayson was deeply religious and that most of his classmates attended church on Sundays. He also surmised, from discussions around him, that Charles Darwin was held to be a close relative of the devil. Mrs. Grayson had put him on the spot, and he was determined to find out what he could about the Theory of Evolution. His thirteen-year-old mind was not equipped to properly absorb the information that was contained in the three library books and the *Life Magazine* articles that dealt with Darwin's theories.

"Monkeys, Caleb! That's what Darwin believes in," his Pa told him when Caleb asked what he thought about the Darwinian theories of origins. "He says that humans came from a piece of slime and, eventually, from monkeys or gorillas. We believe, son, that an all-knowing and infinitively powerful Creator God created the universe and unique humans in His own image.

Caleb soon had enough information to write a twenty-page essay and tried to present the information as accurately as he could, detailing what Darwin was promoting and what he had been taught and believed.

"Stand right here, Caleb, and speak loudly so that the whole class can hear you," ordered Mrs. Grayson. "I want you to read your essay to the class and answer any questions your fellow students may have." Before he started to read, a number of students asked to be excused because their parents did not want them to hear anything that had to do with Darwin. Caleb emphasized in his reading that even when we do not agree with someone's views, we should always reason and listen in a civilized fashion. There was very little response from his classmates after he had finished reading, but Mrs. Grayson smiled at him and gave him an A+ for the essay.

***

Etiquette

The six o'clock alarm never had a chance to ring in Helen Sterrick's bedroom because she always woke at 5:30 a.m. and for years had felt the same small sharp pang of sorrow as she recalled the doctor's verdict: "The news is not good, Helen," Doctor O'Leary spoke. "You will never be able to have your own children, so if you want to have a family, then I would suggest adoption." He'd looked at the thirty-five-year-old compact, neatly dressed teacher and wondered why she and her husband had not decided long ago to adopt a baby. He knew that she loved children and had often seen her holding and hugging small babies at social events.

Helen's thoughts turned to the stranger who lay beside her. There had been a time when their mutual love was fresh and strong, but after fifteen years of marriage, only civility remained. Tom had lost interest in her, and she had been replaced by hockey and golf. He flatly refused to consider adoption. He belonged to the "good ole boys club," and Helen knew that he far preferred their company to hers. Divorce was not an option she considered because of her principles and promises. Tom also allowed her complete freedom to follow her own interests, just as long as she made the meals and kept the house neat.

It could be a lot worse, Helen thought as she surveyed the miserable, violent relationships around her. *It could be much worse.* As she made her morning cup of tea and a soft boiled brown, farm fresh egg, her mind turned to her teaching projects. All her maternal instincts were being channeled to "her boys."

"Can you do it, Helen?" Principal Ken Mugford asked. "Would it be possible to use this innovative new course to bring some civility and grace into the lives of fourteen and fifteen-year-old boys?"

The image of the boy in her mind's eye had intrigued her for some time. Most of the new immigrant students had a "deer in the headlights" look in their eyes, but Caleb was different. Shabbily dressed, gawky, and unmannered, he nevertheless showed an eagerness to learn that appealed to her teacher's instincts. *He will be my litmus test*, thought Helen, *if I can take this awkward, immigrant boy and allow him to fit and be comfortable in a new, strange culture, then I will feel that I have succeeded.*

She had heard that Caleb was one of a family of ten Dutch immigrant children. The parents were followers of a stern religion based on the teachings of the Reformation theologian, John Calvin. *I'll attempt to bring humour and gaiety into his life by teaching him manners and proper etiquette*, she mused. She failed to divine the inconsistency of her own situation as she sought to engineer the happiness of others. Caleb was thin and a head taller than his classmates, but he walked erect and proud. *Yes*, she thought, *I know I can help this boy and the other uncouth boys in the class.* "I'd like to do the course, Ken, but you must let me improvise and have free rein with the course materials," she demanded.

"Of course, Helen. I know that if anyone can carry it off, it will be you. I'll be keenly watching to see if you can make a silk purse out of these sow-eared rubes," he cautioned with a sharp laugh.

Caleb's classmates made a lot of jokes about the Health and Personal Development course before they started it. HPD was taught during school hours for grade eight boys at Sears Junior High. The teacher was a feisty, diminutive Scottish matron called Helen Sterrick, whom the students nicknamed "Brogue."

"Good morning, louts," was her opening greeting to the all-male class. "I've been asked by my esteemed employer to make presentable young gentlemen out of you all, and when you're ready, I will present you to presentable young ladies." Guffaws and hoots erupted from every corner of the class, but Brogue stared at the offenders, tapping her pointer on her desk. Once silence reigned, she began to outline her strategy to obtain the impossible dream. "Manners! Louts, it is manners that I will teach you. Regard! Louts, it is regard that you must have for your fellow humans. Without etiquette and the proper usage of the English language, all the strikes in succeeding in life are against you." Over and over, hour after hour, they practised how to speak-eat-introduce themselves, and how to properly court a young lady.

"Caleb, I will pretend to be Mary-Lou, whom I have noticed you staring at, and you pretend to ask her to go on a bowling date."

Red-faced Caleb began. "Uh h-hi, Mary-Lou. Did you watch the basketball game last night? Did you notice that I managed to score twenty points? Uh h-how about going bowling sometime?" he croaked.

"No, Caleb, nice girls don't care to hear how many baskets you scored," corrected Brogue. "Introduce yourself and then say something nice about her appearance, and stop saying 'uh' with every second word." Brogue patiently coached until Caleb got it right. It was a hilarious sight when the short, petite Brogue grabbed all six-foot-plus of Caleb and guided him through the basic waltzing steps. She harangued, joked, and cajoled all of the boys until the day she said they were ready to be presented.

"Now remember, louts—oops, from now on you are young gentlemen—you will be *coming out*." she purred archly. "On Wednesday I want all of you to wear your best clothes—black shoes, white shirts, and ties will be essential. Then I will pair all of you with one of the grade eight girls, who have prepared a luncheon for you in the Home Economics class. You will greet your partner as I have taught you and present her with a corsage. After the meal, you will escort your partner to the school gym and ask her if she would like to dance with you."

On Wednesday morning, all the grade eight boys showed up in the HPD class in their best clothes, clutching bunches of wildflowers, and stoically enduring the taunts of the laughing older boys. Brogue proudly beamed her approval on them, and all the teachers clapped and laughed as they marched into the appointed class for lunch. Caleb complimented Mary-Lou, who looked very pretty, and asked her to be his partner. Then, as he had been trained, he used knife and fork with a napkin to eat the prepared lunch. After lunch, he escorted her to the gym and they glided over the polished oak floor doing the three step waltz. Dancing was a wonderful way to hold a girl in your arms, and all the more enticing for Caleb, because in his upbringing he had been taught to avoid dancing. Teaching and nature collided, and in this case nature won again. At the end, all the boys thanked their partners, and then they formed a circle around Brogue as she sat on her chair and hoisted her into the air. She was a great gal and all the boys were a bit in love with her.

What a great teacher! Caleb thought, and he never forgot her. That was the only year that Sears High offered that particular course, but the grade eight boys all enjoyed it and benefited greatly! As happened so often in the town of Sears, gifted people usually moved on.

"I have an announcement to make!" proclaimed Caleb's sister Anna as they gathered around the Nachtegal supper table that evening. "Caleb is now no longer a 'lout.' His H.P.D. teacher has given him a certificate that says that he is now a gentleman."

All his siblings broke out into loud hissing and cheers, but his mom looked at him with pride. "Caleb, why are you not eating, son?" she asked. "Did the schoolgirls feed you such a large luncheon?"

"There's nothing wrong with my appetite, Mom," he replied. "I'd just like to ask you to provide me with a knife and napkin when we have our dinner." A crescendo of boos and hisses soon convinced him that a fork was all that was needed at the Nachtegal family table.

***

Enjoying Sports

"Can I count on you to play forward on the junior basketball team?" Coach Cordes asked Caleb with some hesitation. He knew that Caleb lived eight miles out of town, and that afternoon and night practices would be a problem. Winter was basketball season, and Sears had plenty of weather obstacles to prevent him from attending practices. He loved playing basketball, and as he neared his fourteenth year, he was almost six feet four inches tall.

"Count me in, Coach," Caleb replied with a confidence he did not feel. "If I can't get a ride, then I'll run into town. That should get me into good shape for the season."

"Okay, Caleb, the left forward or center position is yours, and I'll be counting on you," he confirmed.

"No, son!" responded his Pa to Caleb's request to have two afternoons off from doing farm chores. "We all have to pull together in order to survive here, and I need you to do your chores." Caleb then presented his case to his Mom, and before long, his Pa relented and gave permission to attend basketball practice. He had become adept at manipulating his parents' penchant to exercise control over each other.

He then asked Tom Jersey, the town dentist, if he could hitch a ride in their station wagon, since his son, Ted, also played on the junior team. The Jerseys were black people who had moved to Sears from Alabama, and they made no secret of the fact that they were glad to live in a town where there was no overt racism. They lived on a large acreage just up the road from Caleb's home, and Ted and he got along famously. He was as tall as Caleb, so they played as forwards together. Ted's younger brother played guard.

Mr. Jersey had no experience when it came to driving in bad winter weather, and if it was windy and snowing, he would not drive. In those cases, Caleb would drive the family's yellow Ford station wagon when it was available. He would pick up Ted and his brother, who were terrified to be in the car with an underage driver. Mr. Jersey never asked Caleb how he, being under aged, was allowed to drive. More than once when the Ford was not available, they ran the eight miles to town in cold, snowy conditions and arrived exhilarated and with energy to spare for the game. This so impressed Coach Cordes that he would drive them home after the game or practice in his Jeep. Sometimes, he would invite them to sleep in his spare room. He had a very pretty wife who appeared to be much younger than him, and she always treated the boys with great hospitality. Coach also drove a red Corvette with a ragtop, which did little to stop the bitter cold. A leather cap with goggles, a large scarf over his parka, and fleece-lined gloves completed his attire. They all thought that he was the epitome of coolness.

"Gather around, boys, right over here," Len Cordes commanded the ten players who comprised the Sears junior basketball team. "We lost the game tonight, fellas, and we shouldn't have. We're a better team than the boys from Caplet, but they had the desire tonight, and they beat us." The team had all just showered, and Coach Cordes was sitting nude on the bench, scratching his head and stroking his thinning hair. Caleb had been brought up to be modest about his body, and the sight of Coach Cordes standing up and pacing around the locker room completely nude, with his ample stomach, was somewhat disconcerting.

"Caleb and Ted, what were you guys thinking about tonight, because it sure wasn't basketball?" he sputtered as he snapped his towel inches from their faces. "Did the sight of all those pretty cheerleaders distract you tonight?" They hung their heads and kept silent, because they knew that Coach had to blow off some steam and then he would be okay. Ted and Caleb had played the entire sixty-minute game, and during the last ten minutes they had just ran out of gas. Together they had scored more than half the team's total points and had nothing to be ashamed of. The Sears Rockets were, indeed, a better team than the Caplets, but the Caplet coach had a better method in how to extract the maximum from his players.

The Rockets played fifteen games that season and lost only that one. They all hated losing, but it is a necessary lesson in life.

Coach Cordes had no children, so he virtually adopted his team players. He was very good to his players in many ways, but he also expected a lot. He would never tolerate a slacker, and those players who were not prepared to give their best effort were soon off the team. When Caleb entered grade nine, his friend Ted and his family moved away.

Caleb was asked to play on the senior basketball team during his third junior year, and he eagerly accepted. "You worry me out there, Caleb," Coach confided. "Most of those guys out there are four years older than you, and you look so skinny beside them. Don't be too aggressive, and walk away from any confrontation." Technically, Coach was not allowed to let Caleb play on the senior squad, but he valued his height and rebounding skills. The Senior Rockets were beaten by the Waneker Rainmakers in the finals of the Northern Division because the Rainmaker boys were definitely a superior team who hailed from a much larger high school. Coach made Caleb warm the bench for most of the game, and when Caleb asked him why, he curtly replied, "You just look too fragile out there."

It was during the long bus rides home from playing in the neighbouring towns that Caleb was confronted with his moral teachings. Many of the players and cheerleaders were eighteen or older and often smuggled alcohol onto the bus. Every trip followed the same routine. Firstly, the games were discussed and then all the old school songs were sung. Then all the chaperones and teachers moved to the front of the bus, and the beer and hard liquor started to circulate among the students in the rear of the bus. Finally, the heavy petting and necking would start and continue until they reached their destination. He was often invited, and many times severely tempted, but at fourteen years old, he was too scared and was also convinced that it was wrong behaviour. He sat behind the teachers and wondered what had become of his friend Ted Jersey.

***

Music Revolution

"C'mon, Caleb, let's hurry home and listen to the radio," begged his sisters and neighbourhood friends. "CBC radio is playing the top forty hits on the 'Caboose' program." The world was being shaken by the rock-n-roll revolution, and tiny Sears, with only one radio station, was not exempt. They all would go to a house where the parents were gone and crank up the music. Elvis Presley, Chuck Berry, Bill Halley and the Comets were leaders in the vanguard of a new musical revolution. "C'mon, Caleb," urged his circle of siblings and friends, "sing 'Jailhouse Rock' for us." And he would launch into a screaming rendition of the Elvis rock song.

It was not only the music that changed. Clothing, hair, shoes, and attitude styles all changed in a matter of months. Girls wore tight fitting jeans or large swirling skirts with saddle shoes. "Please, Mom! Can you buy me a large bottle of Hollywood waving gel?" Caleb begged his mother. "All my friends are using it to create 'Elvis pompadours' and 'flying saucer cuts.'" It was cheap to buy and a liberal application made his hair set up like concrete. Genetics had provided him with a large mop of dark brown hair with streaks of blond. It was perfect for forming into any style he wanted, and he tried them all. The only drawback was that if he outdid his classmate's hairdos, they would waylay him at school and try to mess it up. After numerous altercations, the teachers decided to impose a dress and hair code, which proved impossible to maintain. On Friday afternoons the lights would go out in the hallways and a lot of yelling and giggling ensued. The teachers disappeared from sight and their actions seemed to indicate that it was okay for the students to let off some steam.

After the hair thing, the next cool style for boys was leather jackets and leather engineer boots with lots of chains. Large leather trucker's wallets stuck out from the back pockets of skin tight Levi jeans, which showed four inches of white sock above the boots. A heavy chain from the wallet looped around to the front of the belt and was attached with a strong leather loop. It needed to be strong because it was often required to stop the wallet from being jerked from your pocket. All of these changes were accompanied by a surly look, slurring of speech, and a rebellious attitude.

It took some time, because of the language barrier, for Caleb's parents to become wise to what was happening. When they realized that it was not only the "worldly kids" who were acting up, but that also their own children were being affected, they took strong action. "Children, there will be no more listening to the rock and roll songs on the radio," was their parent's first edict. "You will all be required to dress modestly. Yes, Caleb, you can keep your jacket, but the other garbage must go. You have all been brought up as Christians, and that means that you behave as Christians." The church minister held a series of sermons on "Christian Lifestyle" and what it meant when you were committed to be a follower of Jesus Christ. Caleb listened to all the voices and competing world views and knew that God had His claim upon him. He was just confused about how to work it all out in daily life.

It proved to be a great struggle for him, because he was popular and wanted to be liked by the friends he had at school.

"C'mon, Caleb, don't be a party pooper," teased Mary-Lou. "My parents are gone tonight, and I've invited some friends over for dancing and fun," she giggled. She sat behind him in class and liked poking him with her ruler and mussing up his hairdo. She was dark, pert, and very pretty, and she knew it. "There will be beer, and my dad has lots of liquor," she added. "C'mon, Caleb, we'll have a blast!"

Caleb liked Mary-Lou, but he also knew that her family was easygoing, and her parents allowed things that would never fly in his family. It would not be good for him to hang around with her too much, especially since she was popular with many other boys. He had no desire to belong to the retinue of boys that Mary-Lou liked to have around her. The percentage of girls who became pregnant while attending Sears High was significant, and he was determined to avoid compromising situations. Caleb also liked his neighbour girl, Carly, and she was watching him to see what he would do and say. Carly's family shared the same values that the Nachtegals held dear, and they were values that were not just skin-deep. Carly was also his sister's best friend, and Mirjam was convinced that Carly was the girl for him.

"I'm sorry, Mary-Lou, but tonight isn't a good time. I have other things to do," Caleb lied. "Maybe some other time we can go for a coke and a walk." He felt cheap as he walked away and knew he should have told her the real reason he could not come over. It was not that his classmates, including Mary-Lou, were not claiming to be Christians; they all said that they were. The difference was in the commitment. Claiming to be a Christian and acting contrary to every teaching of Christianity was an empty shell, devoid of meaning. Caleb began to experience strong sexual feelings, but he knew that he had to control them. The locker room talk of his classmates about girls was dirty and demeaning.

The constant use of coarse and vulgar language began to rub off on him, and he had to make choices. He began to withdraw from social contacts who were belittling his Christian values. He tried to explain to his friends that the constant use of obscenities and curse words not only insulted God, but that it would diminish their capacity to communicate effectively.

"Loosen up, Caleb," Coach Cordes interjected as he began to notice his withdrawal. "Go with the flow and enjoy yourself. Remember that we only get one chance to live, and I advise you to make the best of it." Caleb offered no reply but knew that Cordes's wife was divorcing him, and he could only surmise the reasons why. Only a few of his school friends enjoyed the security of a stable family life, and he treasured his siblings and parents.

Caleb began to see a lot more of Carly, but she almost became like another sister to him. "What do you want of me, God?" he earnestly prayed and listened for the answer. "What is my portion? Can I be a part of this wonderfully interesting world, or do I need to hold on to your teachings?" The only voice he could hear was the voice in his own head. Some of his Pentecostal friends claimed that God spoke to them directly, so he thought it might happen to him.

"You are in the world, but not of the world," was the biblical message. Caleb needed to work with that dilemma, seeing that his feet were firmly planted in both worlds. He had to grapple with what he thought were his needs versus a theoretical knowledge that he was called to give of himself for the wellbeing of others. No magic formulae would provide him with answers. He had to work out his own salvation, and he would be held responsible and accountable.

Crush on His Teacher

Grade nine was a time filled with change and adventure. "When will you ever stop growing, Caleb?" asked Miss Muirhead (a.k.a. Bebop) with a smile and shaking her black, curly hair. "Either we raise the doors or have the surgeon cut some bone out of your legs." She smiled as she looked up at all six feet four inches of Caleb, and he smiled back. She was short but very feminine and pretty. At twenty-eight years old and unmarried, she was considered to be an old maid by his fellow classmates. She had a difficult time teaching the rowdy class, and it was obvious that she looked forward to the ending bell.

"Promise to quit bugging Bebop or I'll choke the daylights out of you," Caleb gasped into the ear of the worst offender. Tony had constantly harassed Bebop until she left the class crying. That made Caleb very angry. He had inherited his mom's fierce temper, and it often got the best of him. He endured the taunts and teasing of being "teacher's pet" but allowed no one to be openly mean to her again. He was realizing that to be cowardly was a worse stigma to live with than to not have the group's acceptance. Soon after, Bebop went steady with another teacher, who Caleb deemed to be totally unworthy, and the blow to his crush on her was a humbling and necessary learning experience. The rage of hormones and the conflicting demands and expectations of those surrounding him provided a potent brew for rebellion. Temper tantrums were the external vents for the confusion within. Sporting events provided a welcome relief, and often his lack of skill was compensated for by a fierce determination to compete and win.

Caleb's Rivalry and Affection for His Sisters

"Caleb, you are a complete idiot!" yelled sister Anna as she narrowly avoided the flying ping pong paddle aimed at her head. "You're just a poor sport who can't stand losing. Grow up or play by yourself!"

"You only win because all you ever do is return the ball without ever trying to smash, spin, or try trick shots," he fumed.

"The object is to win, not show off," Anna smirked as she flounced off. "Learn how to play the basic shots before you try the hard ones."

After the smarting sting of four defeats wore off, he realized that she was right. Solid content trumped style every time, but the learning did not come easy. All of his seven sisters were talented, and some showed remarkable literary and artistic ability. Caleb felt proud of them, and they taught him never to underestimate a woman's abilities.

The first boyfriend of the Nachtegal girls belonged to the second oldest sister, and soon a steady parade passed under the critical eyes of Caleb and his younger sisters. "Get off the barrel, Caleb," hissed his sister Anna, "or at least tell us what's going on in the living room." They had rolled the empty forty-five-gallon steel gas barrel to a strategic position where they could look through the porch windows into the living room without being seen.

The two older sisters were entertaining their boyfriends, and Caleb gleefully embellished all that he saw while managing to stay on top of the barrel. "They are stroking each other's hair and kissing and drinking Mom's best wine," he gleefully dramatized to the rapt faces.

They instantly replied, "Let us see! We want to see for ourselves. Get off the barrel, Caleb, or we'll push you off!"

"Okay! you sissies," he smirked as he jumped down, "go ahead and get your free lessons so you'll know what to do when your time arrives."

But love was not all fun and games. A paroxysm of sobs passed through the thin walls of older sister Trina's bedroom and reached Caleb's astonished ears. Trina was usually self-possessed and always in control, so he gently knocked, opened the door, and softly asked, "What's wrong, Trina? Do you want to talk about it?" She lay in the corner of her bed rolled into a fetal position and looked the picture of abject misery. Trina had a boyfriend, and Caleb instinctively knew that this could only be boy trouble. "Are you pregnant, or has Pa told you to stop seeing Rusty?" he asked.

She just shook her head and slowly, amid a cascade of tears, spoke.

"He told me that it's over; no reason why—just that it's over and he's not coming back."

As Caleb held her hand, he sputtered, "He's nothing but a jerk, Trina. He doesn't deserve you, and I say 'good riddance.'"

Anger flared in her eyes, and he narrowly avoided the raking nails. "He is not a jerk. Don't ever call him that again! I love him, and he will come back to me." Rusty, however, never came back, and the time came when Trina said, "Caleb, you were right. He was a jerk." He tried to explain to elegant, fastidious Trina that many boys prefer the earthy, heavy-set girls, and the appearance of Rusty's new girlfriend proved his point.

***

Final School Day,
Look Away, Look Away

The sharp blow from the wooden Tee-square almost knocked Caleb off his feet. He turned instinctively and slugged Mr. Casey in the middle of his chest. He tried to grab Caleb's ear, but Caleb was too big for him, and then Casey tripped over his own foot. "Get out of the Industrial Arts room and go straight to the principal's office!" he snarled. His eyes were bulging out as he held a fist to his chest and used his other arm for support.

"How may I help you, Caleb?" asked the front office secretary as he slowly pushed open the heavy oak door.

"Teacher Casey sent me down to see the principal. He'll be arriving shortly to speak to the principal about what happened," Caleb softly replied.

Mr. Mugford, the principal, slung his left leg over the corner of his desk and lightly hit his left hand with the rubber strap held in his right hand. "What happened, Caleb? Why did a smart boy like you do such a stupid thing? You know what the penalty is for striking a teacher," he warned.

Caleb stripped off his shirt to show him the sharp welts on his back. "That's what he did to me because I'd forgotten to lay my wood plane on its side," he muttered defiantly. Muggsy shut the door, winked his eye, and told him to cry out in pain as he lashed the desktop three hard, loud blows with his strap.

"Mum is the word, right, Caleb?" he smiled. "Take a detention and I'll go have a word with old Casey."

Caleb returned to the next Industrial Arts class and never had any more trouble with Mr. Casey. He even gave him an A at the end of the course. The actions of Muggsy were a valuable lesson in adult diplomacy. Wisdom and deceit often proved to be closely related in the politics of human interactions.

Before the end of the grade nine school year, Miss Muirhead, the homeroom teacher, passed out the course selection sheets to be filled out for the upcoming grade ten year. When she came around to collect them, she asked Caleb why he had not filled his out. When he first told her that he would be quitting school at the end of grade nine, she immediately marched him to the principal's office. Caleb explained to him, as best as he could, why his family needed him to start earning a supporting wage.

"What nonsense are you telling me now, Caleb?" interjected "Muggsy," as the class had nicknamed him. "Do you mean to say that your family's economic survival depends on the paltry wage that a fifteen-year-old boy would generate? Notify your parents that I am coming to visit them this evening," he commanded.

Caleb informed his parents about the impending visitor, and at seven-thirty sharp, both teachers arrived. Kate bustled around offering coffee and cake, and the principal said his piece. "Surely you can't be serious. Mr. and Mrs. Nachtegal?" was Mr. Mugford's opening salvo. "Caleb informs me that he will be leaving school at the end of grade nine because you have ordered him to leave. I ask you to consider very carefully if what you're doing is being fair to the lad? Caleb is an excellent student and can make a choice of any career if he gets the required education."

Peter listened and stared intently at the Savile Row suit, manicured hands, and shiny shoes of Muggsy. "May I respectfully say that you have no idea how immigrants need to fight for survival," he interjected in his fractured English. "We appreciate your concern for Caleb, but he can return to school again when I am healed and able to resume my work. Caleb may seem to be a fifteen-year-old boy to you, but I know that he can do a man's work. I started working full time, labouring fourteen-hour days when I was twelve. In the logging industry it matters only what you can do, not how old you are," he finished with finality.

"Is there no other way to solve your dilemma?" reasoned Muggsy. "What about your church? Can they not support you with financial aid? You must surely also be aware of the high accident rate in the logging industry that Caleb will be exposed to," he countered.

Caleb saw the flare of anger in his Pa's eyes at the mention of charity and knew the discussion had ended. It was heartwarming to see the concern of his teachers for his welfare, but Caleb also felt the same stubborn pride evidenced by his Pa: "The Nachtegals will look after their own needs."

Mrs. Knight (nee Muirfield) hugged Caleb before he cleaned out his locker on June 21, 1960. It was hard to see where he was going with the barely-held tears stinging his eyes. His classmates wished him well, but he could see that many thought his life might as well be over. As the school doors closed behind him, he knew that a whole new beginning was starting in his life. He had enjoyed school, and at times would miss it terribly, but now he was becoming excited at the prospects of new adventures and experiences opening up before him. "Look ahead, look away, Caleb," whispered the voice in his head, "the best is still to come."

CHAPTER V
Neophyte Lumberjack

ODE TO A CONIFER

EONS
OF GROWTH
PROUDLY DISPLAYED
UPON THE MOUNTAIN GLADE.
GRIZZLY SLASHES OZING SAP FROM
THE BRIGHT ORANGE GASHES.TENDRILS,
PUSHING, PENETRATING ROCK, CAPTURED IN
FROST RELEASED BY THE SUN BREAKING LOCK.
BRANCHES EMBRACING THE JAY, RAVEN, AND EAGLE.
THE DESPOILER CAME AND SAW PLANKS AND HOLLARS:
LOOK! THE GIRTH, HEIGHT, AND CUBES; MANY DOLLARS.
NO CEREMONY OF ENDING, THE POWER SAW ROARED, WEDGES
WERE PLACED. SO PUNY A CUT, SO QUICK WAS THE FALL. THE CRASH
WAS HEARD BY ONLY ONE MAN AT ALL. IT HAD REACHED FOR THE STARS;
NOW LAY STRIPPED OF ITS FRONDS AND ITS BARK. DOWN THE HILL A MACHINE
DRAGGED THE TRUNK TO THE MILL. GONE WAS THE SPLENDOUR AND BARE WAS
THE HILL. SHRIEKING SAWS THE PLANKS THEY DID CUT. STRAIGHT AND TRUE WITH
NARY A KNOT.
BRACES
AND STUDS,
BEAMS FOR A HOME.
SO MANY USES
FROM JUST
ONE TREE.
A STUMP
STANDS IN
MEMORY.

Caleb

Caleb's fifteenth birthday was a big deal in the Nachtegal family, and his Pa opened the festivities by placing a large brown parcel on the kitchen table. "We didn't want it to be this way, Caleb, but now that you'll be starting to work, your Mom and I have bought you this present to acknowledge that you have become a man. Open it up and let us know what you think."

Caleb quickly peeled off the wrapping and exposed a shiny yellow tin of Sportsman tobacco, a cigarette rolling machine, and a large collection of cigarette papers. Finally! He was allowed to smoke legally and did not need to sneak around behind his parents' backs. He rolled smokes for all takers, and everyone was soon festooned in wreaths of smoke. The festive occasions were, however, short-lived, and in early July he would begin his new job at his oldest brother's portable sawmill, high up in the Nefelt Mountain Range. On the night before he started, his Mom laid out his logger's clothes. A black and red checkered flannel shirt, with a tough khaki pants, lay beside heavy duty, steel toed work boots.

"Be careful, my son," warned his mom with tears in her eyes. "It's a brutal world out there, and you know how accident prone you are."

"I'll be okay, Mom," Caleb promised with a bravado he did not feel. "I'll be home every weekend and will bring a full pickup load of dry jack pine blocks for the kitchen stove."

Learning the Ropes

During the summer months, sawmill production was slowed by wet forests and boggy roads. Caleb worked short eight-hour days and helped brother Jan with every aspect of the business. Jan was now married with a growing family, and Caleb often stayed in the mill cabin by himself. Road building and timber tract surveys were required preparation for the high production winter months after freeze-up. He had previously spent summer holidays working for Jan at his sawmill, but that had been fun times. Now it was for real. A real paycheque came every two weeks, and even though he gave the cheque to his mom, it still felt good holding it in his hands.

The hot August sun heated the resin that oozed from the lodge pole pine trees and filled the air with a heady aroma. The soft drone of busy bees pollinating the flowers on the wild raspberries filled the still summer air. Caleb grabbed handfuls of ripe berries and gulped down all that he could find. Large, shiny black flies were also busy depositing their eggs on the berries, but the berries were so delicious that he was willing to brave the intestinal problems caused by the hatching fly larvae in his gut.

Mechanical problems with the mill machinery had allowed him a free afternoon. He found a soft mossy spot and had just fallen asleep when a loud yell awoke him. "Where is everybody? I need help!" yelled the sweating, angry truck driver. His yells echoed back and forth from the surrounding hills. He had been contracted to haul away the sawn lumber to the planer mill.

"Yo man! I'm here," Caleb groggily replied. "What do you want?"

"I need a man and equipment to pull my truck out of a mud hole," he sneered with a look that said plainly, "You are not that man."

"Everyone has gone to town," Caleb replied, "so if you want any help, then I'll have to do." Under his breath he muttered, "A--hole."

When they arrived at the stuck truck, he could see that the rear tandem assembly had sunk into the mud right up to the wooden deck. "You'll need to remove the load of lumber in order to pull that baby out of the mud hole," he told the driver.

"Keep your opinions to yourself and listen to what I tell you," he snarled. "Get the D-4 Cat from the mill and follow my instructions."

When Caleb arrived with a loud clanking, the trucker had him park the Cat well in front of the truck and told him to anchor the machine by throwing the dozer blade over a large stump. The truck driver then pulled the steel winching cable to his truck and looped it around the truck's front axle. "Winch away when I honk," he yelled over his shoulder and climbed back into his cab.

As soon as Caleb heard the honk, he engaged the winch into pulling mode. He heard the squeal of the gears in the Hyster Winch and the rasping of the steel cable as an enormous pull was exerted. He stopped the winch and climbed down from the Cat. "What are you doing, you idiot?" yelled the driver. "Keep pulling until I honk again, and give the Cat more throttle."

"Either the winch will break or your truck, but the Cat will not pull your truck out of that hole!" Caleb yelled back. Again he engaged the winch, picked up the motor speed, and pulled the front axle clean out from under the truck. The cab fell down on the ground, and the whole truck looked like it was half buried. The air turned blue with cursing and foul language as Caleb turned and walked away. He stifled the "I told you so" and hid the smirk on his face. How could an afternoon that had started so great have ended up so bad?

Recreation Dangers

The hot working, dog-days of summer were followed by long evenings when the sun would shine until 10:00 p.m. "Please, Caleb," begged Phoebe and Mirjam, "can we go to the lake this evening for a swim?" They all jumped into the Ford, and soon they were all floating in the blissful waters of the sun-warmed Northern Lake.

The girls stayed close to shore, but Caleb was showing off his dog paddle some distance from the shore. It proved to be a tiring stroke and he decided to stand up for a rest at the same time that he was gulping for air. Instant utter panic enveloped him as his head went under and he inhaled a full mouth of water. He was able to jump up from the bottom to get a gasp of air but was unable to get into a swimming position again. People swimming near him were smiling and laughing at his presumed funny antics, not realizing that he was drowning. "Help! Help!" Caleb screamed as his strength began to ebb and his mind flashed back to the awful nightmares of drowning and suffocation in the German bunker so long ago. As he went under for the last time, two pairs of hands pulled and pushed him to the surface. Two ten-year-old boys towed him to the diving platform. He climbed the ladder and retched painfully as he stretched out on the wooden deck. It took a long time before he dared to catapult into the water and furiously dog paddle to shore. His sisters had not been aware of the incident, and the boys were nowhere to be found. They had saved Caleb's life, and he was not even able to thank them.

***

The mountains of the Nefelt range were wild and beautiful. It was one of those warm, hazy September days when there was not much to do. The lofty peak behind the sawmill beckoned to Caleb and his co-worker Bart. "Can we climb it in one day and get back before dark, Caleb?" he asked.

"There's only one way to find out, and that's to do it," Caleb replied. They packed a light lunch and cinched up their *Pierre Paris* logging boots. In lieu of compass or map, they followed the creek bed up the steep slopes and avoided the poison ivy and witch hazel shrubs. When they emerged from the timberline into the low brush area, the first irritations began around their heels. Logging boots are not intended for mountain climbing, and they would pay the price. It was time to slather on copious amounts of insect repellent to ward off the whining clouds of mosquitoes that erupted from the vegetation with every footfall.

"Look to your left, Caleb," whispered Bart. "That's the largest momma Grizzly I've ever seen!" When she reared up on her hind legs with a "woof, woof," they saw the two roly-poly cubs running to the safety of their mother.

"Let's give them lots of room," Caleb cautioned. "Black bears don't bother me, but I don't want to get a grizzly angry with me." They retreated a safe distance, pulled off their boots, and watched the bears while they soaked their feet in the ice-cold mountain water. The ease with which the she-bear upended rocks to provide grubs for the cubs showed the tremendous power in her limbs. It was late in the afternoon when they scaled the final rise to the peak. A wondrous panorama lay below them, sharply revealed by the slanting rays of the westering sun. The dark colours of the conifers were broken everywhere by the bright cottonwood trees starting to put on their fall colours. Small groups of caribou, mountain goats, and rock badgers were visible on the slopes, and after packing some moss padding into their boots, they started down. They missed the creek that had been their guide to the timberline, and long before they entered the logging area, darkness surrounded them. Fortunately, a full moon rose above the horizon and provided enough light under the forest canopy to allow them to keep going.

"Down Bart. As long as we go down the steepest grades, we'll be sure to cross a logging road soon," Caleb reassured him. Bart had only been a logger for a short time and was showing signs of apprehension. The next foot check showed red stains on their socks, and the pain was growing with every step. "Eureka, we have found it!" Caleb shouted as they stumbled onto the overgrown skid trail. It proved to be another two- hour detour, which took them well below the location of their own cabin, but at least they knew where they were. Two hours after midnight they staggered into their cabin. It would take weeks for the blisters to heal, but some pains are worth bearing. That day would always stand out in their memory for its beauty and thrills.

One of the Crew

In November, the logging crew experienced severely cold weather. The roads froze and the logging and lumber trucks were able to roll over the crude forest roads.

"Wake up, son," entreated Caleb's mother's voice as she shook him awake at 4:00 a.m. on Monday morning. "You need to meet the lumber truck in one hour."

It was brutal to leave the warm womb of his bed and steel his body for the blast of freezing air. His Mom had a hot porridge breakfast and three fried eggs on the stove, and his lunchbox contained twelve sandwiches that would last him for two days. Without his Mom, he would not have been able to survive the abrupt transformation from schoolwork to a taxing physical logging environment. How he loved that woman who in every way helped him to meet life's challenges.

The truck dropped Caleb off at the horse barn at 6:00 a.m., and then he watered and fed his old nemesis horse, Nelly. He also fed the horses from a neighbouring mill. After he had harnessed Nelly, he climbed on her back and rode her two kilometres to the mill site. On his very first trip he was falling asleep on Nelly's warm, broad back when a high-pitched scream and an explosion of powder snow caused her to bolt. Caleb almost fell off, and when he looked back, he saw a whiskered lynx holding a snowshoe rabbit in its mouth. The falling, crystalline blanket of pure white snow would soon cover also this tooth-and-claw event. Tears of fright rolled out of his and the horse's eyes. It was a great relief to finally arrive at the mill site. The large fire that burned the waste produced by the saw mill had burned out over the weekend. Caleb's first job was to get a large pail of diesel fuel and get the fire going again.

Technical Stuff

The portable sawmills that operated in the interior of B.C. during the 1940s to 1970s had a short lifespan, since they were very wasteful of the natural wood resources that they used. On average, only 30 to 40 percent of the fallen tree would be manufactured into lumber. The four exterior slabs removed from every log were burned, and every saw cut made by the giant head saw produced one-half inch of coarse sawdust, which was also burned. The stump, branches, and top of every tree were burned or left to rot on the forest floor. At the finishing planer mills, additional wood was shaved from the rough planks, and all inferior wood was discarded and burned in large beehive burners. The burners were made out of sheet metal with an open steel mesh top. The Government Forestry Service soon saw to it that no tree cutting permits would be issued to such operations. The years from 1945 to 1970 were the heydays for this type of logging operation in the interior of British Columbia.

For the interest of those who have had experiences in the interior logging industry, and for all those who are curious about a bygone era in which Caleb worked, this is how this industry operated: A tree cutting permit had to be obtained by the mill owner from the forestry department, and then roads and skidding trails were constructed. A large clearing was made where the sawmill was situated. This required considerable planning, since the slope of the land, as well as the concentrations of marketable timber, would determine the most advantageous location. The foundation for the mill machinery was made from large straight trees that were levelled and prepared to hold the steel logging carriage and tracks. A six-foot diameter saw with removable saw bits was located at the middle of the track run, and a large diesel motor powered the flywheel with rubber v-belts. The sawyer and his helper stood at one end of the platform, and the lumber packers stood on the other side. Logs were rolled onto the carriage, and the sawyer would clamp the log with three steel jaws. Then he would power the carriage past the saw to firstly cut off the bark slabs and then to cut the remaining square into planks. The lumber packers threw the exterior bark slabs into the fire and stacked the rough sawn lumber on jacks that would later allow lumber trucks to load them. A large sucking blower, situated directly under the large head saw, spewed the coarse sawdust onto a large burning pile. Larger operations also included an edger, which enabled the lumber packers to slice off the bark edges on the planks with a separate smaller saw.

The Cutting Edge of Danger

The mill crew, however, was only one component of the operation. In the forest, the most dangerous and complicated work took place. Two men handled the falling of trees and the operation of the tracked Caterpillar, or Cat, to drag the fallen trees to the mill site. Sid Helkenberg was the tree faller who worked with Caleb, and he commanded the largest wage of the crew. Caleb's older brother Jan operated the Cat and supervised all parts of his operation. He would drag from five to ten trees to the mill with each trip that the Cat made. Usually about five trips could be made in a day. This allowed Jan to have additional time to intervene in any disputes that cropped up.

Tree faller Sid was a "prima-donna" and lorded it over all the other crew members. His stentorian yell of "Tim-ber-r-r" was a warning for all who approached that a tree would soon be smashing to the earth. He often used the dangerous but efficient method of partially cutting up to ten trees and then bringing them all down with a strategically placed tree to the rear, which would produce a domino effect. Gusts of wind, or trees that would fail to break, could suddenly whip back and end the life of a careless faller. Trees that were rotten in the center were called "widow makers." They could split and break backwards, impaling the unfortunate faller. Sid was panther-quick and leather-tough and would always dash behind a large protective tree nearby as soon as the last tree began to fall. Safety inspectors from the Workers Compensation Board would issue stringent warnings against such practices, but Sid would smile and suck on his toothpick while he was being warned. When the inspectors were gone, Sid referred to them as desk jockey a--holes. Part of Sid's job was to cut all the limbs from the tree trunks, but this was one part of his job that he hated, and often the tree trunks arrived at the mill site looking like Christmas decorations.

The roar of the Cat signaled that Jan was bringing another load of trees, called a "drag," to the mill. The mill crew always inspected each drag. If the trees were large and straight, it would mean more money in their pockets. All the crew members worked on an agreed dollar amount per one thousand board measure of lumber produced. A large log would produce much more lumber in a shorter space of time than a bunch of small ones. Large spruce trees were prized because they were used to produce scaffolding planks for the construction of skyscrapers in the United States. The planks were all rough cut two inches thick and nine inches wide by thirteen feet long. They were incredibly strong, and four grown men could bounce in the middle of the plank without it breaking. The crew were paid a premium for every thousand board feet, and it was cause for celebration when a truckload of "two-by-nines" would leave the mill.

Labour Negotiations

The winter crew comprised seven workers in total. Before they started production, there was a discussion and muttering among the five experienced new crew members. Soon Jan was confronted by their spokesman, who informed him that he represented the rest of the crew. "Jan, we want a word with you about the kid," barked Bill Street, the head sawyer. "He's only fifteen, inexperienced, and we're concerned about him. We all depend on each other for safety, and since we work on contract, we're worried that he won't be able to keep up with the rest of us and will lower production efficiency."

"I vouch for my brother. Do you hear me, Bill? And to the rest of you, let me make that clear," responded Jan. "If Caleb is unable to do his part of the work, then I'll hire a replacement for him; now quit jawing and let's get back to work."

Low Man on the Totem Pole

Caleb was back to working with Nelly, his old farm horse nemesis. His job was to cut up the long trees dragged to the mill site by the D-4 Caterpillar tractor into usable log lengths. He soon learned the intricacies of operating his Stihl-Lightning chain saw. Often starting a cut with the point of the bar was required, and if done improperly, the saw could kick straight back into the operator's face. After the trees were all cut into logs, Caleb would skid them to the sawyer's platform using Nelly. She again tried the old bite and kick routine, but a sharp blow with his cant-hook stopped her shenanigans. Bill, the sawyer, kept a close watch on Caleb's performance, and if there were less than ten logs left on his landing, he would start shaking his fist at him. The only time that would happen was when the Cat was late, or when Nelly would try to run away. Paradoxically, the worst trouble with Bill started when he was provided a large surplus of logs.

"What's the matter, Bill?" jibed the other mill workers. "Getting a little rusty in your old age? Is the pace to much for your old bones?"

Bill snarled and started to harangue Caleb to help him with doing his job.

Caleb was sharpening his chainsaw when Bill's massive arm came around and his hand grabbed the front of Caleb's shirt. Then he slammed him against the wall of the motor housing.

"Let me go, you bastard!" Caleb sputtered and then kept quiet when he saw the sharp axe in Bill's left hand.

"Know what this is for, punk?" he asked in a low, menacing voice. "It's for cutting off all the branches on the logs that you put on my landing. The last log I cut had a four-inch spike on it that nearly dragged me into the head saw. If that should ever happen, no matter how badly I am injured, I will come after you and get you." The two lumber stackers came running and dragged him away from Caleb as he collapsed onto the sawdust pile. He said nothing to his brother, and when Bill saw that he was not a tattler and did a good, fast job, his attitude changed for the better.

Horses Have Feelings Too

"Whoa, you idiot!" Caleb yelled as Nelly pulled the log too far past the sawyer's platform. She often arched her neck and turned to stare at Caleb with distended eyes. She did that just to show him that he was being too bossy. This time, however, his voice must have conveyed an extra measure of menace, because Nelly kept right on going and then broke into a gallop down the logging road with the log bouncing behind her. Caleb ran after her, convinced that Nelly would soon stop, and then he would teach her that her manners were unacceptable. She would stop and then turn her head and let him come to within ten paces, with his voice dripping dulcet entreaties, but his eyes registered murder. Then with a snort, she would be off again. Mile after mile the same scenario played itself out until Caleb decided to approach her by walking backwards. Then he was finally able to collar the renegade. She could read his eyes and smell his rage, but instead of beating her, he climbed onto Nelly's back and made her pull the log all the way, uphill, back to the mill. The return journey taxed her strength to the extreme, and she never bolted again.

The mill crew was cutting the last log at quitting time, and Caleb had to work a four-hour night shift to catch up again. Something changed forever in that equine brain, because Nelly became the most obedient horse that he ever worked with. After the fateful chase, she would greet him every morning with a gentle nickering noise and rub her nose against his face. Caleb always scratched her ears and sternly would tell her, "No kissing on our first date, you froward wench!"

We're in the Money

It was previously mentioned that the crew worked on a contract basis. For every one thousand board feet of lumber produced, they were paid a fixed price. Caleb was paid two dollars and fifty cents per thousand board feet, and on a good day they could produce ten thousand board feet. Twenty to twenty-five dollars per day was a good wage for a kid at that time, and was more than the wage his Pa made working at the planer mill.

"Well, 'high pockets,' what are you going to do with all that money?" Sid would tease Caleb with a smirk on his face when it was payday. "Got a cute chick-a-dee down in Sears to spend it on?"

At lunchtime the entire crew would sit around the fire, and Sid always made the coffee. A tin can was filled with water and coffee and then suspended from a steel pole over the glowing coals. "Billy Can Coffee" they called it, and Sid brewed it just right.

"Nah, Sid," Caleb teased back at him, "after seeing the trouble you've had with 'wimmin,' I'm steering clear of them." He was aware that a large part of Sid's and Bill's wage was being garnisheed by court order to provide support for previous and present wives and children. They never seemed to learn or heed their own advice, because a large part of the discussions concerned their latest 'wimmin' troubles.

Educating Caleb

"You're smarter than you look, kid, so listen close to what I tell you," Sid uttered his backhanded compliment for the umpteenth time. "Chain saws and wimmin—they are trouble kid. Trouble. Do you hear me? Stay away from them, and you'll be rich and content," he finished as he threw his remaining half-cup of coffee, with a flourish and swirl, into the slab fire. Every imaginable topic under the sun would be discussed as they sat around the blazing fire. Solutions to the political, economic, and religious woes of the world were vehemently proposed and defended.

Often the speaker would turn to Caleb, being the youngest crew member, with the opening preamble of a large brown stream of tobacco juice to punctuate what would follow. "Idiots, kid! All idiots—those educated welfare bum politicians who get paid high salaries with our tax dollars." That would be the final consensus of the older crew members after lengthy arguments about who was to blame for the ills of mankind.

Caleb's brother Jan would laugh and jeer. "Go ahead, Bill, run for Prime Minister; we promise to vote for you." When the discussion veered into religion, it was every man with his own opinion. Sid, the faller, was an avowed atheist and socialist. Bill, the sawyer, was an agnostic, and his helper started as a communist but changed his opinion whenever it suited him. Felix and Luke, the two Native lumber stackers, said they were Roman Catholic but had no idea what that meant. They seldom contributed any opinions but always looked at whoever was speaking, smiling, and nodding sagely. Jan and Caleb were Protestant Christians who held strongly to a biblical viewpoint.

Sid sucked loudly as his silver toothpick explored the many cavities in his ruined teeth. "It's religion and superstition that have caused the misery and wars on this planet," he would opine. "We need to look to the workers' paradises that exist in China and Russia. That's what we need in North America, if it can be done without the bloody violence."

"That's BS, Bill, and you know it!" Caleb would vehemently interject. "Mao and Stalin were murderers and thugs. Everything in Western culture that is noble and worthwhile has been derived from the Christian view that all life is from God. People have worth because they are created in God's image. God will judge everyone for what they have done, be it bad or good. All life from conception matters."

"Mankind will never be free from the curse of violence," Jan would interrupt quietly, with a warning look directed at Caleb to tone down his strident opinions. "After all, Sid, the survival of the fittest entails that the strong will always seek to eliminate the weak."

Sid would look at Caleb intently and then disparagingly remark, "Pretty strong opinions for a snot-nosed kid, I say. Better listen to your brother's advice or you might get a lickin." These discussions, while passionate, were never hateful, and everyone would agree to disagree and to continue at the next opportunity. During the first months, Caleb sat and listened, fascinated by the variety of opinions expressed, but soon he entered into the verbal fray. It was vividly shown here, in this small group as well as nationwide, that Canada was a polyglot society bound by an overriding common interest to advance one's economic wellbeing. Bill sagely ended all his contributions with the remark, "Opinions are like rear ends; we all got one, and everyone is different."

Misery and Counselling

Caleb had just finished sharpening and gassing up his chainsaw when he turned and saw Felix sitting slumped over with tears running down his brown, leathery cheeks. "What's wrong, Felix?" he asked, concerned to see a man who normally showed little emotion being so distraught.

"They're all leaving me behind, Caleb," he sobbed with his guttural voice. "All my friends are either dead or they want to die."

Caleb found it strange that the friends of a man in his thirties were either dying or wanting to die, so he asked, "Why do they want to die, Felix? Do you mean they want to commit suicide?"

"It's the booze and the drugs that are doing it; it kills your mind until there's nothing to live for, and then it's better to end it," Felix explained with a face of pure misery.

"Do you mean that you also feel that way about living?" Caleb asked him, not only concerned about his wellbeing but also wanting him to continue to be part of the crew.

Felix was in his thirties, covered with scars, and missing all his front teeth. He had the same Stanley stainless steel thermos that Caleb had, and when he grabbed Felix's cup by mistake, he instantly gagged on the foul-tasting liquid that he drank. Felix grinned broadly when he noticed Caleb's reaction. He wore the same clothes in cold or warm weather, and when the holes became too large, he pulled another shirt or pants over the ruined ones. He claimed that all the members of his family were dead and that he had never had anybody who really cared for him. "What about God?" Caleb asked. "Do you believe that He cares for you?"

A sly smile creased Felix's mouth as he answered. "God has never given me a wife or a paycheque, and all the preachers from different churches say that they're right and the others are wrong. The Roman Catholic priest told me that as long as I'm baptized and get the holy rites, then I won't go to hell."

"What about suicide?" Caleb persisted. "Did the priest tell you, according to his doctrine, what happens to those who take their own life?" Felix looked puzzled and Caleb realized that the intricacies of theological doctrine were too much for him, so he dropped the subject.

On Friday or Saturday evenings he would occasionally see Felix coming out of the Sear's beer parlours located on Main Street. The alcohol made him loud and bellicose, and Caleb learned to avoid him in town. He felt very helpless as he observed Felix walking the disaster road.

***

Wheels

"She's a beauty, Caleb," purred the Ford salesman as he caressed the vinyl interior of the five-year-old 1957 Ford Fairlane. "Nine hundred and fifty dollars and she's yours. Five hundred down and the balance at 8 per cent over one year."

A cream white top with green bottom panels below the golden curved accent stripe seemed a thing of pure beauty to Caleb. He had completed two years of hard work and had managed to save enough from his thirty dollar per month allowance to swing the down payment. He knew that Frank would not budge on his prices and that he was an honest salesman and would not sell him a lemon. "It's a deal!" he shouted triumphantly as they shook hands. "When can I have her?" When the paperwork was completed, he stepped into his car, and it would have been hard to find a prouder boy in all of Sears.

The warm interior of the A-frame clapboard church and the unaccustomed inactivity for a whole hour caused his latent narcolepsy to surface. As his head bobbed in agreement, he briefly awoke to hear a snippet from the sermon. "Everything that we have we hold in trust. God is the owner of all His created world," emphasized the preacher in his Sunday afternoon sermon. "We are stewards allowed to use our King's possessions." Caleb again jolted awake as a sharp finger poked into his back. He pondered the meaning of what he had just heard. That meant that he really didn't own his Ford. He had not minded working for his family or paying monthly donations to the church, but he had become very possessive of his '57 Ford. According to the preacher however he needed to possess as if not possessing. That car spelled independence for him and allowed him to escape into a world that he believed was controlled by himself. As he polished and maintained it, he grew to realize the powerful attraction that material objects are able to exert over people. The car became an idol that occupied a place that was reserved for someone else.

Lead Hand

"Please, Jan, let me be the sawyer," Caleb begged his brother. "I've watched the technique and learned all the tricks. I know that I can increase production to a higher level than Bill ever would be able to do." Bill had told Jan that he was quitting, and Caleb wasted no time in asking for his job.

"I know you can do the job, Caleb, but I promised Mom to keep you away from danger, and you know how dangerous the sawyer's job is," cautioned Jan. "Eighty percent of sawyers lose some part of their bodies, and you can be a mighty careless boy."

After two applicants failed to pass muster, his brother reluctantly allowed Caleb to become the mill's sawyer. He immediately hired his cousin to replace the two lumber packers. Cousin Karl had a prodigious appetite for work and constantly jerked his hand at Caleb to let him know that he should push him harder. One of the former lumber packers took over his old job, and the other packer became his assistant. Within two months, production was up by 30 per cent, and Caleb became the golden boy of the crew. "Careful, Caleb, please be careful, don't push it too hard," Jan reminded him, over and over. "Money can never compensate for a maimed body or worse—a dead one."

Bonanza

It was during the winter of Caleb's nineteenth year that the mill was placed in a stand of fine straight timber. The forest crew was able to cut and skid more timber than he could saw in a ten-hour day. He had experienced some close calls, but as his mom would say, "Thanks be to God, my Caleb still has all his body parts."

He again pestered his brother. "C'mon, Jan, let me saw during a night shift of four hours so that we can reduce the glut of logs at the mill site." Eventually, as usual, he got his way. That winter proved to be an economic bonanza for all the crew. Caleb could provide his parents with ample money for all their needs, and he received an increased allowance. It also meant that both his younger sisters and brother would be able to attend university and develop the wonderful literary abilities they possessed. The love of money may be the root of evil, but having a sufficient amount to make ends meet was certainly a novel and pleasing experience.

Strange Birds

Cliff Walker claimed to have come from Alabama, and Caleb did not like him. He drove the logging truck that Jan had recently bought, and he drove it hard. Caleb had to share the cabin with him and he was amazed to see the number of guns and knives Cliff had stowed in his trunk. After a supper of instant potatoes mixed with pork and beans, Caleb proceeded to ask him, "What's up, Cliff? Why do you need to have all those weapons?"

Before he replied, he pulled out a particularly large knife and slowly stroked the razor edge with a whetstone. "I keep these just to make sure that people I don't like leave me alone. For instance, I don't like Jews, Italians, or Negroes. I think it would be good for you, kid, if you stay on my good side," he remarked with a leer.

Caleb did not sleep well that night, and the next morning he spoke to his brother. "That guy is a creep, and I refuse to be in the same cabin with him. Please fire him before something nasty happens."

"Nah, Caleb," Jan scoffed. "He's just trying to scare you. Pay him no attention; he's a hard worker and doing a good job, isn't he?"

The following day, their Pa came to visit the mill, and when Cliff saw him, he approached Peter and thought he would be affable by telling him about the curse of integration in his home state. After every few words, he would let loose with a string of curses as he slapped Peter on the back. Peter pushed hard against the chest of this obnoxious fellow and told him to be ashamed of his racism and blasphemy. Jan and Caleb watched in horror as Cliff pulled down his fly and started to urinate on their Pa's boots. Jan kicked him as hard as he could and then told him to clear out. Jan ordered the rest of the crew to prevent Cliff from getting to his trunk and Jan informed him that he could pick it up at the RCMP detachment in Sears. Thankfully, they never saw or heard from that despicable person again.

Intersection and Collision

Jokes and horseplay often served to break the tedium of the long winter working days. The crew took along well-read, dog-eared copies of the *Readers Digest* and improved their vocabularies, as well as enjoyed the telling of the funnier jokes. At the start of employment, Jan would warn the new employees that burlesque girlie magazines were not allowed on site. "What's up with that brother of yours?" Sid asked Caleb when he was first hired. "What's wrong with looking at pictures of good looking women?"

"Nothing," he replied, "just as long as they got all their clothes on. We believe that pornography degrades women and ruins relationships and marriages." Sid shook his head in disgust and muttered something about "uptight Calvinists." He, however, never broke the rule, and with the passage of time his choice of language steadily progressed beyond the four letter word variety. Much that happened in the lives of the mill crew was the same, but there were divides in outlook and morality that bespoke of completely different world views.

On the edge

The January blizzard howled outside the rude cabin, but inside, the cherry-red, airtight stove made an oasis of warmth. Caleb, left by himself, was made keenly aware that one mistake could rudely alter the situation. "Be careful!" Jan had warned as he left for a four-day break. "If you injure yourself, it could be too late before help arrives. Remember that one kick or squeeze from the horses could put you down for good."

"It's okay, Jan," Caleb reassured him, "I'm not a greenhorn or a kid anymore."

When the accident happened, it came from a completely unexpected quarter. Caleb had cut four tinder dry, jack pine trees into sixteen-inch (40 cm.) lengths and proceeded to split them with the steel maul. The task was a mundane exercise for him, and his mind was busy with thoughts of eternity. Suddenly, a chunk of steel broke off the maul and imbedded itself into his thigh. A gout of blood darkened the front of his pants and quickly froze solid in the -35 F. degree temperature. *It's not your fault, but you're in serious trouble*, was his first thought. His second thought was, *Think carefully or you may not be around much longer.* The First Aid kit was above his bunkbed, and he had to get there quickly to staunch the flow of blood. Praying all the way, he got to the cabin and first cinched his belt around his thigh, above the wound. The blood flow slowed to a trickle, and then he removed the jagged piece of steel. The First Aid kit had an ample supply of surgical gauze, which he tightly wrapped around the wound. After ten minutes, he slowly released the pressure from the belt and cried with relief when the bandages stopped the flow of blood. He had only completed two days of his four-day horse care watch.

The loud neighing of the two thirsty and hungry horses jolted Caleb awake, and he realized that he had slept through their evening food and water feeding. The wounded right leg was sore and stiff, but he found that it would move and, with the aid of a corn broom, he could get around. It usually took him about twenty minutes to attend to the feeding routine, but this time it took over an hour. Nelly nickered and nuzzled him when he limped into her stall, and somewhere in that equine brain she knew that all was not right. Caleb's every move had to be planned as he realized that there was no more room for mishaps.

During the fourth night, the fever started and a wonderful kaleidoscope of images coursed through his brain. A being appeared who held the periodic table of the elements in his hands and kept yelling, "Chemicals! Caleb, that's all you are—disintegrating chemicals."

"No!" he yelled back at the fell creature. "Stir the brew all you want, for all eternity, because there will never be another me." The being dissolved and was replaced by the image of Moses as he was drawn in the children's Bible that his Pa used to read to him in his childhood.

"You will always be here, Caleb," Moses reassured him. "There is an infinite amount of work to be done." He reached toward him, and then Caleb awoke in Jan's strong arms as he bundled him into the warm pickup truck.

After four days in the Sears hospital, he could go home, and soon Caleb was pulling the logs through the screaming head saw again. The images and hallucinations had a powerful effect on him, however, and often his thoughts pondered their meaning.

Tragedy

"What a fortunate, blessed family we are," was the refrain that repeated itself in Caleb's head as he gunned the 1957 Ford up the farm hill and spun a perfect 180-degree parking manoeuvre. The work week was over and he was looking forward to a relaxing weekend with his friends. The hot July sun made his eyes squint into narrow slits, and he could barely discern the two small figures with their white shirts walking up to the farmhouse. "Must be some salesmen who heard that Pa was an easy mark," he mused as he watched their slow approach.

His Mom was not at home. She had travelled to Holland for the first time since emigrating to visit with her family. Her parting words still rang in his ears: "Be careful all of you, because I won't be here to watch over you." Peter was hoeing in the potato field, so Caleb greeted the two approaching church elders and invited them in for coffee.

"Please go and get your father," were the first words they spoke. "We have terrible news."

"Not my Mom! Please Lord," Caleb begged as he raced to get his Pa. "The plane must have crashed, or she's had a heart attack. Don't let it be her."

"Sit down, Pete," the older elder asked when Caleb and his Pa returned. "Your son Brock has drowned in Carson Lake, and the police have just retrieved his body. They asked us to bring you this terrible news, and we are so terribly sorry."

Caleb had never heard such a terrible keening cry erupt from his Pa, and he blocked his ears and ran away. His prayer for his mother's safety was answered, but not in a way that could ever be imagined. Never again would he consider that in relation to other families, the Nachtegals were blessed and fortunate.

When his sedated Mom was carried home from the airport, she asked one question: "Why was it him?" According to witnesses, Brock had gone under the water without a struggle. A simple game of retrieving a thrown inner tube, played with a friend, triggered a renegade gene and caused the beginning swimmer to lose his life.

The grief that Brock's death caused his parents in their senior years never completely disappeared, but "faith" came to the rescue. They and Caleb would never, in this life, understand the why, but they accepted that God is in control. There is a purpose and a reason, but humans only see through a darkened glass.

> *He grew strong and sturdy to delight a parent's eye,*
> *Full of bright life, intelligence, and ambition,*
> *We/He had dreams, made plans, but life passed by.*
> *New realities, works are now his, by divine condition.*
>
> *Caleb*

Stir Crazy

"Why, Caleb?" Jan pleaded, "We get along so well. Why do you want to leave just when the lumber business is making us a lot of money?"

I need to strike out on my own, Jan," Caleb replied. "I'm twenty-two years old, and Sears is choking me. I want to go to the big city and resume my education. I also want to find the special girl of my life, because I can't find her here."

"That's a bunch of BS, Caleb, and you know it." Jan angrily retorted. "You're a skilled tradesman, not an egghead, and there are plenty of nice girls here that you could marry."

"The writing is on the wall for you too, Jan," Caleb continued. "Soon this way of making a living will be over. We're not making efficient use of the tree resources, and the waste will no longer be tolerated by the government. Get out while you can and start a new enterprise." Any further words were choked off by the welling of emotion that he felt for his older brother/father.

Life Finds a Way

Brock's death crystallized Caleb's desire for a new beginning. The chasm he left behind scarred over, and after two more years of support for his parents, he bundled his gear into the Ford and headed south. Babylon was beckoning.

CHAPTER VI
The Gene Pool Asserts Itself

For generations, the descendants of Pablo and Trina stayed, contented and employed, in their sturdy houses, tending to their flower fields and corner grocery stores. Descendants were conceived that became increasingly phlegmatic and quiet. The fiery Spanish spirit lay quiet and latent in the thinning gene pool. Once every second generation, a child would show the flashing eyes and aquiline features that stood out so sharply from the blond, plump faces of his or her siblings.

The huge windmills turned slowly in the soft spring breeze as they powered the pumps that lifted and spouted the excess water from the drainage ditches into the North Sea. Diego laid down the heavy plank across the drainage ditch to the next flower plot and looked, with some envy, over to his younger brother. Steve was using a sturdy pole to vault across the ditch, and his smile told Diego that he was falling behind. "Got a bit of arthritis, old man?" he ribbed as he vaulted back again, just to show off. Diego flexed his huge arms, and his deep-set eyes flashed as he lunged at Steve in a playful attempt to dunk him. Both men worked for a large bulb grower, and their burning ambition was to lease a plot of land for themselves. One-hundred-year leases were common in the area of South Holland, and it was almost like it belonged to you—but not quite.

Tulip Fields in Bloom

"Let's be fifty-fifty partners, Steve. Is it a deal?" asked Diego as he looked at the twenty-hectare plot of land with the waving tulips. He stuck out a calloused hand with black crescents of polder dirt under each fingernail.

"Sure," Steve replied with an outstretched hand only slightly smaller. "It's the only way we can financially swing it. You and I both have growing families, and it's hard to make ends meet on a labourer's salary."

After one year, the profits were divided and the brothers separated. A strong desire to "run the show" ran in each brother's veins and made any long-term partnership unworkable.

"Beautiful! Isn't it, Rita?" Diego intoned in his deep voice as they drank in the rich red and yellow colours of the tulips. He held her close and solicitously supported her growing womb. "After I sell this year's crop of bulbs, I'll have saved enough to buy our own house."

"It's sad, Diego, that you cut all the lovely blooms when they're in their prime," Rita replied. "Why do you do that?"

"I'm not a flower grower, dear," Diego explained. "I sell the bulbs, and they need to be nourished rather than the flowers. I am sorry to remove such beauty, but it cannot be helped. Your beauty is my delight, and we will share everything together." Life was full of promise and beauty for Rita and Diego, but after a number of children were born, it all changed.

The ominous clouds of coming war forced the young couple to be separated. Diego was called up in the draft and soon joined his brigade. Cramped and dirty bunks with a bare minimum of hygiene led to outbreaks of typhoid and meningitis. "My back," moaned Diego to the camp physician as he curled into a fetal position. "My head is splitting, and I'm burning with heat. What's happening to me?"

Doctor Geiss saw the symptoms so common in the camp and uttered the dread diagnosis. "You have meningitis, Diego," the doctor replied. "There's not much I can do for you. You're in God's hands."

Diego survived, but a broken and bent man returned to his Rita—a man who could do no more physical work for many years. A clerical position was found for this formerly strapping giant, in The Hague, where he settled with Rita and his young family. As he slowly improved, he began to run a corner grocery, ably helped by his Rita.

At the end of the terrible 1940s, Rita, in her forties, gave birth to her last baby. It took all her reserves to bring her baby to the light. "It's a girl, Rita," Diego spoke proudly, holding his daughter.

"A beautiful, dark-haired girl, and she has my nose." They called her Tirzah.

It was another day of hard work for Rita. With baby Tirzah precariously dangling from her hip, Rita entered their small store. Housekeeping duties and working in the store were beginning to wear her down. A blast of damp, cold air entered the store when Diego came in and left the door open. "Put down that flour scoop, Rita, and put the baby in her crib!" he excitedly exclaimed.

"What is it, dear?" Rita worriedly responded. She was not used to seeing her man so agitated and excited. Diego's trials had made him become a silent, sorrowful man.

"I received a letter from brother Steve. He tells me he is doing great in Canada and wants us to come and join him in the far west of British Columbia. Quick, Rita, get the world globe and let's see if we can find where that place is located!" he enthused. All of Holland was gripped by emigration fever. Shakespeare said it so well in the play, *King Henry V*:

> "Now all the youth of England are on fire. They sell the pasture now to buy the horse. For now sits Expectation in the air."

Plans were made, changed, and made again. Major decisions did not come easily for Diego, but the lure of Steve's rosy gushing's about Canada proved to be the clincher. "Lots of cheap land available for growing flowers," was the final come-on that decided Diego. The Atlantic Ocean was crossed in the old troop carrier, *Volendam*, and unbeknown to one-year-old Tirzah, she was followed four months later by a skinny six year old boy who travelled in the same boat.

Diego rented a large house and was again able to resume a physical, hard-working life. He even slogged for months in the peat bogs, cutting the water logged peat into neat squares with a sharp-edged shovel. He saved every penny he could but did not neglect his offering to the Lord in the church where the Teelharts worshipped. Rita did all she could to help her man. If a dime could be stretched, she did it, and she ranged far and wide for "good deals." As soon as he could afford it, Diego purchased land so he could return to growing flowers. He became known as the 'Dahlia King'. They purchased a second-hand panel van that they used only when necessary. To save gas, Rita would often hitchhike in order to take advantage of grocery and clothes sales.

"Hop in, lady, and take a load off your feet!" yelled the affable, grey- haired stranger. Rita threw her shopping bags in the rear of the dilapidated Ford. She looked carefully at the driver and then used her hankie to clean the dusty front seat before she sat down. She introduced herself in her broken English and provided the driver with a written destination. He laughed and responded, "No problem, pretty lady, I can drop you off there. Are you new to this country? You sound like an immigrant?"

Suddenly the car lurched into a side street, and a terrified Rita noticed a whole new look on the driver's face. At the next intersection, when the car slowed, she opened her door and rolled into the gutter, yelling at the top of her voice. The car stopped momentarily and then sped away as people came to investigate the yelling. A passing police car stopped and two officers comforted a distraught Rita. They took down a description, provided by Rita in broken English, and brought her safely home. It took a long time before she left the comfort of Diego's arms, and it took even longer before she hitchhiked again. She always ended the story of her terrifying ordeal with the remark, "*Het was en rot vent* (he was a rotten man), and I lost my nice shopping bags."

Soon they purchased a house that not only housed their large family, but they were able to take in boarders. "We make a good team, my Rita," Diego told her, his deep-set blue eyes gleaming. "We both want a good, safe, Christian life for ourselves and the children." Soon they bought a larger property and opened a flower and garden shop. "Canada is a good land to live in, Rita," he would often tell her. "I think we made the right decision to come here." Rita would smile and laugh in agreement and gaze with love at the last of her eight children. God was again smiling upon her family, and the house was filled with good cooking smells and Rita's mirth-filled laughter. She had great delight in loving and spoiling her little Tirzah. Every morning she placed two large hair ribbons in Tirzah's hair and provided her with lots of Dutch licorice.

It was simply amazing. Traces of the imperial hidalgo characteristics were evident in some of the Teelhart children, but Tirzah was all Spanish. She blossomed into womanhood with deep-set, magnetic blue eyes, a beautiful curving mouth, and an imperial hidalgo nose that gave the face strength and character. Maybe Pablo was looking down and smiling. She was the joy of her mother and the worry of her father. He hoped that her beauty would not attract wild, irresponsible boys. His misgivings were not without foundation. During her eighteenth year, Tirzah introduced her parents to her new beau: "Dad and Mom, I'd like you to meet Caleb Nachtegal."

***

Big City—You Mean More to Me

The seven years of service were finished. "I want you to stay here with me, son, and expand the farming operation," commanded Pa. "We'll buy the adjoining 160 acres, you'll marry one of the Jong's daughters, and we'll both have a good life."

"No, Pa," Caleb replied firmly, "I've worked for you and our family faithfully for seven years, and now it's time to seek my own fortune. I couldn't continue my schooling because you needed me to work, so now I want to go to the Lower Mainland and get a part-time job and go back to school."

Peter's initial look of anger was replaced by resignation. "Okay, Caleb, if you must go, then go. Just remember that when things don't work out, you'll have only yourself to blame." Caleb offered no response, because there was a whole new world out there that he was aching to see. He was determined to go.

Caleb put all his essential possessions into the trunk and back seat of his 1957 Ford and kissed his weeping Mom goodbye. "I'm not going to the end of the world, Mom," he comforted her. "Two of my sisters already live in the 'big city,' and I'll get to see you often. But before I settle down, I'm going to visit the place of my birth."

"Remember, Caleb my son, to be sure and visit all the relatives from my side when you travel to your birthplace. The Nachtegals will try to monopolize you, but tell them that you are coming to visit all your relatives."

"Don't worry, Mom," he reassured her, "I will visit every last one." Caleb had saved enough money to go on an extended vacation to Europe, to visit the land of his birth, and travel on to fabulous Paris.

After Paris, the Farm Won't Do

The old chartered DC-8 lumbered into the rain-laden clouds above Vancouver's airport with all four propellers biting into the darkening sky. Loaded to the max, with every seat filled, its destination was over the North Pole to Schiphol Airport, located near Amsterdam. It was the first time Caleb had ever flown in an airplane, and he was eagerly looking forward to the adventure. Four young adventurers, including Caleb, occupied the rear seats, and the stewardesses provided ample libations. A mellow anticipatory mood enveloped him as he imagined what it would be like to see the land of his birth and to walk once more over the dykes on the island of Goringa. It had been sixteen years since six-year-old Caleb Nachtegal had left, and vivid, childlike memories remained: leaden skies filled with seagulls driven by gusting winds and sharp rain pellets were among the memories. Labouring men driving huge work horses among the waving flowers and sugar beets were also imbedded in his memory banks. Aunts and uncles providing ice cream and candy were enveloped in the rosy hue of a cozy, safe world.

Trouble

The cribbage tournament was going in Caleb's favour when he felt a small shudder through his seat. A bright starry sky shone down on Great Slave Lake in the Northwest Territories far below. A sharp reminder from his fellow players forced his attention on another sixteen-point crib hand that would give him the best out of a seven game tournament. A loud "splat" sounded, and the window view became obscured by a thick film of oil. "Hey, Stew!" Caleb excitedly asked the girl standing in the galley. "Why is there oil coming out of the motor?"

"Please, sir! Lower your voice, and do not alarm the other passengers needlessly," she responded with evident irritation. "There's nothing to be worried about."

Maybe not, Caleb thought, but he knew enough about motors to know that the stopped propeller spelled trouble.

Soon enough, the captain's voice rasped over the speakers that the plane had lost the use of one motor and there was concern about a second one. "We'll be turning back to the closest airport, which is Edmonton," the captain informed the passengers. "We're able to maintain altitude with three operational motors, and even go a long way with only two working motors."

That would be highly optimistic, Caleb thought, *especially when the plane is loaded to capacity and carrying full tanks of fuel.*

Keening wails broke out among the approximately two hundred passengers after the captain's speech, and the stewardesses provided sedatives to all who wished to use them. Caleb and his seatmates fixed their gaze on the three revolving props that were becoming more visible in the murky morning light. Two hundred miles from Edmonton, a second motor stopped turning briefly and then started again. Cheers broke out when the captain announced that they were going to make it, and they did.

Thank you, Lord, repeated itself over and over in Caleb's head after the screech of the tires reaffirmed his connection with solid earth. It wasn't an auspicious beginning to Caleb's flying career, but of the many flights taken since, that one stands out. During the entire tense situation, he had been certain that his portion in this life was not over, and an emotional relief with an undefined longing surged through his entire being.

Ill Winds Also Carry Benefits

"Listen up, folks!" yelled the charter flight representative at the front of the transport bus. "You'll be provided accommodations and meals for four days until another plane arrives to bring you to your destination." Lodgings fit for a king greeted the weary passengers at the four-star Edmonton hotel. The concierge handed Caleb a key and a thirty-five-dollar allowance chit for three meals a day. After he entered the posh bedroom, he dropped his bag and bounced onto the huge bed and turned on the TV. Everything was new and amazing, and the liberated farm boy was determined to experience everything that was available.

Goringa Revisited

The remainder of the journey proved to be uneventful, with a brief refueling stop at Reykjavik, Iceland. Amsterdam's Schiphol Airport was ablaze with blue runway markers as the old plane hit the tarmac with a hard bump. As he walked across the landing strip to the terminal, Caleb felt a thrill of anticipation to be in the land of his birth.

"Can you tell me how to get to Goringa Island?" Caleb asked the bored, overweight, blonde girl in the information booth.

She laughed at his use of antiquated Dutch words and spoke in clear English. "It's too late for bus and train service to Goringa. Just go to the taxi stand and make a deal with someone willing to take you."

Caleb grabbed his battered suitcase, hoisted the heavy backpack, and asked the first taxi driver he saw for a ride. "Where are you going?" he asked.

The driver replied with a curt "no" when Caleb told him that he needed to go to Goringa. "You must be a joker or a nut (*niet goed wisj*) to think that anyone is going to take you to Goringa at this time of night," jeered the sixth driver that Caleb approached. "Take my advice; hop in my taxi and I'll bring you to the Amsterdam Hilton. Enjoy a hearty breakfast and then go with the bus in the morning."

As he entered the ornate lobby of the Hilton, Caleb knew that this was not a good idea. "That will be one hundred and twenty American dollars for the night sir," smirked the supercilious desk clerk as he looked at Caleb's battered suitcase and rumpled clothes.

"You are joshing me (*gek*)" Caleb replied. "That's a week's wages for me, and I only have Canadian dollars."

"Oh—that will be one hundred and fifty then," he unctuously demanded.

Caleb stormed out of the lobby, and since the rain had stopped, he tied his suitcase to his wrist and lay down on the bench outside the hotel. As he dozed, he was suddenly awakened by a loud, "*Hey jongen!*" that jerked him upright. "You could get mugged out here. Would you be looking for a ride?"

Caleb put his glasses on and focused on the red-haired youth who hailed him. He was getting cold, and beggars can't be choosers. "Will you drive me to Goringa?" he asked.

"I will drive you to Spain if you can pay," Red chortled, poking his pinky into the tuft of hair protruding from his ear. "Hop in *jongen*," he invited. "They tell me I drive like the biblical Jehu." Truer words were never spoken.

After a wild, high-speed drive, Caleb soon arrived in the center of Polder, his birth town. It struck him, used to Canada's distances, what a small country Holland was.

"That was not the amount you quoted me," he angrily responded to the amount asked for by the extortionist-robber baron called a taxi driver.

"The extra is for the rapid delivery," Red smirked as he dropped Caleb off at midnight in the center of the village. His request for a tip was greeted with a stare that convinced him to quickly leave.

"Tante Lena Nachtegal," Caleb repeated over and over to the old shaking and deaf burgher who finally answered the peremptory knocking on his door. "Where do I find her house?"

"Over there," he finally quavered, pointing to an old brick house at the top of a long dyke. "Are you the Canadian who is coming to visit her?"

"Yup!" Caleb yelled over his shoulder as he made tracks lugging his heavy suitcase up the hill. After a lengthy knocking, the door was opened by a huge, dark-haired man.

It was his Pa's youngest brother, Oom Flip, who greeted him with a bone crushing hug. "Put your shoes there, boy," he ordered as he was shoved aside by Tante Lena. She was his Pa's younger unmarried sister, and she lived with her brother, Flip, a 250-pound giant whom she called by the diminutive name "Flipje." She had long ago adopted Caleb's family as her own. She had visited twice in Canada, and the joy she expressed at seeing Caleb brought tears to his eyes.

"Step into the light, boy, so I can see you," she repeated while circling him like a mother hen. "So tall and thin," she clucked. "Well, we will soon fix that!" A hot stew of smoked eel was simmering on the stove with a side dish of pork hocks swimming in fat. During Caleb's ten-day stay, she managed to chunk fifteen pounds onto his lanky frame with a diet that did not allow her to grow old.

The old, yellowed photograph on the blackened oak mantel showed a shapely, good-looking, young woman beside a young man. Caleb asked his Tante, "Who is that girl?"

"Don't you recognize me, boy?" she smiled, looking pleased and teasing him. "That was taken on my twenty-second birthday."

Caleb, wisely, did not mention that the years had not been kind to his Tante. "But," he stammered, "you never talked about a boyfriend. Who is the man?"

"He was my intended," Tante replied with pain in her voice. "We were engaged, but he was unfaithful to me, and I never wanted to go through that again. Besides, the thought of having babies repelled and frightened me. God has given me so many nieces and nephews to love and spoil. Just look at your mom, boy. Ten times she experienced the misery of being in the family way."

Caleb compared the physical form of his Tante to the image of his mother and concluded that bearing ten children had not diminished the beauty of his mother. *Truncated, hurting, and bitter lives strewn everywhere*, Caleb thought as he hugged his Tante. "I shall try to be as good for you as I can, dear Tante."

Caleb's good intentions were soon sorely put to the test. "I was never fond of your mother," Tante remarked in answer to his inquiry about how his Pa and Mom had met. "She was forward and arrogant and put on airs. She used to bike all the way from the neighbouring town just so she could meet your dad coming from his work. All her family had their noses in the air, because at one time they were land owners."

"Not true!" Caleb remonstrated hotly, cut to the quick at the criticism of his beloved mother and barely containing his temper. "You always seemed to get along so well with Mom when you visited with us. Was that all just an act?" He now understood why Tante called him "boy" instead of Caleb. "Caleb" was the name of his Grandpa Bedard. She harboured a deep dislike for his mother's family and felt that all the boys needed to be called after the Nachtegal male names, like Caleb's brother Jan. After that initial skirmish, they avoided the issue of the maternal French mother's family and enjoyed many good days exploring the island.

Goringa is a beautiful small island that the hard-working Dutch and French ancestors wrested from the sea during the past millennia. It produced a cornucopia of fruit, vegetables, and flowers that were exported to the mainland. The inner circle of dykes was encircled by outer circles of dykes as population growth necessitated. Painstakingly, shovel full by shovel full, the early settlers built their guardian dykes. Their history was full of the instances when the wild North Sea breached the defenses and caused human tragedies. In the flood of 1953, almost 500 people lost their lives when most of the island was under water. As Caleb walked and rode over the landscape, it was evident what his Pa had so often said when he talked about his birthplace: "Nowhere have I found a place so verdant and productive as my birth island. History has shown, however, that 'The Sword of Damocles' always hovered over us."

Caleb pondered the reasons why a man who so loved to farm would leave such a lovely place, and he found the answer in his own entrepreneurial character. Always a renter and never a chance to truly own your own land would be a galling blight for any entrepreneur. Living among people who had many good qualities but were unmoving in their implacable traditions and superstitions would be hard for his father's ranging intellect. His religious beliefs separated him from the old traditional church-goers who viewed him as a heretic. The deep divide between Caleb's mother and her in-laws also contributed to the discontent. He could hear the siren's calling to his Pa: "Away, away across the sea to new beginnings where I can be free." Sunlit propaganda pictures of endless, waving wheat fields, peopled by smiling, happy Canadians, were a powerful lure.

"No, boy, please do not be foolish but listen to your Tante," was the response when Caleb told her that he would be leaving for France and Paris on the morning bus. "Have I not been good to you? And you are just beginning to put on some weight," she cajoled.

Caleb laughed, kissed, and hugged her and told her she was the best cook in the world. "Everyone needs to see Paris before they die," he teased her.

"Boy—boy, don't go! I never did, and I am glad. That city is like Sodom and Gomorrah, full of sin and corruption," she warned.

Next morning, stuffed with a huge breakfast, Caleb barely made it to the bus on time. "Bye, Tante Lena," Caleb yelled as he waved from the bus. "I'll see you before I fly back home," he promised.

City of Light and Darkness

The towns and villages of Belgium and Northern France passed by in dun-coloured clusters. A day in Brussels made it apparent that Belgium's colonial wealth was spent in the cities. Imposing edifices and many statues sought to impress, and did. It did not prepare him, however, for Paris. To his small-town eyes, this was a city like no other. His destination hotel was in sight of the Arc De Triumph, and after he had wrestled his way through the crowded sidewalk, he found a chair and fell asleep in the lobby of the Amsterdam Hotel. The lineup to the concierge stretched out the entrance door, so after a power nap, he finally got the key to his room. It was a tiny alcove with a wash basin. There were two toilets and one shower for the entire third floor. Well, Caleb was used to making do with rustic surroundings, and a quick washing under the armpits with a dab of underarm deodorant prepared him for exploring his surroundings.

"New in the city, are you, lad?" was the greeting Caleb got from a white, short, sturdy South African as he entered the lobby.

"Never been here before, Mac. Can I buy you a beer while you tell me all about it?" Caleb responded with his most engaging look. That turned out to be a fortuitous meeting. Jack Krieger was a pilot in the South African Air Force and had been in Paris on previous vacation leaves from duty.

"You want to see Paris, Caleb? Then I'll make you a deal," he offered. "You pay for the drinks, and I'll be your guide, plus I know some cute girls who would like to come with us. Is it a deal?" Even though he was a rube from the sticks, Caleb knew that right up front he needed to let Jack know that as a Christian, his idea of fun had limits, so he told him. When Caleb explained to him what those limits were, the man laughed and responded, "No problem, mate. My parents brought me up strict, but you're only young once, righto!" He laughed with an engaging wink. "Let's be Voortrekkers, as we say in South Africa."

Voortrekkers love to explore, and Caleb was glad that it worked out great. Jack's alcohol intake did not break his budget, and Jack's girls were nice, eighteen-year-old girls who were on holidays and looking to explore Paris with boys who would share the cost but not be demanding. They came from the Dutch province of Brabant and had been brought up in Roman Catholic families.

The first street-smarts that Jack taught Caleb was how to exit the Amsterdam Hotel. In 1967, the Algerian and Moroccan guerilla wars for independence from France were in full swing, and Paris was full of wounded victims reduced to begging. Men whose legs had been blown away manoeuvred on wooden roller platforms with steel-pointed sticks. A request for money, accompanied by an upraised pike, was hard to ignore. Right outside the hotel entrance, a phalanx of prostitutes was surrounded by a larger circle of maimed beggars, and Caleb could not imagine how they were going to exit. "Follow close behind me, Caleb, and do as I do,"

Jack ordered. Interlocking his fingers with his arms stretched out in a frontal vee, Jack divided the tightly packed crowd with Caleb right behind him. When they picked up the girls at their hotel, they repeated the manoeuvre coming in and going out. No one objected to the dividing push, and for three days Jack guided them to the sights of Paris.

Caleb was spellbound by the massive public buildings, museums, and architecture. Paris had beautiful buildings. All the public buildings were made of large quarried marble, granite, and other durable, huge stone blocks. Amsterdam seemed to be made of small red bricks, but Paris was built for the ages. The next four days, Caleb toured by himself, since Jack did not care for the museums and park tours that Caleb enjoyed. He was a great friend who Caleb intended to stay in touch with. He later somehow misplaced Jack's address, so he couldn't send him a note of appreciation. They had been ships passing for a brief duration, never to meet again.

For hours Caleb wandered through the artistic boroughs of Montmartre, boated over the Seine River, and visited the immense structures commissioned by Napoleon at Fontainebleau. The palace of Versailles and the Louvre Museum proved to be an endurance test. So much to see, but aching feet and burning eyes allow only so much. The grim details of the killing of King Louis and Queen Marie Antoinette were a grim reminder of the ferocity of the French Revolution, another tributary contributing to the oceans of spilled blood on this planet. Caleb in later years was able to visit other great cities of the world, but Paris remained forever the "City of Light and Darkness."

After returning to Tante Lena's house for two final days, Caleb noticed that she was determined to explore what he was about. She rejected all his views on politics, history, and the technological advances of science. "Lies, boy, all lies," was her response to man walking on the moon, that the earth was round, or the immensity of the universe. She finished with, "The devil is able to twist anything and everything, boy. Do not believe everything you see or hear." Caleb was tempted to continue but then thought better of it. With the arrogance of youth, he initially thought, *Lies and deceptions are everywhere, I will put my ignorant Tante straight*—but then what purpose would it achieve to upset his old, loving tante? It was time to return to his Canada and begin a new adventure in the Mediterranean of Canada, the Lower Mainland of British Columbia in the city of New Westminster.

"That taxi fare amount that you paid, arriving from Schiphol, was a robbery, boy," Tante scolded when Caleb told her what he had paid to get to her house. "I'll get a taxi to bring you and me to the airport for half the price you paid," she smirked.

"How is that possible?" Caleb retorted. "This is a socialist country, and all taxi fares are supposed to be regulated."

A sly smile crossed his Tante's face as she taunted, "Just wait and see."

The battered Chevy pulled up to Tante's house, and the portly owner-driver managed to pry his large stomach from behind the steering wheel. Tante greeted him with a cheery, "Good morning, Bram, how are your wife and daughter today?" Not waiting for a reply, she immediately followed with, "My nephew has foolishly spent all his money and now needs a cheap ride to the airport. What can you do for a lovely day trip for the three of us?"

Bram plucked at his waistband and sucked on his metal toothpick for a while. He swung his massive head and peered at Tante from under bushy eyebrows before he stated his price. A scream of protest immediately erupted from Tante. "You know what your nickname is Bram? Well, do you? It's not very nice, and your generosity to my poor nephew will help to make people forget it. Now if you show some common sense, I'll do my best to put a stop to it." Some more toothpick sucking ensued before Bram reluctantly agreed to Tante's price.

They all piled in and proceeded to Schiphol Airport at a torturous pace. Farewell hugs and kisses were done and then Caleb asked his Tante one last question just before he boarded the plane: "What was Bram's nickname that you used to threaten him with?"

Tante's lips curled in her trademark smirk and she replied, "Something for you to find out, Caleb, know-it-all." Caleb barely arrived at the check-in gate on time. He clambered aboard for a long, boring trip back to his new home. His encounter with destiny was waiting for him.

***

The Twain Did Meet

It was a warm, sultry June afternoon as Tirzah walked home from her school. Her books weighed heavy as she felt the stifling heat waves radiating from the pavement. The closely-spaced horn beeps of the car behind her stiffened her back. The loud wolf whistle caused her to quicken her step. She had been bothered a number of times by older men asking if she needed a ride home, and her mother had advised her to ignore them and keep walking. The sudden loud laughter accompanying the remark, "Hey, stuck-up!" caused her to turn, and she ran to the boy who jumped out of his car to embrace her.

"Please, Caleb," she pleaded, "don't ever scare me like that again!"

"Well," Caleb teased her, "if you'd wear a long skirt to cover up those legs of yours, then I wouldn't be tempted to do so." Tirzah had given her heart to the tall, lanky boy who courted her, but at times she was frightened. There was a wildness in him and an arrogance that was the exact opposite of her quiet nature. He bewildered her with his compliments, and she constantly worried that he would find her boring and move on.

Caleb Has Found Her

Pledged to Each Other

"Talk to me, Tirzah," was the oft repeated request Caleb made. It sometimes annoyed Tirzah that he demanded it, because her upbringing had been so different from his When she saw and heard the Nachtegals' constant chatter when they were among each other, and heard how they took note of the characteristics of the people around them, she often felt left out. Caleb's sisters could be witty, sharp, and critical, and Tirzah felt very different. Emotions and feelings were deeply felt but not discussed in the Teelhart household, and father Diego was famous for his brevity of speech. Mother Rita's laughter and humour were the bright spot in the family upbringing but did not include wise and sensitive discussions with her children.

"What am I to do?" Tirzah agonized. "Caleb knows I love him, but he wants me to confide in him at a level I've never experienced. I have no one to confide in and ask advice from. It's been two weeks since he left, and he's probably not coming back." As she probed her memory, she recalled the many times that the tension at the Teelhart dinner table was at times unbearable. Her older siblings radiated their unhappiness but never verbalized it. The spiritual treasures that were accepted or rejected were seldom discussed. Tirzah realized that her insecurity about her appearance, lack of confidence, and her feeling of being unloved all stemmed from never having had anyone tell her how lovable she was. Discussing intimate emotions just was not done in the Teelhart home. "Please, Caleb, come back again and I promise to do my best to talk to you," was her unspoken longing. When her Caleb bounded up the porch steps and hugged her so hard that it hurt, she knew it would be for good. With her lovely, tear-streaked face turned to him, she whispered, "Teach me, Caleb, how to express my feelings. I want to."

"You're my girl, Tirzah. I will never leave you again," Caleb promised. For many years it was still difficult to overcome the reluctance to communicate, and often Caleb would misunderstand the silence as avoidance.

What a change in life one other person can make, Tirzah thought. *My previous life seems like another time period.* She knew that biology was calling and hated to part from her Caleb. It was time to get married, have babies, and be a mother. Even though they had little money, they went boldly ahead in faith.

The wedding day was the happiest day in the lives of Tirzah and Caleb. The minister intoned from seemingly far away, "Do you, Tirzah, take this man to be your lawfully wedded husband?"

"I do," answered Tirzah, with a brilliant smile that made Caleb's heart want to jump out of his suit.

And They Two Shall Be One

***

The huge, orange Boeing 747 stood parked at the boarding gate, and the newlyweds had never seen such a gigantic aircraft. The generation of jumbo jets purchased by Canadian Pacific Airlines for overseas flights seemed to come straight out of a science fiction story. Friends and relatives were hugged and waved goodbye as the honeymooners departed. After boarding, Caleb and Tirzah walked to the back of the airplane, and the friendly stewardess immediately asked if they were newlyweds. She giggled and told the couple that the plane was only one quarter full and that they would get the special newlywed treatment. Economy fares never had it so good. Food and libations were pressed upon them, and Tirzah soon felt stuffed, while Caleb did his best to let naught go to waste.

Up, up and Away

They had just saved and received enough money for airfare and car rental to have their honeymoon on the fabled Hawaiian Islands. "Where will we stay, Caleb?" Tirzah asked as they looked at the accommodation prices on the hotel marque.

Sun-Drenched Interlude

"Never fear, sweetheart," Caleb enthused. "We'll rent an old beater car and then go shopping in the Army and Navy surplus store." Tirzah knew that Caleb had signed up for the triple island tour, so that would mean three car rentals and accommodations. "How much will that come to?" Caleb asked the perspiring clerk as he dumped the pup tent and large sleeping bag on the counter.

"Twenty dollars, sir, and that includes free hand wipes and glow sticks." Tirzah, who had been entrusted with the money pouch, peeled off a crisp Canadian twenty dollar bill and was met with a stolid stare. "We don't take funny money," rasped the clerk. "You better go to the bank and rustle up some good ole United States greenbacks.

The breeze had stopped and the old Datsun was as hot as a furnace inside. "Where is the AC?" asked Tirzah.

Caleb replied, "Right here," as he peeled off his shirt and rolled down the window.

"No fair," Tirzah complained, "you men have all the advantages."

"Not all," Caleb replied with a grin that Tirzah was beginning to know.

The Bank of America was located and the Canadian Dollar bankroll was decreased by 15 per cent in the resulting exchange. The pile of purchases was waiting on the counter when they returned, and Caleb wheedled a free hatchet into the deal.

The beaches! The glorious Hawaiian beaches and flaming sunsets were the stuff of dreams. Suntan lotion was slapped on and into the warm water Tirzah and Caleb played, swam, and surfed.

"Come over here, haole!" yelled the butternut Hawaiian teenagers who laughed as Caleb tried, over and over, to catch the wave. "That's it!" they all yelled as Caleb paddled furiously and stood up on his board. It seemed the ride lasted forever to Caleb, but Tirzah told him it was only a few minutes. After three rides, a coral bruise ended the fun, and the lovers lazed the day away.

Queen of Kalapana

"That looks like a lovely spot to set up camp!" Caleb exclaimed as the Datsun jolted over the lava rocks.

"It sure looks lonely out here," a worried Tirzah replied, but Caleb teased her and ran into the water.

"You've got a lumberjack to protect you, my wife!" Caleb yelled and then ran back and cajoled Tirzah to join him in the warm, blue water. After a sparse dinner, augmented by split coconuts, Caleb set up the canvas pup tent, and after the sunset, the honeymooners crawled inside and fell asleep."

A sudden poke in his back woke Caleb up from a deep sleep. "Wake up, Caleb, please wake up," begged a distraught Tirzah. "I'm itching all over. There are creepy crawlies in our sleeping bag."

Caleb reached over and hugged his Tirzah. "Nonsense, girl," he soothed. "We're sleeping on clean, white sand, and there are no mosquitos in Hawaii. Just go back to sleep."

"No, Caleb, I'm not imagining it," Tirzah firmly replied. "Give me the car keys, because I'm not sleeping in this stupid tent any longer! It doesn't even have a floor covering to protect us."

Caleb gave her the keys, heard the car door slam, and then promptly fell asleep again.

Tirzah yanked the tent flap open, and the bright morning light blinded a half-asleep Caleb. He was unprepared for the gale of laughter from his beloved. "What's so funny?" he snapped with irritation.

"It's your face, Caleb. Come to the car mirror and look," Tirzah teased as her face changed to concern.

"How can it be?" Caleb yelled. "I don't feel anything, but my face and body are covered with fine red welts."

A passing Park Ranger came by to check out the disturbance. One look at Caleb's face brought out a barrage of laughter. "Slept out in the open without a floor covering in your tent, didn't you?" he chortled. "Thought there were no pests in Hawaii, didn't you?" he continued. "Sand fleas are the worst, and they're everywhere, boy. Quit being a cheapskate and buy a decent tent or stay indoors," he finished with an air of superiority.

Caleb found a cheap plastic sheet, and all future campouts were only interrupted by irate property owners who would ask pointed questions about his reading ability. Tirzah asked Caleb why he didn't heed the "No Trespassing" signs.

"Rules—rules are made to be broken, sweetheart," objected Caleb with a look that Tirzah knew boded no good.

"Isn't that what the hippies are advocating?" Tirzah argued. "I thought you didn't agree with their world view."

Caleb ended the discussion by chasing Tirzah and kissing her so soundly that she had no more breath to argue.

No! No! Caleb thought as the time for leaving was approaching. *Why do the best times of life go by so quickly?* He had just snapped off the radio as the depressing news about the Vietnam War interrupted the halcyon mood of the sunlit evening. The "Hawaiian Wedding Song" had been interrupted by the latest setback for the American war effort. *What a bizarre situation*, Caleb thought. "A mile south of where I live, American boys are drafted and sent to Vietnam to die, while I as a Canadian have never fired a gun in anger."

Tirzah was a vision in her figure-hugging jump suit, and Caleb was entranced by his bride. There are times in life so special that they should never end.

Two twelve-year-old, or thereabouts, Hawaiian keikes were skim boarding in the shore surf, and Tirzah asked if they would like to have our boogie board and camping stuff. Baggage costs to bring the stuff home were more than the value of the items, so they had been looking for a worthy recipient. "Really! Do you mean it?" the bronzed duo excitedly asked.

"Have fun and enjoy," responded the honeymooners as they headed to the Kona airport.

Leaving from Kona, a short flight landed them at Honolulu, and then a six-hour flight brought them back home to start a whole new life.

Surf's Up

CHAPTER VII
Dreams Do Come True

Caleb Rewind: Return from Europe
to Finding His Place and Going Steady

That familiar tightening of the stomach began before the plane touched down on the tarmac of Vancouver airport. *What now, Caleb? The money's all gone, and you need to find a place in an entirely new environment. No job. No place to stay. Where and how do you begin?* Ah, the wonder of insouciance as it replaced the stressful whys. Caleb mentally ticked off the points of profitable contacts available to him and soon found a job, as well as boarding with meals provided.

"You need to be aware of a few rules that I insist upon," rasped gaunt widow Marla Jensen, owner of the boarding house. "Keep your room neat and tidy; no abusive or profane language allowed; show up for meals on time; and put your dirty laundry in the proper place before Thursday morning."

"Not to worry," Caleb assured her with his best smile pasted on. "My Mom taught me all about neat and tidy, and punctuality is one of my many virtues."

"Humph!" Marla snorted from a lipless mouth. "We'll see if actions match your smooth tongue."

Caleb's fellow boarder across the hall soon put his resolutions to the test. "Hi, my name is Jed," he aggressively stated as he plopped down and bounced on Caleb's bed with no offer of a handshake. It was apparent that he was firmly resolved to establish his ascendency in the boarding house pecking order. "Country boy, I reckon," he sneered as he took Caleb's pictures from the dresser where he had just put them. His following derogatory remarks about the people in the Nachtegal family picture brought out the beast in Caleb.

"Do not ever do that again," he raged as Jed lay on the carpet with blood spurting from his mouth and nose.

"Marla, help me," croaked Jed. "I've been attacked by your insane new boarder." After a quick First Aid job on Jed's nose and mouth was finished, Marla called Caleb and outlined her further conditions for Caleb being allowed to stay.

They were terse and simple. "If you want to stay here, Caleb, you must apologize to Jed, promise to not fight here again, and pay for the carpet cleaning or replacement."

After four hours of cooling off, Caleb agreed to her conditions with one demand: "Please remember, Marla, that family is very dear to me and that you need to remind Jed about that."

Finding a job was the next challenge, and "beggars can't be choosers."

"Fifteen hundred dozen eggs delivered door-to-door, every week, will provide you with a good living," proclaimed Ed Cruden, who was in charge of Polster's fresh eggs door-to-door delivery service. He continued with, "You also need to provide your own reliable vehicle, capable of holding enough product for each day. I recommend a station wagon."

"It's a deal," Caleb enthused, wondering how he would ever get a station wagon.

"Deals on Wheels" was the come-on ad at the Dodge/Chrysler dealer, and he soon drove away with his new Dodge station wagon. The five hundred dollars garnered from selling the old Ford provided the down payment, and three-hundred-dollar monthly payments for eighteen months put the financial noose around his neck. Long legs and physical stamina proved to be great resources for running door to door with cartons of eggs and the odd poultry order.

After a month of deliveries, with one hour per day devoted to gaining new customers, it became apparent to Caleb that he was unable to budge above thirteen hundred cartons per week. "Not to worry, Caleb," enthused Ed with his smooth-talking motivation speech. "On Monday, I'll go along with you and show you how to deliver three hundred plus cartons per day, every day." Ed was true to his word and nearly wrecked the Monday route. Every customer who was not home received an extra carton of eggs.

The following Monday, 15 per cent of the Monday customers told Caleb not to bring any more eggs. "Thanks for nothing, jerk," was his reply to Ed when he asked how it was going.

Then the top selling egg salesman that worked for Polster allowed Caleb to accompany him on his route, and there he learned invaluable lessons. "You need a good product, son, which you have, but you're mainly selling service. The customer is King—always, always King." With that advice, Caleb reached a peak of sixteen hundred cartons per week.

Vicious dogs, brutal traffic, and complaining customers who constantly asked why the eggs were priced higher than the Safeway Store were the order of every day. Caleb would finish his route by 2:30, which allowed him to go back to school and finish his grade twelve matriculation.

After a year of diminishing returns, it took one final incident for him to pack it in and look for other work. Mrs. Cronin was a sweet, frail lady who lived by herself with her French poodle,

Mitzi. "Come on in, Caleb," was her standard greeting from her wheelchair. "I want four dozen eggs today with a chicken. Please put them on the kitchen table and tell me how you are getting on." Usually Caleb would find a short humorous comment to brighten her day. He always complimented her on her choice of scarves and the intelligence of her little dog. Mitzi was cute as a button with her bright eyes and wagging tail. She always looked as if she wanted to talk. Then on one delivery day, Mrs. Cronin was bedridden, and the little poodle dutifully brought the money for the usual delivery. However, this time Caleb went to the fridge himself to store the eggs. From top to bottom the refrigerator was stacked with unused cartons of eggs. Mrs. Cronin refused to accept a refund, so Caleb left it on the table. At the end of his daily deliveries, he told Ed that he was quitting.

***

And Then It Happened

Sunday was always a great day. Going to church and hearing God's Word was always a good mood-lifter. The chance to meet young people and form friendships also played a part. It seemed to Caleb that the Reformed church he attended attracted the prettiest girls he had ever seen. One girl in particular left him weak in the knees. He replaced, "Could I? Should I?" with "What have I got to lose?" His mom's saying that, "My Caleb is not a shy boy," proved to be true. He decided to ask that certain dark-haired beauty out for a date.

"Hi, Tirzah," Caleb greeted the soft voice that answered the phone. My name is Caleb Nachtegal, and how would you like to go out on a date with me tonight?"

A frosty silence was followed by a terse, "Who are you? And for your information, I have other plans for tonight. Goodbye!" Wow! That was a strikeout for his inflated ego, so he solaced himself by dating a number of other girls. Months passed, but every Sunday when he saw Tirzah in church, his infatuation with her increased.

Brad thumped Caleb on his chest and commanded, "Thursday night at 8:30 p.m. I'm having a great party at my place. Stop your moping around, bring a case of beer, and let's rock." As soon as Caleb entered Brad's place, he saw that she was there. Quiet and beautiful, she paid little attention to the chatter around her. She also seemed not to notice Caleb, but before the evening ended, he determined to catch her eye. There was no coyness or flirtation in her level stare from beautiful, deep-set blue eyes.

Her look was friendly and emboldened him to go and talk to her. "I know that I was presumptuous when I asked you out some time ago, but may I take you home after the party?" he asked.

"I'd like that," she replied, and Caleb's heart flipped in his chest. He drove Tirzah to her house as slowly as possible, and before he brought her to the door, he asked, "May I see you again?"

She replied, "I'd like that, and I have Wednesday evenings available." This was wonderful for him to hear. Before too many Wednesdays had passed, Caleb started showing up for Saturdays and Sunday afternoons. Caleb soon asked Tirzah if she would be his steady girl. Her hug and kiss and joyful, "Yes!" made him a happy man. She was eighteen and he was twenty-two. She was delicate and shapely, and her soft, fine hair blew like an aureole around her face. Caleb loved her fragrance and never tired of hugging her. What a great time to be in love.

There was also the matter of asking Tirzah's father for her hand. Diego Teelhart was an imposing man. Deep-set blue eyes in a granite face looked Caleb over critically as he crossed his massive arms. Tirzah and Caleb sat on the edge of the living room couch, and his first attempt at speech was a croak. Another attempt, accompanied by a shot of bravado, worked better. "Mr. Teelhart, I would like to ask you if it's okay for me to date your daughter."

A long silence ended when he asked, "Who are you? Where do you come from? Are you employed? Are you a faithful churchgoer?" Caleb responded to all his questions as well as he could, with some embellishments. Diego ended the conversation with, "You may see Tirzah twice a week, and she must be home by eleven o'clock."

"Yes, sir!" Caleb exulted. "Your daughter will be safe with me," he assured him with relief flooding his stomach.

Caleb soon pushed the boundaries. Tirzah looked worried when he airily said, "Rules are made to be broken." Two dates a week soon became three, and 11:00 p.m. meant that they would park for some more time in Tirzah's driveway. They soon fell deeply in love, and every morning awakening brought Tirzah's beautiful face into his mind's eye.

Caleb's sister Mirjam had enrolled at Simon Fraser University (SFU), and they decided to share an apartment together. Caleb had saved enough money to attend SFU for a first year Science semester. Attending university had always been an unobtainable dream to him, and now it was happening. Another cherished dream was to become a veterinarian. The years spent on the farm in Sears had formed in him a desire to work with animals. When he told Marla that he was giving notice to leave, she said, "I'm sorry to see you go, Caleb. I was just beginning to turn you into a decent boarder." A thin grin appeared for a moment on Marla's taut face. Her mention that another fellow had applied to fill his departure was welcome news, since Caleb knew she needed the money.

When the SFU application was sent back with a terse refusal, Caleb was outraged. His grade twelve matriculation did not include credits for French language courses. He wrote a letter of appeal to Chancellor Gordon Shradum, who notified Caleb that he would be accepted under a special senior student provision.

To attend university had been Caleb's dream, but the reality of being there soured that dream. How he had longed for the chance to be in those hallowed halls of learning! He enjoyed the studies and did well in all his courses, especially the liberal arts courses that were not part of his intended major courses.

The social atmosphere at university during the 1960s, however, was another story. Maoist posters in the Concourse Mall informed him that you could only be a member if you were prepared to kill your bourgeois parents. Blasphemous and obscene posters were pasted in many places. He closed his eyes and took no more notice, but other challenges soon presented themselves.

"Why are you sitting in that chair?" demanded the long-haired hippie as he blew marijuana-laced smoke into Caleb's face.

"Did you pay for the seats?" Caleb angrily retorted. "I thought the seats were free! This is the restaurant eating area, correct?" He forced down the rising pitch in his voice, which warned him to control his quick temper.

"This whole corner is reserved for the Gay Club," Hippy menacingly responded. "If you like, you can join."

"No thanks. If I bug you, then I'll sit someplace else," Caleb responded. It took all of a month of riots, beatings, and mayhem to ruin any idealism Caleb had ever entertained about the noble university environment. University campuses all across North America were in full riot mode to protest American involvement in the Vietnam War.

One free day from his courses allowed Caleb to ask Tirzah to join him for a day at the campus. It was a beautiful spring day, and the SFU campus on top of Burnaby Mountain was stunningly breathtaking. A riot of daffodils and crocuses had turned the mountain campus into a visual delight. English Literature 101 was the first lecture for the day, and they sat close to the front because a prominent Canadian literary mogul was doing a lecture presentation. It was bad. It was very bad. He started with vulgar anatomical references and threw in a dozen F-bombs for effect. He then proceeded to parody a religious revival meeting, and when Caleb looked at Tirzah's stricken face, he quickly took her out of the hall and tried to tell her that this was not the usual fare of an English lecture. What an awful way to end a morning that had begun so well. All was fair, but only man could ruin it.

They drove to the beach and had a good talk about morals, upbringing, and environment. Tirzah looked directly at Caleb and asked if he wanted to continue studying in such a toxic place. "It affects you, Caleb," she softly whispered, grabbing his hand. "Look at your smoking habit; your breath stinks and your clothes reek like stale smoke. Please don't use vulgar language when you get upset while driving, and control your temper." Caleb was crushed, but when she hugged him, he melted like a big baby. He would have walked through fire for that girl, and she cured him of some very bad habits.

After one year at SFU, Caleb had had enough. The final blow came when his biology professor informed him of the following: "You're colour blind, Caleb, because you're not recognizing the colour changes in your laboratory titration tests."

"Just in the blue-green spectrum, sir," Caleb replied.

"A doctor or veterinarian needs to have a keen sense of colour, Caleb," he replied. "Tissue sample colours and chemical dye tests are necessary for determining what's wrong with the health of animals and humans."

Continuing car and rental payments brought Caleb back to the reality of getting a job and earning enough income to pay the bills. One dream was not to be realized, but Caleb never regretted his decision to leave the university. He vowed that if he and Tirzah would receive children they would all have the chance to attend higher education if they should want to.

***

Back to the Joys of Physical Work

A light punch on his shoulder at the hockey game made Caleb turn to face building contractor Bert Paradis. "Heard you were looking for work," was his opening remark. "I have an opening for a framing carpenter."

"Well, you've found your man," Caleb replied, having never framed before in his life. "How much are you paying, and when do you want me to start?"

"Monday morning," barked Bert. "I'll pick you up at seven, and your pay will be determined by your ability."

Caleb had thought that working as a lumberjack had been hard, but framing houses was harder. The agility, balance, and dexterity required in wood framing large custom houses was a challenge, but he loved it. Before the era of pre-fabricated roof trusses, framers would cut and custom frame all the roofing members by hand.

After Bert had made three trips up two storeys to re-cut his hip and valley joists, Caleb told him the following: "Hey, Bert, there are mathematical formulas that allow us to cut all roofing members on the ground with perfect accuracy."

"Pretty mouthy for a greenhorn," responded Bert, "but what the heck, my hip is hurting from all the climbing that I am doing, so go ahead—give it a shot."

Caleb checked his rafter square against the notations in his rafter and joist guide book with the house measurements on the architectural plans. "I can do this, Bert!" he yelled up to him. "You stay up on top and I'll hand up all the precut rafters and hip and valley joists from the ground." The only inaccuracies were caused by the error of having framed the floor plan three inches out of square.

"That saved us a lot of time, Caleb," Bert remarked over coffee. "I'd like to offer you a substantial raise in pay if you continue to stay working for me."

"Sure thing, Bert," Caleb responded. He knew that building was in his blood, and a builder he would be. He worked with Bert for four years.

***

His Dream Girl Said Yes

Tirzah's father had told Caleb that he would like to speak with him. Without preamble, he asked, "What are your plans regarding my daughter?"

Caleb responded, "I love Tirzah, and we hope to marry."

"When, Caleb? When do you plan to do that?" he asked. "It has almost been four years that you've gone steady together, and it's obvious that you want to be together."

"Well then, Mr. Teelhart," he responded, "may I marry Tirzah with your approval?"

A slow grin spread across Diego's face before he replied. "Tirzah's mother and I approve, but you will need to get Tirzah's approval also."

That night, after tears and tenderness, Tirzah responded with a joyful "yes" to Caleb's proposal. It was hard after such joy for Caleb to leave her and go home.

On August 21, 1971, they were married, and it was the happiest day of their lives. Dad Diego provided funds for a glorious Hawaiian honeymoon, and they have loved going to the Islands ever since.

The newlyweds had arranged to rent the house of Caleb's married sister and brother-in-law for one year, as their entire family was off to Europe on an educational family tour. When Caleb and Tirzah got back from their honeymoon, they moved into a spacious, furnished home. Tirzah was soon pregnant with her firstborn, and she bloomed like a Rose of Sharon. All was connubial bliss until they received a phone message from their landlord. "We're cutting our European tour short and will be arriving back home in two weeks. We intend to keep our agreement and you can live with us until the year is completed." One week after their return, it was soon apparent that it was not working out.

Caleb scrambled to find other accommodations, and they moved into a basement suite in Surrey, B.C. Tirzah did her best, but Caleb could tell that his beauty was not happy in their new location. He held her tear-streaked, lovely face in his hands and laid out their plans for the future. "We need to get our own place, Tirzah, and there's only one way that I can see how I can do that. If I work a double shift, we can make the income to buy land, and I can build our own house."

Tirzah had saved enough money to put a down payment on a lovely acre of land in South Surrey, and Caleb doubled their earnings during the next six months. It was very hard for them both when Caleb would leave at 6:00 a.m. and returned at 8:00 or 9:00 p.m.

Tirzah missed him terribly, and the landlord lady constantly invaded her privacy. Frequent gossip and enquiries about private matters offended Tirzah greatly. Oh, happy day when Caleb told his beloved that they could move into their new home!

The Beautiful Gift of Children

On June 17, 1972, God gave Caleb and Tirzah the wonderful gift of a daughter, and they named her Hannah. Tirzah was overjoyed that she could bring their daughter into the home they would live in for over forty years. Much of the house still needed to be finished, but it was home, sweet home. Free from the burden of a crippling mortgage, Caleb soon made a successful career building and selling houses. Amazingly, a son and then another daughter were soon born. Beautiful, fragile Tirzah bloomed in pregnancy and birthed lovely, strong children. Caring for this sudden threesome in diapers was another matter. "You always said that you wanted a large family, Caleb," Tirzah said as she nursed their second daughter. "However, at the rate of three children in five years, I don't think I have the energy to care for them." The door slammed as Caleb hurried out to put in an evening shift at his construction site.

Large black houseflies entered the house every time five-year-old Hannah opened the screen door. The hot August afternoon sun created a hazy patina over the dusty yard. Tirzah put a clean diaper, for the umpteenth time, on Brock's butt, and then with a weary sigh, put him to bed. She looked forward to a couple of peaceful hours reading and resting, but the sudden wail from little Delphine put a stop to that fantasy. "My ears hurt," whimpered the two-year-old. A quick thermometer check showed a temperature of 104° F, and it was off to the hospital emergency again. First, the two older children were awakened and bundled into the GMC van. Caleb was waiting at home when Tirzah returned at 10:30 p.m. After listening to the chronicle of events, he asked if there was anything to eat.

Tirzah watched him for a sympathetic response, but Caleb kissed his sleeping babies and tumbled into bed. It took a long time for Tirzah to control her sobbing. *It wasn't supposed to be like this*, she thought as she lay beside her sleeping husband. The constant demands of being a wife, mother, and keeping the business accounts for her husband drained the little energy she had. Caleb could fall asleep instantly as soon as he lay down, but she could not. *I can't go on*, she concluded. *Caleb must stop his long working days and help me raise the children he has fathered.* Tirzah replayed the day's events for a long time before the sleep of exhaustion closed her eyes. Silence, beautiful silence, and sleep alone could heal the burden of her exhaustion.

Possessed of boundless energy, Caleb was hurt that he had not realized Tirzah's desperation. They had drifted apart bit by bit, and now they had to face this challenge together. Hurt feelings and selfish interests were discussed with many tears flowing as they slowly, with many stumblings, found their way back to being a team again. As their second daughter Delphine grew, she became a wonderful second mother for her younger siblings. Caleb stopped his "being with the guys" routine and spent every spare hour helping Tirzah and playing with their ever-increasing family. Tirzah's delicate constitution was no barrier to becoming pregnant. With each baby after the first three, she became stronger and more confident in her role as mother.

"PUSH, TIRZAH. PUSH!" Doctor Reagan's voice ascended into a stentorian bellow as her almost ten-pound baby resented being ejected into the cold, cruel world. Tirzah insisted that no drugs and no gas be used to assist her labour. Her determination to never take anti-nausea drugs during her pregnancies resulted in never having to recriminate herself after the Thalidomide debacle. Many families suffered the birth of deformed children resulting from using that anti-nausea drug. With lips compressed and muscles straining, no scream came out as the terrible separating pain of delivery happened. Caleb watched in fascination as the quiet and delicate women he had married became a tiger. When baby, swabbed and cleaned, was placed at her breast, she exclaimed, "All praise be to God who has made it so well!" Never did Tirzah look more beautiful to her Caleb than shortly after giving birth. A smuggled bottle of Liebfraumilch wine was opened, and Caleb and Doctor Regan toasted and saluted mother and newborn daughter Cassie.

Caleb was filled with joy when Tirzah grabbed him by his lanky hair and whispered in his ear, "I love being your wife and a mother to our babies." They all grew to be taller and larger than Tirzah, but they always remained "my babies." God gave them wonderful years, and when Tirzah's eighth pregnancy was confirmed, they were both elated when their doctor told them that it could be twins. That was not the case, but Tirzah delivered a beautiful third son for the whole family to enjoy.

Both Caleb and Tirzah were united in their desire to be faithful to God as revealed in the Bible. Shortly after birth, all eight children received the sacrament of Holy Baptism. For generations their ancestors had done the same. They made a solemn promise to raise and instruct their children to know and love their God. Accepting Jesus Christ as Lord and Saviour was not just a Sunday thing, but occupied the central place in their hearts. They knew with certainty that the gift of their children would be the most significant events in their lifetime. God blesses through the generations of believing families.

Generational Independence

It is a hard thing for parents to realize that children are new, unique people. Caleb and Tirzah were no exception. They often viewed their children as growing copies of themselves. Both had limited educations, but all their children enjoyed the privilege of extended education with professional degrees. As they grew, it was often apparent that they thought they knew life's lessons better than their parents. "Aww Dad/Mom, that's just your opinion," was often the end of a discussion when they attempted to bypass discipline or admonition. It was soon apparent to both that all eight of their children would carve out their own distinct path in life. However, the life lessons of love and faithfulness to Jesus Christ as their Saviour would not ever be compromised or remain unspoken by their parents.

***

Caleb struggled in a tangle of sheets and a daze of confusion. The hot, fetid air in the bedroom pressed on him like a steel sheet. He sensed there was evil in the room, and he tried to remember where his defense hatchet was. He flailed with his arms and struck Tirzah a glancing blow on her head. He had never believed that there were still demon possession attempts, but abject fear filled his every fibre. "Please, Lord, protect me and mine," became a consuming mantra as he fought his way back to consciousness. Serious disagreements with older children the previous evening had led to a series of dreadful nightmares. He cradled terrified Tirzah in his arms as he realized what had happened, and together they consoled each other. They discussed the frailty of the human condition and how easily life can be snuffed out in an instant. Five of Caleb's siblings who had died early deaths had made that plain. I, Lucius, took command. "There is only one constant on this broken, dark, and beautiful planet. The Creator God has the whole world in His hands."

"It makes no sense now, but it will. One day, darling Tirzah, it will," Caleb consoled as he dried her tears from her face.

Making a Living

"Jack of all trades, but master of none," was the self-initiated taunt that rankled in Caleb's head. He had done many jobs, but the most satisfying work was when he could imagine, design, and build. "And make money, Caleb," insisted the alter ego voice that was a part of all his decision- making. "You enjoy making a healthy profit for the least amount of work," continued the taunt. Building custom houses for well-off retired Saskatchewan wheat farmers, as well as borrowing money to build starter, finished houses for first-time buyers, proved to be a lucrative venture.

Increased demand necessitated adding a partner and larger purchases of building lots. "Don't do it, son," warned Caleb's aged retired father. "Be happy with what you have, since it provides you with a good living." Caleb had informed him that he intended to purchase a large inventory of building lots in order to increase capacity. Peter Nachtegal shook his large, silver-haired head and muttered as he walked away. "Too much risk; no good will come of it."

Soon after the purchase, the real estate market in the greater Vancouver area collapsed during the 1980s. When Caleb saw his father after the collapse, the large head was shaking and the eyes broadcast, "Didn't I tell you not to do it." Caleb and company lost all previous profits and narrowly avoided bankruptcy. "Shake it off, Caleb," said the Caleb voice. "Go for it and borrow to the hilt to get back in the game." Hard work and persistence paid off, and many good years followed, but a change was in the wind.

**

Labour Is Worth an Ounce but Trade Is Worth a Fortune

Caleb and his brother-in-law and partner Jared, had been working for weeks in the pouring rain and mud of their construction site. A sudden shout from above startled them.

"Boys, boys, what foolishness is this?" yelled the large, florid man wearing a raccoon coat and standing on top of the dirt pile above the muddy excavation. It was Jared's uncle, who stood there grinning at them from ear to ear. The cold, dampness, and relentless rains had taken their toll as Caleb and Jared toiled in the sticky clay. During the halcyon days of summer, building homes was a sheer pleasure. Browned by the temperate West Coast sun and physically as fit as they would ever be, the partners would not have been enticed to enter any other enterprise. Uncle Jed reached down and, with his patent leather-gloved hand, gave a sharp tug to the partners to help them out of the mud hole. "Remember this, lads," he continued, "one pound of work does not equal even one ounce of wheeling and dealing. Come let me buy you a coffee and discuss a proposal I want to make to you both." Summer days were but a distant memory. This was the difficult present, and Caleb and Jared were eager to listen.

"In Alberta, we've developed a fantastic manufacturing system using aluminum extrusions," enthused Uncle Jed. "My partners and I would like you boys to start a manufacturing plant on the West Coast and join us in this fantastic business." The motel room was oppressively hot, and Uncle Jed poured out another stiff whiskey and doled out expensive cigars. His impressive bulk and bulging eyes exerted a hypnotic effect. "We're willing to allow you to use our patented technology, if you're able to provide financing and build or rent an appropriate facility. What do you say to that, boys?" He ended his pitch with the following plum: "I'll even start your sales by working for you at the beginning."

More meetings followed, and Caleb and Jared decided to enter the world of manufacturing. When they showed the contract details to their accountant, he cocked a quizzical eyebrow. "Do you realize that you're taking all the risk?" he queried. "They risk nothing and get to equally share in the ownership and profit." Uncle Jed had done his sales pitch well, and Caleb and Jared ignored financial advice and signed on the dotted line.

They first acquired property and then built a roomy manufacturing facility. "What shall we call the company?" Caleb asked Jared.

"Alumastar Manufacturing Ltd. B.C.," Jared replied. "Just like the Alberta plant, except for the B.C." he finished.

***

Family in Second Place

"Remember, Caleb," I encouraged my alter ego, "let us be loving in what we say about our family. After God, they are first in our heart."

The hot July night and the many things to do jolted Caleb wide awake at 4:00 a.m. Every morning was the same: so much to do and so little time to do it. Tirzah's soft, even breathing made him lie rigidly still so he wouldn't awaken her as she lay cradling her unborn baby. Sleep was precious for her, and the slightest noise would awaken her. She was beautiful in her pregnancies, and baby number six was growing rapidly. Caleb needed to see her face, and his love for her drove the last wisps of insecurity away. His working days were not as long as before since Alumastar had become profitable and he had been able to delegate more of the work to others. After Tirzah delivered her last child at age forty-one, the wonderful fertility was over. By this time the links of love forged together were stronger than steel. "We're a team, Tirzah," Caleb whispered, cupping her smiling face in his hands. "You are my wife, lover, partner, and soulmate. and I hope that we can always be together."

God Gave: Patience, Wisdom, Understanding

Tirzah smiled with some apprehension as she watched her husband and boys play roller hockey together on the tennis court. The fencing wire at both ends showed large bulges where hard body checks had thrown hard bodies into the meshed wire. Caleb had lost his brothers to drowning and cancer, and she realized how much it meant to him to have three sons with strong bodies and spirits. They all enjoyed competitive games and winning. She enjoyed watching the minor hockey games, but as her boys grew into their teenage years, the games changed. Fighting and hard checking resulted in bruises, torn ligaments, and concussions. She no longer wanted to watch and urged her boys to stop playing.

Tirzah enjoyed the family's day-boating trips to the Fraser River. When the river was low enough, long sandy beaches provided endless fun and games. All her children and Caleb loved water sport, and she cheered as the roar of the boat brought another beginner up on skis. Her mind remembered the last hot summer at the lake. Every chance they got, when the water was calm, her boys and sometimes the girls would be water skiing and enjoying the holidays. She smiled inwardly as she saw her girls enjoying their music, reading, and play acting. It made her mother's heart glad to see all of them healthy and strong. "Please, God, take care of them when I can't," she often prayed. She knew that Caleb always laboured with apprehension over their children because he had lost so many of his own siblings. Tears came quickly when she recalled that, "I too, Lord, have had to say goodbye to brothers who are still alive but have chosen to forsake you."

"What's for supper tonight, sweetheart?" Caleb greeted Tirzah before he kissed her hello. She always reminded him about what comes first and was annoyed that he often forgot. Caleb was ravenous after a long day of work and had just finished spading their vegetable garden.

"You will just have to wait and see," she teased, "but you can be sure that it will be delicious." It always was. She liked it when Caleb would compliment her. He would hug her, smell her soft hair, and whisper, "You look good, you smell good, you cook good, and you are good."

Tirzah had a great ability to listen and provide comfort and support.

"Calm down, sweetheart, it's okay," Tirzah soothed as the sobbing of her first-born child filled the room.

"I am so alone," Hannah lamented, "so all alone." Talented, artistic Hannah was in the throes of a down day. Her parents always noticed the signs. Ebullient and frenetic activity usually preceded the blues. "Dad always tries to tell me what to do," she complained. "I will not be dictated to by any man, and that includes him."

Nor any of the boyfriends that you could not accept, thought Tirzah. "Jesus taught us that before God, men and women are equal, but we have different roles in life," she patiently explained to her daughter.

"Well, I feel that there is no role for women in the church we attend," Hannah replied bitterly. "I am leaving and going to a church that gives women more say in church life."

"You need to speak with your father about this," replied Tirzah with worry in her voice. She knew immediately that discussion would not go well. Caleb was unbending when it came to keeping vows and promises made before God. She would bring her concerns to her Lord, and she always added a special request for each child, including her car-racing sons.

Brock gunned the three-cylinder Sprint up the steep road to Simon Fraser University. He was in his last year of engineering studies and had whittled the twenty-kilometre trip through city traffic down to thirty minutes. The whine and flashing lights on the cruiser of the pursuing traffic cop brought this trip to a sudden halt. The resulting fine, as well as a damaged front bumper from rear ending a dump truck, had put him in a foul mood. "Slow down, son, and live," admonished his father, and Brock waited for the rest to follow. Caleb looked at his sturdy son, who was named after the brother he had lost. He had dreamed of the son that he had hoped to have, and from the first day of his life, Brock was it.

He was a jolly and aggressive tot who loved to roughhouse with his dad. At seven years of age he would join Caleb, when school was out, on the construction site. "We got to go home now, Dad," he reminded Caleb when five o'clock had come and gone. "Mom is going to be angry if we're late and her dinner goes cold."

"Righto, son," Caleb replied as he looked over the neat piles of reclaimed nails that Brock had found. He swept up his boy in his arms and noticed the red welts on Brock's hands from using the hammer. Long rows of nailed boards on the sloped roof showed where the persistent boy had been busy.

Slowly and subtly, things began to change. Ever since the teenage years began, Brock had started to withdraw into himself. "All study and no play makes for a dull life, son. You're in your twenties now, and I would hope that you would notice and maybe date some of those pretty girls you grew up with."

The angry, "It's none of your business. I do not need to follow your example," retort caused Caleb to realize that some barriers are necessary for independence to grow. The love was always there, but the communication was gone. He remembered the expressive eyes of his father-in-law, who rarely spoke of what he felt.

She was the smallest of Tirzah's babies, but Delphine was an absolute joy. Dark and beautiful like her mother, she laughed and smiled her way deep into her parents' hearts. "Me too, Daddy, me too!" she would squeak in her high-pitched voice. "Let me do the same acrobatics like Hannah and Brock." Smart and meticulous in her schooling, she was the delight of her teachers and showed rich imagination in her playtime. One day early in the morning, Delphine was looking out of her bedroom window at her dad's garden. The sudden sharp bang of her dad's gun was followed by the jump and fall of the wild hare feeding on her dad's vegetables. She watched as her dad appeared, shovel in hand, to bury the small animal. After he left, she scurried outside and dug up the dead animal. Assured that it was dead, she reburied it and put a small marker over the grave. When Caleb noticed the marker, he knew immediately who had done it. The sobbing little girl gave her dad a look that ensured no more killing of wild hares.

After she finished grade school, she went to university to become a teacher. "It's not fair, Mom and Dad!" she would exclaim whenever she detected government hostility toward her Christian university. "I'm joining a group that's going to Ottawa to protest government bias." Male bullies and domineering persons were soon confronted when detected by Delphine. Her heart melted, however, when courted by the Ontario engineer whom she married.

"Wow, almost ten pounds," remarked the nurse as she held the glistening, chubby baby girl by the ankles. Cassie was Tirzah's fourth baby, and when Caleb saw the two together, he was amazed that such beauty existed. Tirzah's loving care for her children and man showed in every way.

"Why are they all so different?" Caleb remarked to Tirzah. "Remember when we used to joke that if we were to be blessed with kids, they most likely would resemble each other like peas in a pod?" As Cassie grew, she changed from a tomboy into a shy but determined woman. All her talents and studies were directed to accomplishing her goals. She seemed not to need or want male attention, and no suitors came to claim her. "You've got to smile and notice the boys if you want them to notice you," Caleb would tease her.

Cassie would smile her enigmatic look and reply, "It's okay, Daddy-O." She became a loving and true blue woman who was very much appreciated by all who took the time to get to know her.

Caleb junior was born in the veil and looked nothing like his older brother. He fussed and complained when Caleb would roughhouse with him as he had done with Brock. "Don't neglect your boy!" Tirzah would scold Caleb when she noticed that he gravitated to his oldest son. "He's not only named after you, but he looks like you. Just give him some time."

The Alpha four motor on the Nachtegals' speed boat sputtered on takeoff, and Brock yelled as he sank into the turbid waters of the Fraser River. "Drive much?" he yelled again as his dad wheeled the boat around for another attempt.

"How about you, C.J.?" Caleb asked his second son. "Are you going to give it a try?"

"Don't feel much like it," C.J. replied. "Maybe some other time."

"C'mon on, give it a try," Caleb persisted. Reluctantly, his namesake slid into the icy water and fastened on the slalom ski. "Don't you think you should start on two skis," advised Caleb.

"No! It's too much work to put two on," C.J. replied.

Caleb eased into the throttle to give his son an easy start. Spotter Brock yelled, "Hit it, Dad! He's up already." Caleb looked with amazement as his son skied as if he had done it many times before. That proved to be C.J.'s style: little fanfare, but great performance. He ended his high school years by being male athlete of the year and went steady with the girl he would marry, who was also the female athlete of the year.

The sixth Nachtegal baby was a lovely girl, perfect in every way. Caleb had always hoped for a girl who would mirror the beauty of his Tirzah. Eva Tirzah came close. She grew strong and determined and reminded Caleb of his father. "Ouch, Eva!" Caleb yelled. "I asked for a shoulder massage, but please don't injure me," he joked as Eva's strong hands eased the pressure points.

"Horses, horses, Eva. Is that all you think about?" Tirzah asked as her young daughter ran around the house pulling the reins on her make-believe broomstick horse. It was more than a fad. Eva spent many years with her younger sister working at the thoroughbred horse farm close to her house.

It was a statement, not a request: "You need to buy me a horse, Dad," Eva demanded. "I want a horse of my very own. I know you can afford it, so what about it?"

"Okay," Caleb responded. "But you'll need to find a boarding place for your horse, because there's no way I'll have our beautiful acre stomped into mud and looking and smelling like a barn yard." Eva chewed on that for some time before the competing demands of school, friends, and her burgeoning musical lessons scuttled the idea of caring for a horse on a remote site far from where she lived.

She was fully aware of the time commitment required to care for a horse, as well as the time for exercising that a horse required. That however, did not stop her endeavour. "Come, Dad. I want you to look at this fabulous property especially set up for horses," she cajoled in her final attempt to convince Caleb. "Five acres, three stalls, and lots of cross fencing," she continued in her most persuasive tone.

"No, Eva Tirzah," her mother objected when she noticed that Caleb was waffling. "I am not moving from our lovely acre to live on a horse farm." That closed the request, and no more was spoken about it.

The back-breaking work of placing concrete was done, and Caleb collapsed into his dirty yellow upholstered chair with a cold beer. The soft strains of Pachelbel floated across the room, and Caleb glanced at his young daughter as she played the harp. After all the piano players, youngest daughter Neeleah had chosen to play the harp. Caleb had ordered it made and then had lovingly finished and painted it with a lustrous silver-pearl colour. She played her harp with skill and feeling, but it was always too short.

Neeleah glowed with health right from birth, and after her third birthday she exhibited the strong spirit of her grandmother, Katherine Nachtegal. "I don't like it," she complained as she arched her spoon above her head and threw broccoli all over Tirzah's clean kitchen.

"Into the corner you go!" yelled Caleb. "You can come back to the table when you say 'sorry.'"

After a period of time, Tirzah asked, "Are you sorry, Neeleah?"

"No sorry," she responded, "and no prayer." During kindergarten years she spoke very little, and her teacher asked Caleb and Tirzah if they would consider testing for autism. They knew their daughter intimately and were confident that her rich imagination would break out when she was determined to be ready.

"We present the Bachelor Diploma of Liberal Arts, with great distinction, to Neeleah Nachtegal," resounded through the auditorium as Caleb and Tirzah watched their tall daughter receive her university diploma. It was a proud day for her parents when Neeleah achieved what her six older siblings had also attained.

Her love of literature showed itself in the omnivorous reading of books from many differing genres.

"Now that you have your degree, what are you going to do with it?" Caleb asked his daughter.

"I want to become an English professor and eventually become the head of an English department at the university of my choosing," replied Neeleah.

Caleb never doubted that she would, and often he retreated, verbally bruised from disputes with his daughter. The arched eyebrows and the "Oh, Dad!" usually signaled the end of any contentious conversation.

Last of the Nachtegals

"*Push, Tirzah! Push-hhh!*" Doctor Regan bellowed as Tirzah gave birth to her last baby. Caleb grew concerned as he saw the doctor, scalpel in hand, enter the birth canal. One final huge push and Caleb saw their son emerge, large and blue. "Why is he not breathing?" he loudly asked as he saw the oxygen mask being slapped over the baby's face. Doctor Regan, with a dismissive gesture, took no notice of Caleb's question. He grabbed the nine-pound boy by the ankles, hoisted him up, and applied a firm smack to his bottom. An indignant howl was followed by rapid breathing, and the blue colour faded to rosy pink.

Tirzah was overjoyed as her beautiful son was placed at her breast. "Praise be to God who made everything well. We have received a son." Caleb was amazed that after such an ordeal, Tirzah's face radiated contentment.

"It was a close call, Caleb," Doctor Regan rasped as he stripped off his medical garb and eagerly accepted a glass of chilled Liebfruamilch wine. The baby was born on his day off, so he was allowed to imbibe. "Baby's umbilical cord was wrapped tightly around his neck, and the heartbeat was fading fast. I had to cut it off in the birth canal. We had to jolt him with enriched Oxygen to get him breathing." Caleb and Tirzah looked at the heavy set, jowly man who had delivered seven of their children. He was profane and unorthodox, but no doctor had ever been more trusted by Tirzah and Caleb in difficult circumstances than he had been.

They called him Peter Dylan John, and immediately he caused an uproar among his siblings. "Three first names!" Brock yelled, "Why three? You only gave me two!"

"What about me?" interjected Hannah. "I only have one name."

"It all has to do with family history," Tirzah gently explained. "Granddads and some uncles who died were remembered." She did not elaborate to the children why none of the first four were not named after family. Later she smiled at Caleb and remarked, "We never used to worry about family name traditions, but the times have changed, eh boy?"

Petey, as the family called him, was a rascal. He idolized his big brothers and teased all his sisters. Sneak attacks and trying to overhear private conversations were his forte. "One more time, you miserable little cretin," yelled Neeleah as Petey tried to pull down her jogging pants. "One more time and I will smack you so hard that your head will spin."

Petey smiled and bided his time for the next covert operation. "Hey, Dad!" he would ask. "Do you want to know what Brock and Caleb Junior are up to?"

"No! I am not interested," Caleb teased. He enjoyed sparring with his rascal son and watching Petey's intense disappointment when he failed to show interest in his son's latest spy revelations. Caleb also sought, by disappointing him, to discourage his youngest son's KGB spy activities.

Intense grunting and the toppling of furniture brought Tirzah running from the kitchen to check out the commotion. Her husband and youngest son were engaged in an age-old ritual of testing strength. "Bring it on, old man," was the taunt from Petey that caused Caleb to engage in a session of arm wrestling.

Perspiration beaded Caleb's head as Petey laughed. "Is that all you got, Pops?" It was indeed all that Caleb had as he went down for a third time to the burgeoning power of his growing son.

Tirzah smiled as she recalled the previous times that her Caleb was overpowered by the two older boys. "It took a long time for Brock to beat you, husband, but now eighteen years later you are older and declining." She had always known that her man was intensely competitive. He was also very proud that their sons were growing up healthy and strong. She knew that his family was a precious heritage and treasure to him.

Building houses, fabricating recreational trailers, roofing projects, and completely restoring a vintage 1962 Corvette were all projects that her Caleb and her sons completed and enjoyed. They have grown up as independent men who love their Lord. What a blessing.

CHAPTER VIII
Trying to Heap Up Worldly Riches

... and does not favor the rich over the poor (Job 34:19).

Is Loving Money Evil?

It was one of those beautiful September days when the slanting sun bathed everything in a golden glow. Caleb swung lazily in the hammock tied between two cherry trees on the property where Tirzah and he had enjoyed so many good years raising their children and loving each other. Life was good, and life was sweet, but still a gnawing discontent worked away under the contentment. He had always realized that feelings and states of mind were never permanent. Most humans are fickle creatures with short attention spans. Acquisition was imprinted in his genetic code, and money meant power and possessions. With a force of will, Caleb shunted aside the lure to think about money stuff, but he knew that it would return. Caleb knew his Bible, and especially the warnings about making an idol out of worldly possessions. Lucius would make acerbic comments in the background, which were often ignored: "What would it be like to be truly rich?" he obsessively wondered. "Rich like Croesus. How did the ancestors fare and cope?" He had a large notebook of his imaginings, and the reel in his mind spun back to a time long ago.

The Roman Attempt

Lupernicus swatted at the swarm of blackflies that attacked his face and tormented the team of mismatched oxen pulling his plow. The pulling traces had been repaired and patched many times. Sharp edges had left rub marks on the oxen's flanks. Buried rocks would hook and snare the plow's point, and the sudden shock would rip apart the rawhide belts attached to the plow. No matter how often he goaded the larger ox, it refused to pull equally with its smaller mate. The squat, broad-shouldered Italian never had imagined that farming would be so difficult.

The rolling hills of northern Hispania had attracted many young Romans, including Lupernicus. He had taken his bride and growing family to the former Carthaginian territory and was determined to become wealthy. The promise of cheap land came with an obligation to serve in the Roman militia. His experience and training as a naval cadet worked in his favour to gain title to a twenty-five-hectare farm.

"By Jupitar," he moaned in the stifling heat. "I never expected it to be so hard to earn a few miserable sesterces." The oxen lumbered to a stop, glad to have a moment of relief from the relentless drag of the crude plow. Their long ears and whip-like tails swung in a steady rhythm to dislodge the large horseflies and stinging gnats. Hard crusts of dried feces protected their rear flanks, but the large liquid eyes were an open target for the aggressive insects. Lupernicus turned to watch his wife, Alsa, and his two older boys planting wheat, barley, onion, and celery seeds in the crooked furrows he had just made. He remembered the beauty of the young girl who had caught his eye when he saw her dancing during the Roman harvest festival. Now covered in sweat and dust, with a cartwheel midriff, little remained of what had once attracted him. She was, however, a good mother and knew when to be quiet.

A portion of the farm was covered by grape orchards and olive trees. The cool shade beckoned, and Lupernicus unyoked his oxen and allowed them to graze under the olive trees. "Let's have some food!" he yelled to his wife and boys. "I'll water the oxen and then we can sit under the shade of the olive trees."

Alsa smeared the bread she had baked that morning with fat and honey. She provided milk for her boys and wine for her husband. She winced as he greedily reached out his hand. Often as not, a cuff would also be coming her way.

She weighed her opportunity to speak and decided that after having eaten, her husband would be more approachable. "It is not working, is it, Lupernicus?" she tentatively asked.

"What is not working, foolish woman?" he replied to her with irritation in his voice.

"The money they promised you," she asked. "To buy our produce, where is it?"

Lupernicus snarled, "When I get through with that sniveling Marius, he'll wish he'd never lied to me. Tomorrow I will pay him a visit."

***

"Here, Lupernicus, have another drink," urged the swarthy purchasing agent for the Hispania Ninth Legion. He tried to calm the angry man who had barged in, but with little success. His close-spaced eyes shiftily rotated, looking for the nearest exit if things turned ugly.

"Marius, you lying pig, son of an accursed brood!" raged Lupernicus. "You promised to buy all the produce I could raise for an agreed price. So far, all you've taken are a few bags of wine at a ridiculously low price. My wife, children, and I are working from sunup to sundown with nothing to show for it." He gripped his calloused hand around the hilt of his short sword as he edged slowly closer to the cowering agent. Marius had not attained to his position, however, without often having resorted to glibly provided excuses. Rob the ignorant and poor and kowtow to the rich and influential people had proved to be his route to riches.

"Listen to me, Lupernicus, and I will make you rich," he promised again. "Can I help it if the bottom has dropped out of agricultural products? There hasn't been enough fighting, and many soldiers have had time to grow their own vegetables. It's not my fault, but if you want to make big money, then have I got a deal for you."

Lupernicus took his hand off his sword and tossed down another large draught of the cheap red wine provided by Marius. "I'm listening, you slippery eel! Go ahead and tell me about your get-rich scheme."

He listened carefully as Marius detailed the huge signing bonus that was being offered to trained naval soldiers for service in Northern Gaul and the Northwest Lowlands. "Two thousand sesterces to sign, and a further five hundred for every month of service. After five more years are added to your already-served naval service, that will allow you to retire with a sizable pension," promised a relieved Marius as he watched the anger subside in the dangerous man before him.

After a long pause, Lupernicus finally spoke, causing the fat man to lean expectantly forward. "It's a deal, but remember this: if you lie, I will come after you, and you will regret it. I promise."

Alsa listened with mixed emotions when Lupernicus told her about his plans. He had been cruel to her on many occasions, but he had always protected his family from predators and provided for them. "In five years, I will return," he promised, "and then we will never want for money again." She felt her fifth child stirring in her womb, but the promise of the bonus money did much to allay her fear. Her sons were growing fast, and who knew what would happen in five years?

After three years, Alsa was notified that her husband had died a glorious death in service to the Empire. Three weeks later, she married Marius, who had become a frequent visitor.

***

The Viking: From Beast to Christian Husband and Father

"Gold! Gold and plunder, that is what I will risk my life for," roared Rorik. "Is there anything else better than that?"

His mother stopped her entreaties as she saw the determination and fire in her son's eyes. "It has been five years since your father left our home, and we must presume that he has died in some forsaken place. If you're determined to go, then I will resign myself to also losing my only son," she ended. The remote Scandinavian settlement that was Rorik's home was located at the end of a deep fjord. Since only a few older men and young boys remained, it was fortunate that it was virtually impenetrable and impervious to attack. His mother, Lakasa, would never understand why men would leave their families and snug settlements to heed the siren lure of gold and adventure. Abandoned by husband and son, she would be forced to depend on others for her subsistence. She looked at her image in her treasured burnished copper plate and wondered what remaining eligible man would still find her attractive.

Rorik's father had been the chief in his village, so there was no question as to who would command the Viking longboat. He plied the oars with his men and was at the forefront, leading every raid. He regarded compassion as a weakness. "By Thor! Leif," he upbraided his eldest crew member after a brutal raid on defenseless villagers, "stop your mewling and puking! Did you think that they would meekly hand over their goods and women? Remember, we can leave no witness to inform others about what we have done here."

"Why the women and children, Rorik?" protested Leif. "Are we butchers, or warriors?"

After the raider's bloodlust had faded, Rorik divided the loot taken from the hapless villagers among his crew. What they could not stow, they buried close to familiar landmarks for future retrieval.

"Do you ever grow tired of all the hardships and killings, Rorik?" asked his bodyguard, Alfred.

"Not when I think of the boring alternative," laughed Rorik. "Do you want to grow fat at home with a brood of young ones around you and a wife to nag you? Not me, Alfred; I plan to become as rich as I can, and then I will go home, settle down, and live like a king."

The raiders were surprised when Rorik turned the longboat to the southeast. They had heard the stories about fierce warriors who sailed in huge ships with iron battering rams. Two other longboats joined them on their first raid on a lowland settlement.

The Roman galley appeared out of the mist and immediately drove its battering ram straight at Rorik's Viking longboat in order to aid the threatened village. The Vikings were ready but paid dearly for their victory. It was the reinforcement of the two other boats that turned the tide of battle in favour of the Vikings. Rorik's ship was smashed, and the two other boats had no room for him and his men. They decided to go ashore to wait for a relief vessel. None came, and after some years, the raiding party found a new home.

Crossing the Great Divide

"A cross! Peter, my grandson, I have traded my ill-gotten gains for a cross," softly spoke the white-haired, stooped Viking to the sturdy son of his oldest daughter. Rorik had done penance by giving most of his stolen loot to the poor people of the village. Peter had become a willing, albeit not a very useful, helper during the harvest and had difficulty listening to his instructions.

"Why, Bestefar (Gramps) Why do I need to listen to you?" he obstinately ... endlessly asked. "You told me before that I'm a good worker, am I not?" Rorik stopped the angry retort that sprang to his lips as Peter split another cucumber and gently explained how to separate the cucumber from the vine.

Every day Rorik was still aware of the terrible crimes he had committed and the redemption in Jesus that God had given through the means of his wife. He often crooned a paraphrased line from the Psalm Katje had taught him: "*My sins of youth remember not, and please forgive committed transgression.*" He still missed the wild mountains and forests of his youth but had found contentment in working the solid clay of the lowlands. Lush crops and an ever-increasing number of progeny gave him a contentment that his forbearers had never known. In the setting evening sun, he smelled the good food that was being prepared. He entered his rude home and gathered his beloved Katje into his arms and kissed her as she stood over the peat fire broiling the hare that Roric had snared for dinner. "Thank you, God, for allowing me to have a portion of your riches, in this life and the one to come." Successive generations lived, loved, and died until another special son was born.

***

The Crusader

The scorching heat of the opened oven door reddened the fair face of John, son of Epie the baker. Every morning at 4:00 a.m., the oven had to be up to temperature to accept the lumps of rising dough prepared the night before. Epie was the sole baker in the small village and was appreciated for his fine bread and pastries, and reviled for his high prices and undersized loaves. "They think that I should match the prices of the bakeries in Dordt," he muttered to himself, but was overheard by John. "People don't realize that living on an island incurs extra costs. I don't intend to slave away forever for a mere pittance. No siree, I am going to get rich if it's the last thing I do."

Ten-year-old John knew that what he was hearing was not in line with what the minister preached about in the kerk. He noted that his father spoke and acted piously on Sundays, but often cheated and lied during the week. "Please, Father," he asked. "would it not be good to give Widow Rense some free bread and a few pastries?"

The hard slap that immediately followed his appeal threw John against the hot oven. "Never expect me or yourself to give charity to those who have only themselves to blame for their misfortune!" roared his father. "No buts or ifs. Put some butter on those burns and get back to work."

After five years of relentless work, John rebelled. He could no longer abide the crass selfishness of his parents. He had learned to read and had memorized large parts of the Bible. He knew that money was more often a curse than a blessing. His parents were a living proof of what the love of money resulted in. Jesus had said;

> *What good will it be for someone to gain the whole world, yet forfeit their soul?" (Matthew 16:26); "Man shall not live on bread alone, but on every word that comes from the mouth of God. (Matthew 4:4)*

The house was deep in slumber when John stole down the stairs, gathered his clothes, and stuffed his rucksack full of bread, cheese, and butter. He placed the pitiful wage his father had given him in his pocket and then penned a short note to his mother with a promise that he would someday return. It was a short run to the dock, where he cajoled the ferry operator to give him free passage across the strait to the mainland. On the road heading eastward, a farmer offered him a ride on his heavy farm wagon, which was heading east to Dordt. In 1212 AD, boys and girls his age were gathering there to join the struggle to liberate the Holy Land from the Arab infidels. Streams of young people from all over Europe were coalescing into a mighty stream. "Leave your material goods behind and join us!" they shouted at the curious or jeering bystanders. "Leave it all behind and join us as we go to liberate the Promised Land." Ideals had since met reality, and now a mature John was ready to settle down.

The racket made by the thrushes under the roof tiles woke the returned crusader from a deep slumber. He was momentarily disoriented in the garret room, but the sound of his mother downstairs brought him back to reality. He had spent so many nights outdoors on his long journey that sleeping indoors was still strange for him. Now that the idealism of being part of the children's crusade movement was crushed, he needed to figure out what it was he wanted to do for himself and his growing daughter. He listened to the racking cough of his stepfather and knew that his earthly time was short. His mother was becoming old and forgetful, so John decided to find himself a wife.

Cornelius tamped down the hemp seeds in his large ceramic pipe, which constantly had to be relit, and warily sized up the blond giant who had asked for the hand of his daughter. His fingers roughly tugged at the mass of his unruly beard and he yelled to his wife, "Jantjie! Bring some more beer." This was followed by the beginning interrogation. "Marrying is a serious business, John, and I want to know how you are planning to support my Truus? She has two older brothers, so there will be no inheritance for her if she should marry. Do you understand that you can expect no help or money from me?"

John waited until his temper had cooled, and then with an even tone replied to the cold, stolid burgher. "I promise to take very good care of your Truus, and I will inherit my own farm when my mother passes on."

He opened his mouth to speak again, but Truus entered the room, gave him a warning look, and then looked sweetly at her father. She settled her ample bulk onto her father's lap and stroked his head. "I want to marry John, Father, so break out the wine bottle and let's celebrate."

Truus proved to be bossy and barren, and John often thought of his beautiful Tonia, but he treated his wife with respect. Truus and her stepdaughter grew very close. Many townspeople assumed that she was the actual mother. Truus also had the Midas touch in business. Her advice to John when he was selling his crops or purchasing seeds and equipment was shrewd and valuable.

"It's just not right, my daughter," complained her father many years later. "John owns more land and is far richer than I and your brothers. I know it's not his business sense that has accomplished this. He is much too easy going. It is you, my daughter. Your worth is far above rubies, and I hope your husband appreciates you." Her final economic triumph was the nuptial arrangement between her stepdaughter and the son of the mayor. All of life for John and Truus began to be centred around their social obligations. They became much too busy to tend to their spiritual garden.

***

A Toi La Gloire (Thine Be the Glory)

The song bubbled in a joyous stream from young Chloe's mouth. Spring had cast its soft beauty over the Normandy countryside as Chloe picked daisies and chased butterflies until she collapsed in a tired heap.

"Come, Chloe, time for supper," caressed the voice of her doting father as he swept his precious girl into strong arms. Calvin Viljoen had made it no secret that he had longed for a son. His frail wife had poured all her physical energies into producing a healthy daughter. Unable to bring the baby forth herself, the final entrance into the world by Chloe was accomplished by the intervention of the capable midwife. Calvin noticed that the ethereal qualities in his wife soon eclipsed her desire to participate in the rugged life of a French peasant woman. He also knew that no more children or sons would ever be born to him and this wife.

"I somehow never seem able to catch my breath, my darling man," Chloe whispered to her husband as she lay dying. "Please take good care of our Chloe." After the burial of his wife, Calvin's only desire was to provide his daughter with everything that her mother had missed.

Chloe noticed the deep mahogany-hued lines in her father's face as he slowly chewed the goat meat and potatoes she had prepared, lines so deep that the day's dirt had not been removed by the washing at the well. "Marry a rich man, my precious girl," suddenly erupted out of her father. "Escape this incessant labour that drags a human down. Get money. It gives one the power to make choices."

"The Lord will decide whom I will marry," Chloe interrupted. "But whoever it is that I shall marry, it will be because I love him … just like you loved my mother." Father Calvin was, however, not to be dissuaded.

Every Sunday evening he would invite one of a coterie of the most well off bachelors in the village to dine at their home. "Cook the best meal that you can, Chloe," he would encourage his daughter. "Wear that dress your mother left you … you know, the one with the lovely pink and red colours. I ask only one promise from you, my daughter. Should God grant a son to you, then will you please call him Caleb?"

"I will, Pa. I surely will," Chloe teased as she showed another prospect, chosen by her father, the door. What kindness it was that Calvin did not live to see the suffering and misery experienced by his lovely Chloe. After her marriage to Henri Bedard, Calvin died a disappointed man. He would never know that not one but two Calebs would be born to Chloe to honour his request.

Caleb Bedard, grandson of Chloe Bedard, loved his farm, his mother, his wife, and God. The Reformed preacher in his village had tried many times to rearrange the order of priority without success. "You attach too much importance to worldly possessions, my son," admonished both the preacher and his mother, Katherine.

Caleb deigned to reply but slyly thought, *talk all you want, preacher man, but those who minimize goods and money end up in debtors' prison. The rich parishioners sitting in their private pews are secretly envied by the poor backbenchers in the church. It's the landowners and aristocrats who are looked up to.* Katherine divined her son's thoughts and admonished him. "My son! Seek first God's kingdom, and the rest will follow."

After the Roman Catholic mobs had chased the Huguenots from their villages, Caleb's world collapsed as he left all his possessions behind. Before he walked away, he once more allowed his calloused hands to touch the fine handcrafted implements, and his eyes to linger on the stone boundary walls of his precious farm. He turned his hands with palms facing him and muttered, "My hands will win me the victory once more." No prayer crossed his lips as he subconsciously expressed rebellion against his Maker. One cart, pulled by the family milk cow, contained all the possessions of Caleb's mother, unmarried brothers, and his wife. They survived days of slogging over the muddy roads and driven by the relentless goads of hunger and thirst. At the end of their resources and energy, they finally reached the last stage of their journey.

"I do not take French money; only guilders accepted here," was the laconic reply to Caleb's attempt to purchase passage on the decrepit ferry to Goringa Island. In frustration, Caleb began to berate the wiry Dutchman, but he took no notice as he ejected his nose contents and then rolled a cigarette.

"No, Mother, please don't part with your silver wedding service," begged Caleb as his mother offered the heavy plate to the suddenly-interested bargeman.

"It has to be done, son," spoke Katherine in a dejected voice. "There are still papist troops in this area. We need to get to a safe haven on the island. The Reformed minister told us we'd be safe there."

It took many years of back-breaking work to once again have his own home and to rent a small piece of land to grow his produce on the Island of Goringa. Prejudice against the Huguenots was strong in the beginning, but slowly the taciturn islanders accepted the newcomers.

The brown stream of tobacco-stained spittle narrowly missed Caleb's boots as Hans educated him on the traditions of the island. "Work for the rich farmers during the day," he advised. "Work for yourself in the evenings, and if your wife is thrifty, you can slowly become rich."

Caleb looked at the slack-jawed, dirty little man in front of him and narrowly stopped the French curse that rose in his gorge. "Thanks for the good advice," he lied as he turned away. *As if I need a backward islander to tell me how to farm*, was what he really thought.

"Ten per cent," spoke the fleshy lips twitching in the huge head of the Goringa landowner. "I will rent three hectares of land to you for ten per cent of all the crops you grow."

Caleb knew that the going rate was between seven to nine percent, but he agreed to the usurious terms. He evenly divided the remainder of the crops with his extended family, and no one went to bed hungry. Never again would the consuming desire to become wealthy dominate his life. "Teach me your ways, Lord

Jesus; *Je t'aime.* (I love you.)" It was the final meditation of his heart as the reliable but mortal pump pushed its last liquid load.

***

Pablo the Spaniard

Seville was a good place to live. Pablo turned twenty in 1560 AD and was proud that his country, Hapsburg Hispania, was the dominant empire of the day.

"My son, when are you going to be concerned about your future place in life?" warned his father. "Life is not a lark, and you should be busy making money and buying property in order to raise a family."

"I will only be young once, Father," Pablo replied. "But don't worry, Pater, I am planning to enlist in the army and make my fortune as a soldier."

"How many rich soldiers do you know, son? Only the generals and officers get rich, and you have no high up connections to grease your path. Stay with me and we will join the House of Trade on the Guadalquivir River and make our fortune together. Juanita, daughter of my good friend Jose, has been looking at you with undisguised admiration, and you should be nice to her."

Pablo remembered his father's advice as he ruefully scraped the mud and manure from his boots. Beautiful, sunny Seville had been replaced by the soggy cold Dutch lowlands. Fine silk shirts and pants were supplanted by steel chest corselets, puffy leather pantaloons, and weapons that had to be constantly polished to keep the rust away. The damp lowland air in the fall and winter months not only caused metals to rust but also spoiled food and drink. The conquered lowlanders deeply resented the cruelty inflicted upon them by the "Iron Duke," who established the Blood Councils to root out Protestant heretics. *I should have listened to you, Father,* thought Pablo. *It would have been so much better to stay home, marry Juanita, and make a lot of money trading in Seville.*

"Do not be stupid, Pablo!" shouted his commanding officer. "You'll get a bonus for every heretic you arrest or kill." Pablo had refused a direct order to chase and kill the escaping family that had refused to kiss the sacred relic placed before them by the priest. Pablo had been raised to revere church and Pope, but the sickening sight of burned and strangled peasants revolted him.

"No amount of money offered can ever turn me into a butcher," protested the elegant, fun-loving Spaniard. "I will not be a party to such evil."

The world is indebted to such men as Pablo.

"I love you, my man," murmured Trina as she put patches on the long woolen underwear that Pablo needed to keep warm as he worked in the tulip fields. "You did not become a 'Judas' to accept money for cruelty. Arrest and jailing could not bend you, and I love you for that." The sharp homesickness for remembered Seville was healed over as Pablo dandled his bright, dark-haired daughter, Maria, on his knee.

The Stolid Dutchman

Adam Smith, the great Scottish economist, would have loved Marinus Nachtegal. He embodied all that Smith had theorized about.

> *"It is not from the benevolence of the butcher, the brewer, or the baker that we expect our dinner, but from their regard to their own interest."*[1]

---

1 An Inquiry into the Nature and Causes of the Wealth of Nations by Adam Smith 1776, Book 1, Chapter 2
Of the Principle which gives occasion to the Division of Labour

Work hard, make money, and mind your own business, comprised Marinus's philosophy of life. He lived his life in the moment and had little interest in anything beyond the immediate. His ingrained prejudices against the French did not extend to pretty Huguenot Betje Bedard, whom he doggedly courted until she gave in and said "Yes." The French troubles were past, and it was best to forget about them.

Betje gave birth to one son, and Marinus named him Jan. It was not due to lack of trying, but Betje was unable to have any more children.

Marinus was a good provider for his wife and expected her to be obedient to his viewpoint. Often he would say, "Am I not a good provider for you, Betje? Could you have married anyone else who would have looked after you better than me?" Outwardly Betje submitted, but inwardly she often had trouble containing the lively intellect so superior to her husband's. Whenever Marinus would launch into a verbal tirade against French morality and customs, Betje would try to sidetrack him into a different direction. She was aware of the terrible massacres perpetrated by the French Romanists against the Huguenots, but she also loved the elegance and beauty of French culture.

At age forty, Jan Nachtegal, descendant of Marinus and Betje, married Sophie Ruiter, who was the daughter of the largest landowner on Goringa. He entered a loveless marriage to gain access to her money. Like his father, he only had one son, and he settled into a life of disappointment. Bitter arguing and differing spiritual views between the parents led to a disconnect that resulted in a failure to agree on how to raise their son, Peter.

Krom Houtje

Peter Nachtegal reached into his pocket to supply his friends with another round of stout ale at the local tavern. The money he had stolen from his mother's purse had somehow disappeared. "Sorry, boys," he muttered as he caught the barmaid's eye, "that will be all for tonight."

"Ah, come on, Pete," joshed his friends, "quit chasing girls and buy us another round." He hoped to find Greta waiting as he pushed the door open into the blustery evening. She, however, was long used to Peter's manipulative ways and had hurried home to her parents. Everyone in the village knew that Peter was a scoundrel, except for his parents and on-and-off again girlfriend, Coby.

The answer to enjoyment is enough money, thought Peter as he schemed and planned his next escapade. He could only steal so much from his parents without it being obvious. He hated physical work and was too mistrusted to get a clerical job.

"What? No money, Pete?" exclaimed his friend Seth. "That's a bummer, man. Let's fix that right away. Come with me tonight and we can poach eels by lantern light and snare hares in the marshland."

"That's private property, Seth. You know that policeman Vosje runs patrols there," objected Peter in a worried voice.

"Not to worry dumkopf," laughed Seth. "I have it all figured out. Join me at eight tonight, and I'll teach you how to make some extra cash." The lure of money quickly overpowered Peter's fear, and since his morality had been compromised long ago, that also was no obstacle. The evening's poachings provided the thieves with a large cash credit from the local tavern owner, who was eager to barter for the prized delicacies.

The obsessive desire for ever more money soon led to Peter and Seth's arrest. Constable Vosje caught them red-handed with a pail full of eels and three large hares. The pair begged and cajoled to no avail. The policeman's formidable bulk and holstered pistol also dissuaded any thought of running to escape. The judge, however, listened to the pleas from Peter's parents and felt inclined to give him one more chance.

Before pronouncing sentence, however, he was outraged by a disturbance at the rear of his court room. "Order! Order! I shall have order in my courtroom," he yelled to the bailiff.

"Throw the scoundrel in jail!" yelled Coby's father. "We've just found out that our daughter is pregnant by this degenerate."

"Place him on the next boat to Indonesia and see to it that he enlists," pronounced the judge.

Peter's army stint in Indonesia proved to be his final undoing. The primal beauty of Bali had no effect on him. The selfless love of Coby was not appreciated. The end of those who have known and then exchange truth for dross was clearly evident in Peter's final years. He angrily waved with a dismissive gesture as his wife Coby read to him from the Bible: *"Such are the paths of all who go after ill-gotten gain; it takes away the life of those who get it."* (Proverbs 1:19)

The 1900–1999 French/Dutch Generation

Peter Nachtegal and Kate Bedard's marriage conjoined all the best and worst attributes of the French and Germanic heritages on Goringa. Intelligent, passionate, quickly jealous, and suspicious were deeply ingrained traits that both shared. When it came to money, however, there was deep division. Peter wanted to save every dime that he made, and Kate thought that money was for spending. The list for spending was endless with their large family. "Peter, the children need clothes, shoes, organ lessons, and healthy food," was the never ending demand by Kate. Peter knew that most of Kate's requests were reasonable, but his ambitious plans required that money be saved.

"Money, money, Peter. Why must you always go on about money?" lamented Kate after she had listened to another diatribe from her husband on how to be a thrifty housewife. "Does Jesus not say that we should not worry about possessions and money?"

"Planning for a prosperous future is not worrying, Kate," defended an exasperated Peter. "In order for me to make you a queen, we need to save," he slyly riposted.

"You do not fool me for a minute, little man," laughed Kate as she shoved playfully against his huge bulk. "I'll make sure you never turn into a money-loving miser." And so the battle was joined with never a clear victor in sight. Peter laboured diligently, collected what he could from wage-earning children, tried to save, and reached a comfortable end. Kate indeed became a queen, but her fortune was comprised of a multitude of spiritual, god-fearing children, grandchildren, and great-grandchildren.

The 1900-1999 Spanish/Dutch Generation

Diego Teelhart gasped in amazement as he studied his ancestral tree. He had always presumed himself to be of solid Dutch stock, but the record clearly showed that the Spaniard Pablo was his forefather. "I always told you, Diego, that you looked like a fierce Spaniard, just like your father," teased his wife, Rita. "You could have been a brother to Hernan Cortez."

"Well then, if that's true, then I shall conquer an empire like Cortez," replied Diego with a twisting smile of his lips.

***

"Yes, Diego, I know your flower business is doing okay," flattered Diego's brother on the telephone, "but you're talking peanuts compared to the opportunities to be found in Canada. Emigrate, Diego, and your fortune will be made." Diego's temperament was not accustomed to quick decisions. But when Rita agreed, all the Teelharts, including baby Tirzah, went to seek their fortune in exciting Canada.

Diego Teelhart was not your average Dutchman. Deep-set eyes and a large Roman nose accentuated the purpose and seriousness of his nature. His friends would tease him with nicknames: "Good morning, hidalgo; Hey, conquistador," were sobriquets that would greet him as he walked with a forward stoop. Meningitis had nearly killed him during his army service and had left an indelible imprint. For many generations, the Teelharts had been flower growers. Tulips and Dahlias were Diego's passion. Diego had hoped to emulate his younger brother's financial success, but it was not to be. His hard work provided a good living for his family, but his desire to be rich was not fulfilled in monetary results.

Seven healthy children were born to Diego and Rita, but none of the seven showed the Spanish heritage so evident in their father. In her fortieth year, Rita gave birth to her eighth and final baby. They called her Tirzah, and she was the image bearer of a long previous Maartje. She was a lovely baby and became a beautiful girl who was very aware of her Spanish nose.

"Save your money, Tirzah, every penny that you can," advised her father as he handed her the approved application to start working at the local bank. She had noticed through all her growing years how important it was to her parents to have money. She had been able to cover her deep sensitivity with a layer of passive acceptance. Conversational skills did not come easy to her, but she showed great adeptness in organizational skills and in being diligent in her tasks. She also had the rare ability to listen and focus completely on the person speaking to her.

***

Caleb and Tirzah Nachtegal

Caleb awoke to the delightful giggling of his six-year-old second daughter, Delphine. Her brown face and dark hair formed a picture of health and beauty as she prodded him with her stethoscope. "You fell asleep, Daddy, during your checkup, but I finished it anyway." That moment, a photographic plate engraved in his mind of one of those precious moments that are remembered forever. Tirzah and all the present children were all laughing as Delphine squeaked in her high voice, "Daddy's in perfect health, because I wore my nurse's cap when I checked him."

"Do you realize, Caleb, that our tenth wedding anniversary is almost here," reminded Tirzah's soft voice. "It's time for you to slow down and spend some more time with us, your family. You can be so obsessed with work and making money, and you never refuse requests for help. Please don't let your absences allow these precious growing years of our children to slip away."

Caleb worked through the emotions of being hurt and feeling under-appreciated. He knew that Tirzah often spent evenings and weeks alone as he worked to establish enterprises in other cities and to help his brother Jan during his farming harvest. He had promised her that they would be a team as they raised their large family. Almost imperceptibly, he increased his moneymaking enterprises and his involvement in church and outside activities so that he was rarely at home during the weekday evenings. The excuse that, "I'm doing this all for you and the kids, Tirzah," was no longer ringing true. He had to confront the question: "Do I have the money, or does the money have me?"

Caleb had never considered himself to be greedy. Making money was an enjoyment, much like playing Monopoly. Construction, land development, real estate, futures, stock market investing, and manufacturing, were all pursuits he was good at and enjoyed. He disliked controlled markets and government intervention, and he was a true free enterpriser. Every time he set a goal and attained it, he would move the goalposts further ahead.

Caleb loved his five daughters and knew that he should be more involved in their inner orbit. All of them did well at school and loved literature and music. An open door was soon provided. "Could I ask a favour of you, Father?" asked the eldest daughter. Hannah had obtained a number of university degrees and was busy teaching. She had grown to be stubbornly independent, and it was unusual for her to request any favour.

"Certainly, daughter," Caleb replied with a wary grin. "To the half of my kingdom, if you so desire."

"Well, I won't require that much," Hannah laughingly responded. "I'd like you to give a lecture to my English as Second Language class at the university. They all want to know how to make money and become rich quickly. I thought to myself, *Maybe Dad would like to help me out with that.*

No getting out of it now, thought Caleb. This time he needed to let Hannah know that he would make time for her. He feverishly set to work, and on the appointed day he presented his lecture on how to make money as part of the pursuit of happiness.

"Good morning, students and hopeful entrepreneurs. I am a Christian, and I believe that free market capitalism is the economic system that gives ordinary people, like you and me, the best opportunity to make money. If your prime goal in life is to make money, or to be a materialist, then you will likely succeed, but you will become a very unsatisfied, one-dimensional person. Life needs a spiritual dimension, and wealth can aid or encumber that journey. I'd like to tell you how my world view determines my attitude about money. Money is simply an agreed upon exchange for goods and services. The exchange can be in shells, beads, paper, or metals, but the value of money is set by the society that uses it. In Canada, a person needs dollars in order to buy goods, services, and assets. Please note the following points:

1) **How do you get it?**
2) **How much do you need or want?**
3) **What will you do with it?**
4) **What will it do to you?**

"**1a**—unless you get an inheritance, win the lottery, or rob a bank, you'll will have to work and invest in order to get an appreciable amount of money. People generally fall into three groups. Most people are satisfied with an eight-hour work day, doing work that requires average skills. They hopefully make enough money to pay the bills and enjoy some leisure time. If you're content with that goal, good on you, but then the rest of my presentation may have little interest for you.

"**1b**—A second category of people are the professionals who have invested in their education. They command higher salaries and better job opportunities. If this is your goal, that's great. Go for it!

"**1c**—I belong to the third group of people who earn enough money for their needs and have extra to buy assets so that they're able to start a business. Hard work and building up a credit rating can be used to buy one very important asset: your own home. With the equity in your home, used as collateral, you can borrow and work with the bank's money to start your own business or invest in good money-making enterprises. This approach takes discipline and commitment to a long-range goal. You need to assess your ability to take risk and find out what you do well. It means that you may first have to do without in order to save up some capital.

"**2)** Set your personal goals and find out how much money you need. The person who works to have $100,000 in his account will have different goals than someone who wants $1,000,000. The more money a person wants usually means that they are willing and able to take more risk. Highly profitable businesses usually require more money to buy or start. It's the same for investments. Stocks, over time, produce a high rate of return. However, if you have a weak stomach for risk, then stocks may not be for you. The roller coaster stock market prices are proof of that. The most profitable markets of all are the futures and forex markets. In order to trade profitably in these markets, one needs nerves of steel and the instincts of a predatory animal. These markets are definitely not for the faint of heart, and one should never use money needed for living expenses in these high-risk markets. In order to begin making wealth, try not to purchase eroding assets. I know that most of us require a car, but it's probably the worst eroding asset you can buy.

"**3)** Setting goals for making money is a good thing. Deciding what you will do with the money you make is also necessary. Discipline is essential. Many people who try so hard to obtain money are destroyed when they succeed. That is proven by the vast majority of lottery winners and people who get large inheritances. Providing for a comfortable life is good, but selfishness and greed eat away at the human soul and make us less than human. When we give money and time to charities and good causes, then it will provide more enjoyment than the effort we put in. It is a win-win goal to have in your life. As a Christian, I believe that God is the owner of everything, and that I, as a steward, am to use responsibly what He gives to me.

"**4)** While the 'obsessive love of money' is evil, responsible possession of money is a blessing and a worthwhile goal. Free market capitalism allows us to use our skills and energy to build a worthwhile future for society and ourselves. I want to leave you with one last thought to remember: *Strive to possess, as if not possessing,* and then your money will not make a slave out of you."

As Caleb looked closely at the facial expressions of Hannah's pupils, he could almost predict what most of them would choose for their life's direction. Rapt attention for the methodology and a blank stare for the spiritual discipline were evident. He ended with, "Thank you for the opportunity to speak to you today."

***

It was a proud day for Caleb and Tirzah as their oldest son, Brock, presented his oral thesis. They watched as their handsome son spoke with confident knowledge. Brock had elected to become an electronics engineer and graduated after five years of diligent studies. Many prayers for his safekeeping during those years had been answered. He drove his three-cylinder Sprint like a race car driver up Burnaby mountain day in and day out. One small rear-ender against a gravel truck was his only mishap. He soon landed a well-paying job with an international company, which allowed him to save a substantial amount of money.

"Dad, what do you think about me moving out and living on my own?" Brock suddenly asked.

Caleb was startled but carefully responded. "What are you planning to do, son? Are you going to rent, or do you have a purchase in mind?"

"What would you advise, Dad? Rent or buy?"

"Don't waste money on rent, son," Caleb advised. "Renting only makes sense when you can't afford to buy. Find a quality house that you like and then go for it. You know that your parents would backstop you if you ran into financial trouble." Brock heeded that advice and it became his cornerstone to financial success. All the Nachtegal children were taught to never go into debt with the purchase of non-essential things. "You should only borrow in order to buy a house or set up your own business," warned Caleb. Most of his children followed that advice.

Tirzah watched in astonishment as her Caleb traded commodities, equities, and other investments on his online computer. She had always thought that buying and selling futures and stocks and bonds was a gambling venture that Christians should avoid. They were equal partners in everything, and Tirzah thought it was time to give her husband a warning. "The only time I ever owned any stocks," she whispered worriedly to Caleb, "it did not go well. I was wiped out completely. Every three months I received a notice telling me how well the stocks were performing and splitting. One fine day I was informed that they were worth nothing."

"There's always risk involved in buying speculative goods," Caleb replied as he hugged his true treasure. "No risk and pain, no gain. It's my knowledge pitted against the market. Trading is true, free enterprise compressed into short time frames. Sometimes I lose but more often I will win." After thirty years of trading, Caleb had become wary of the hype and had learned to spot real opportunities. He saw no difference between buying a stock, commodity, or purchasing real estate for future gain. The entire North American economy functioned around, and needed, speculative trading.

Cassie was the third daughter and fourth child of Caleb and Tirzah. Even tempered, disciplined, and cautious, she was a delight to her parents. Steadily she forged ahead toward her goal to becoming a Registered Occupational Therapist. Silently Caleb's heart ached for his daughter, who seemed not to attract male attention. To think that a daughter of his beloved Tirzah would never hold her own baby seemed so impossible to consider. "God does not call all His people to the married life," counselled Tirzah, but Caleb knew that inwardly she also sorrowed that such a talented and delightful daughter would miss what she had so loved to receive.

"Shall I buy a condominium or should I rent?" Cassie asked her father.

Caleb replied with his stock advice: "Buy, Cassie! You have a good job and salary, so there's no reason why you wouldn't buy." Another child was on her way to financial security, and her parents would later appoint her as a financial guardian for their estate. The formulae to financial success was really so simple. Develop your talent, stay away from chronic dependencies, and maintain good health to the best of your abilities. Simple ... but so impossible for so many. All the other factors are in God's control, and He will ultimately decide what is good for His children.

"Do you still remember that old Beatles song, "Will you still love me when I'm sixty-four?" seventy-five-year-old Caleb asked Tirzah with a wide grin on his creased face. He looked at his bride of forty-nine years and wondered how the time had flown so fast. He knew that age would have its way with all of them, but Tirzah had remained lovely well into old age. "Standing right beside me through everything I've done," was a favourite ditty that Caleb would sing to her, and he meant it.

Having a wonderful partner who shared common goals and a world view was a blessing that extended into the financial realm. To possess as not possessing meant that Tirzah and Caleb realized that they were only stewards. God had always provided, and they trusted that He always would. Frugal living partnered with Kingdom giving was their financial golden rule.

It is telling and revealing that the connection between material wealth and spiritual wellbeing is so often mentioned in the Bible.

CHAPTER IX

Caleb's Theory of Nearly Everything

Now I Understand in Part

"I hate growing old, Caleb. I should have turned on the gas jet long ago," commiserated ninety-two-year-old Butch. Caleb stooped beside the stocky old man who was trying to fit a new belt onto his dilapidated old mower. He was lying on the oil soaked cracked concrete floor and didn't realize that the belt was the wrong size. Oil and grease smears covered his arms and face as he tried to figure out the convoluted loops around the pulleys.

"Let me show you why it's not the right size," Caleb offered as he looped the V-belt around the mower's pulleys. He glanced gingerly at Butch as he worked, not wanting to put a dent in the old man's pride. *Old man*, he thought, *that's what my own children's eyes express when they look at me.*

"Forty-two inches is what I need; that's what the book sez, and the man at the hardware store told me that this belt is forty-two inches," retorted Butch angrily. "Who can you believe anymore?"

"Look here, Butch … look at my tape measure. What does it read as I measure your belt?" Caleb patiently explained. Butch grabbed his reading spectacles, adding more grease to the already opaque lenses, and read the length of his belt.

"I'll be ##$$**," Butch swore. "It reads forty-six inches, Caleb. You can't trust anyone anymore. Sorry about the language. I know that you are a Christian, but habits die hard when you get to be as old as me." Caleb worried, looking at the engorged red face, that the old man would blow an artery right there. "I'm sorry, Caleb," Butch apologized again.

Caleb spoke to the old man about the great trustworthy Saviour for all people, but Butch's eyes remained blank. The self-reliant, feisty Scotsman was not about to go soft in the head at this stage of life. A steady stream of door knockers over the years had tried to get the old man to repent and pay. "I like that skinny, hardworking Dutchman," Butch told his daughter. "I just wish he'd stop talking about religion."

***

Taj Mahal #2

"Careful, boys, careful," repeated Caleb as his three strong sons gingerly lifted the heavy beam onto the prepared placement saddle. He knew they could do it, because otherwise he would have had to hire a crane truck to place the heavy beams.

"Not to worry, pops," teased youngest son, Peter. "Any time you can't handle it, just call." That boy never missed a chance to tease or play a joke on his Pa.

Every time Caleb looked at the sons that Tirzah had birthed, he felt the pain of losing his two brothers diminish. Time had gifted him to be able to play with them and build cars, trailers, and house constructions. He would watch them with pride as they grew from tots to smart, big, handsome men. Often harsh pride and frictions developed as they asserted their independence, but he had been a present father as they grew up. The wonderful part of the world where they had grown up provided all the opportunities to snow ski, water ski, fish, play tennis, hike, and enjoy other outdoor activities with their dad. All his achievements paled when compared to the miracle gift of his children, and he murmured, "Thank you, my God."

"Bloody millionaires," muttered the spattered concrete worker as Caleb and Tirzah skirted around the freshly poured concrete sidewalks in the new neighbouring subdivisions being built around their home. "We, the workers, get peanuts, while the home owners rake in fortunes." He had a point! Capitalism rewards investment smarts. Most labourers lived from pay cheque to pay cheque.

Greed and desire held the neighbourhood gathering in its grip as the land developer agents outlined the large amounts of money that owners could expect to receive for their properties. Caleb knew the mantra from experience: "Sell now while prices are high, because tomorrow the bottom could fall out of the market." It would take many more years before Tirzah and Caleb agreed to sell, and the initial promises were never realized.

Caleb held Tirzah close to him as the giant claw bit into the home in which they had raised their eight children. Development had finally invaded their neighbourhood, and they had realized that all the acres would be zoned into small lots. He had worried that it might be too traumatic for Tirzah to witness, but she insisted. For over forty years that home had been a pleasure to live in and contained so many happy memories. Emotion flooded their minds as the excavator destroyed in one hour what Caleb had taken months to build. "This is not our final home, darling," whispered Caleb to his Tirzah. "We are sojourners on our way to heaven. In the meantime, I've built a far finer home for both of us to enjoy as a temporary gift from Him."

Caleb found it ironic that nearly all of the houses in which he had lived in Canada had been demolished while the home he was born in, on the Island of Goringa, was still standing. There was a completely different *zeitgeist* in Europe when it came to preserving the old-style buildings. Renovating and restoring houses hundreds of years old cost more money than to simply demolish and replace with new construction. Nothing could be constructed or changed without going through a bureaucratic maze of regulations. Caleb looked up and hoped his father could hear his words of appreciation for emigrating to Canada so long ago.

"Why? Why?" Tirzah lamented. *We were so happy and content on our lovely acre. When we moved there, we were surrounded with a rural environment. Twelve thousand people lived in Sunnyside, Surrey, and now there are 100,000. Caleb says we need to move because if we stay here, we'll be surrounded by condominiums. I guess he's right, but I hate to be uprooted from this, my lovely home. I hope that the new house he's is building will be cozy and homey. I find it hard to understand those large plans he has drawn. I nod my head in agreement, but I find it hard to envision what it will actually be.*

The morning rain beat a harsh tattoo against the south-facing bay window alcove that Caleb had designed so carefully. He had thought it through carefully, because Tirzah loved to open the curtains to allow the morning sun to stream into the bedroom. He had loved building their final retirement home, and it was nearly perfect, except that all the West Coast storm winds drove their fury right at the southwest corner toward the bedroom windows. He had planned the home for two years and then was able to build it in one year. Situated on a beautiful property with a small lake to row his boat on, it was nearly perfect. The first home Caleb had built for his Tirzah was nicknamed, "The Taj." Their children dubbed their retirement home, "Taj #2."

Destruction of Taj #1

"How do you like it, sweetheart?" Caleb asked his Tirzah after they had lived in their new home for some time.

A long silence from Tirzah was followed by a tentative, "It's very fine, husband, but I would have liked it smaller and cozier."

Caleb was crushed. He had been so sure that Tirzah had understood the plans that he had made. He should have realized that two dimensional drawings meant very little to most people, and that included Tirzah. They had lived for forty years in their first home, and Tirzah had loved that home completely. It took some years before Tirzah felt at home and was happy in Taj #2. The design of the home was a radical departure from Taj #1. He had tried to ensure that living there would be possible even if they became handicapped. Caleb ruefully thought, *Oh to be able to communicate effectively and to understand what people are saying or trying to say. I'm so limited in so many ways, emotionally and physically.* The warring phlegmatic and emotional parts of his character were a source of bewilderment for him. His alter ego was always intruding. Memories of his mother and father's turbulent life flooded into his consciousness.

Taj #2 Retirement Home

Many Questions; Few Answers

The hot August sun burned on Caleb's deeply tanned skin as he stretched out in his rowboat. Two rowing circuits around the lake had soaked his body in sweat. It was time to relax and think. Dragonflies maneuvered amazingly all around him, darting with their double set of wings. The small, blue, iridescent ones perched on his arms and legs for brief moments and as quickly darted away. A pair of bald eagles carving endless circles in the blue sky communicated with piercing calls to each other. The lifting gyres of hot air allowed them to float with motionless wings for long periods of time. At seventy-three years of age, Caleb was at peace with himself and very glad to enjoy partial retirement with his Tirzah. He was humbled that God allowed him to be healthy and strong. *Enjoy it while it lasts*, he thought. *Tomorrow it could be different.* His father had been an untutored, mystical philosopher and poet, so Caleb rummaged in the storehouse of his recollections and queried what to distill and leave to his descendants. Lucius assured that they would look for and narrate anything worthwhile.

The big questions to ponder for Caleb were nothing new or startling. **"What is it all for"** was the question that formed the backdrop, and it broke into three parts. Who am I? Why am I here? Where am I going? He would never forget the scene in the movie, *Doctor Zhivago*, when the father-in-law of Zhivago learned that the Bolsheviks had murdered the imperial Tsarist family. Actor Ralph Richardson used just the right poignant inflection as he brokenly asked, "*What is it all for*?" All the vicious cruelty and the millions murdered in the twentieth century, during which Caleb lived, were encapsulated in that wrenching question. Caleb did not ask God, "Why did You let it happen?" He did wonder why God had not put an end to all the brutality and evil much sooner.

"Why should I even bother to ask the big questions?" queried Caleb. "What insight do I have that is even worthy of any consideration? My children will say, 'Oh Dad!' My surviving, inquisitive siblings will offer pertinent criticisms: 'Come, Caleb, it will be one more addition to a world full of the musings of crack-pot philosophers and theologians.'"

Lucius remained insistent. "We have every right to have our say."

The other voice spoke clearly: "You belong to Me, and your life has been full of love, sin, forgiveness, challenge, adventure, refinement, and blessing. I have given you My book of truth, but you are still learning the miracle of grace. Leave something of the beautiful love story of yourself and Tirzah behind. You had few idols and copied no one. Your story is allowed to be told. Just do not let it be all about you." Caleb had no doubts about the source of the inner voice. He realized that his Lucius conscience, refined by the Spirit of Jesus, provided the insistent voice. The mystery of the great WHY would never be fully solved in the shadow lands of the tarnished, beautiful, broken planet on which he lived. Some great day, however, there would be an answer ... and a reckoning. Of that he was sure.

> "What a day, O glorious day, that will be."
> There'll be no more sin,
> No more tears the eye to dim.
> When he takes me by the hand
> And leads me to that Promised Land.
>
> Author Jim Hill
> Copyright 1955

666—The Number of Man

As Caleb slowly finished reading the book based upon the lectures, *The Theory of Everything: The Origin and Fate of the Universe*, by twentieth and twenty-first century cosmologist Stephen Hawking, he concluded that it was not an easy read. Surely a man who was recognized as one of the world's great intellects would provide him with some great wisdom and insight. Hawking was optimistic that physicists and astronomers who have come up with partial theories are working toward a complete, unified, and consistent theory that can take into account all of the partial theories and produce a unified theory of the origins, history, and ending of our known universe. An all-powerful and omniscient God is not acknowledged as having played a part. Hawking contends that when we achieve this unified theory, 2-"*then **we** shall know the Mind of God*." Caleb concluded that he must have a very limited intellectual capacity, since he could find nothing in himself to provide answers to the big questions.

2-Stephen W. Hawking (28 February 2006). The Theory of Everything: The Origin and Fate of the Universe. Phoenix Books; Special Anniv. ISBN 978-1-59777-508-3.

777—The Number of God

Trinity Western University Professor of Mathematics, John Byl, has written a cogent and powerful rebuttal to the theories presented by Hawking. He presents the case for God in his book, *God and Cosmos*. Byl contends that by equating a unified theory with the Mind of God Hawking overestimates a unified theory and underestimates God. Byl states that the Bible is the source of superior knowledge about the origins of our cosmos. He counters the bleak, mechanistic outlook of secular cosmology with a vibrant and refreshing biblical account. The intricacies of our solar system and life demand that there be an intelligent designer. "Wonderful," concluded Caleb, "that I can read the humble acknowledgment that mankind needs God to provide the answers. Wonderful."

PhD. William Dembski authored the seminal book, *Intelligent Design*. This book is dismissed by skeptical scientists as "creationism in disguise." He postulates that divinely created, intelligent design is legitimate and can be placed firmly into the scientific model.

All the opinions and theories that Caleb pondered on in the scorching August sun begged the question: Can we find out if there is *objective truth?* One person drifting on his rowboat and wondering about the possibilities. One infinitely tiny speck in a vast universe. The very fact that he could even ponder such issues produced its own avenues of wonder. In a world of, presently, over seven billion people, every culture and discipline had given birth to thousands of isms; all human originated and subjective.

He began his reasoning process with "I know that I am conscious and real. One infinitesimal speck in a macro universe beyond comprehension." Scientists estimate there are between fifteen to seventy trillions of cells in a mature human body, each one microscopically complex. He rejected the notions of multiple physical universes as he sought to find the answers in himself. "If I'm real and irreducibly complex, why is my intelligence incapable of trying to source how life came to be? I don't know, from myself, where I came from." The hypothesis that random chance was the instrument that formed life and ultimately him was, to him, absurd. Probability mathematics had proven that even for the protein molecules to form by chance is impossible. He continued, "If I could land on an alien planet and find sentient or nonsentient biological or material complex structures, then I would look for the makers." His survival instinct felt the burning of his skin in the hot August sun, and he started to row the boat to shore with long, lazy oar strokes. Just like Michael across the Jordan! He would postpone his quest for truth for the moment and resume it another time.

"What are you doing out there, Caleb?" asked Tirzah from the shoreline. "You'll get a sunstroke in the dog day heat. Come! I have a cool one waiting for you." She knew the look when her husband started daydreaming. All the pressing busy world receded far away.

"I've been trying to solve the great questions of our day, sweetheart," teased Caleb, not letting on that that was exactly what he had been trying to do.

"Leave it up to the great thinkers, my husband. Hitch up the power boat and let's get down to the river for some cooling water fun." Caleb smiled at the wonderful girl who had entranced him for more than fifty years and pulled his skiff on the shore.

Brock gunned the engine on the power boat and, with a gout of spray and foam, jerked his father up onto his slalom ski. He saw that the old man still had the desire, but the turns were becoming shorter. Caleb had named the boat *Nefertiti*, after the famous Egyptian queen. He sometimes called Tirzah by the same name. The icy cold Fraser River spray arced into his face, and Caleb felt ten year younger as he negotiated the sharp turns. After thirty minutes, the muscles in his arms started to burn, so he signaled to go to shore. Brock pulled a sharp turn toward the shoreline and then quickly turned back to deep water. Caleb leaned back on his ski to allow a dry shore landing. He miscalculated and the ski skeg hooked on the silty bottom, providing him with a humiliating face-plant. All the children and grandchildren howled with glee at the mishap. His portion in this life was being physically diminished, but no less pleasurable. He ended every ski with a silent, *Thank You, God, for still allowing me this*. What a simple joy it was to give all his beautiful, growing grandchildren the chance to skim over the water, free as a bird, with the water spray in their faces.

His mind was often like a dog with a bone. It just could not leave an issue alone. Sleep would not come, so Caleb got up carefully, so as not to wake Tirzah, and hunkered down in his La-Z-Boy chair. He had to wrestle with the broad acceptance of Darwinian evolution by most of the scientific community and the masses that followed them. He found it hard to accept that so many gifted and intelligent people could be wrong, or would not even countenance the idea that there could be an intelligent, all-powerful designer. Was there a manipulator of delusion who was able to control masses of people? He had to accept that there was a paradigm shift in the culture in which he lived. The theory that random chance is the creative force that brought forth matter and life was receiving wide-scale acceptance, no matter how implausible. The social engineers, supported by secular science and most major news media, were replacing Christianity, with its claim of exclusionary and objective truth. The predominate World View in the postmodern western world is that there is no single truth.

Objective truth is to be rejected, and the search for subjective, ever changing, possible truth was to be the only worthwhile search.

Then the Decartian idea struck Caleb with force: "If we know we exist, but do not know from where, then a Creator must surely exist."

Plato opined that "God is Truth and Truth is Divine." Ontological reasoning, according to critics, can be used to prove the existence of anything. As Caleb continued to sink into his semi-conscious pool, he found nothing more. "The answer to my questions lies outside of my reasoning capacity," he decided. "I must look elsewhere, but where?"

"Look to the heavens, puny man," God told Job.

> *"Where were you when I laid the earth's foundation?*
> *Tell me, if you understand." (Job 38:4)*

"Use all your senses, Caleb, to find evidences of My power and glory," insisted the voice. "Your very temporal existence proves that I have made you."

Today we are told that the universe is still expanding, if our instruments are truly capable of such measurements. Science predicts that there may not be sufficient mass to generate the gravity to cause it all to collapse back into the primordial mass of the original Big Bang. Theoretically existing, but so far undetectable, Dark Matter is the theory used to explain the expansion. What is that force we all experience called gravity? The Bible tells us:

> *"sustaining all things by his powerful word." (Hebrews 1:3)*

This passage strongly suggests that gravitational attraction is the power of God, which holds the universe together. Only the Creator truly understands the forces that hold, in the micro, the atoms together, and in the macro, the universe together. Only the Creator truly creates matter from nothing (*ex nihilo*). We can alter and rearrange but never create. Caleb had found part of the portion he had always been searching for.

World Views in Collision

Caleb's mind rolled back to memories of fifty years ago as he listened to his favourite professor, Jed Dorsa, committed biologist, who was a man with a mission. After some years of prospecting in the mountains around Sears, he had returned to his studies and had obtained his Ph.D. He now lectured at the university also attended by former Sears residents Mirjam and Caleb Nachtegal. He was imbued with a mission to remove religious superstition from the minds of his students. There was no unchallenged opinion in his science lectures or tutorial hall for metaphysical jargon.

He had been attracted to, and dated, undergraduate Mirjam Nachtegal a few times and also had her brother in his lecture hall. He liked Caleb Nachtegal, and Caleb liked him. They shared many stories related to the years both had spent growing up in Sears. He liked Caleb's beautiful sister, Mirjam, even more. During Biology 201 lectures, Professor Dorsa was irritated to discover that Caleb made many remarks that disputed the course materials. Initially he ignored the insistent impertinence, but then he decided to confront it. After class, he approached Caleb and asked, "How would you and Mirjam like to come over to my place and we can have a frank and open discussion about your objections to my course materials?"

"That would be great, Prof," enthused Caleb. "Are you sure that it's a good idea to have Mirjam along? She may prove to be a distraction from focusing on and engaging in an in-depth discussion."

"Do not come without her, Caleb," smiled Jed. "Her knowledge will only add to the discussion. I'd consider it quite a coup if I were able to convince two fundamentalist, stubborn Nachtegals to get with the times."

That evening after pizza and beer had been consumed, the gloves came off quickly. "Really, Caleb, why are you continuing to call Darwinian evolution a theory in class when I have shown the biological factual proof that evolution is a proven fact? Add to that the geological record shown in the earth's strata and it's plain that what was once a theory has now become a fact."

Mirjam smiled at her impetuous brother as he rose to the bait. "Fact! You're joking, Jed. None of earth's sedimentary layers have ever shown any fossils that show the links between species. All suppositions remain theories until they are verifiably demonstrated by repeated factual observations of the events reproduced. If life started in the primordial soup, then it should be fairly simple to batch a concoction, with attendant energy sources, in pristine laboratory conditions and form just one simple single-celled bacteria. Furthermore, what gives you the right to not even consider the question that there is the possibility of a great and intelligent Creator? If you exist, then He can exist. We call him our God."

Jed slowed his voice to a soothing level as he patiently explained how, according to serious science, evolution is the engine that brings forth new species. "You have a good inquiring brain, Caleb," he flattered. "Do not shut yourself out of a promising future. I have nothing against religion as long as it remains private and doesn't interfere with factual evidence."

"That type of religion is no religion at all," Caleb protested. "If God is able to create a universe, He is infinitely more capable of creating all life. He is in control over everything. Don't allow your life to be directed by a mechanistic, causative explanation for all origins. All that is beautiful, worthwhile, and moral comes from and shows us a tiny bit of the mind of our Creator. He provides a completely unified theory of everything in the Bible."

Jed shook his leonine head and bantered, "Let's drop it for now, Caleb. We can resume at a later time." The fervent reasoning of

Caleb left an imprint, and Jed enjoyed the later polemical sparring matches that ensued.

"Got time for a beer, Caleb?" Jed asked one afternoon after he had finished his lectures. "I want to hear from you, in a cogent manner, how you continue to deny logic."

As they entered the smoky pub, Caleb found a seat that had some privacy and forced his voice into a lower octave. "I object to you calling a theory a fact, Jed, and I intend to hoist you on your own petard. Atheistic evolution is a theory that rests on the assumption that the first life forms came about by spontaneous chance. Theoretical mathematics have proven that to be impossible. If even the simplest living cells require one thousand simultaneous events to occur with all the correct chemicals and energies in place, for life to occur, then the order of magnitude makes it impossible. It could possibly happen that mankind, using super computers and continuous mixtures of chemical cocktails, may form a living cell. That would only prove that it takes a high degree of concentrated technology and intelligence to use existing materials to form life. You couldn't even call that 'creating life!'"

"I appreciate your line of reasoning, Caleb," rejoindered Jed. "But if as a scientist I should acknowledge intelligent design, then every crackpot theory gains credence. The idea that the earth and universe were created in six days is ludicrous. Have you never seen the movie, or read the book, *Inherit the Wind*, about the Scopes Monkey Trial, where Darwinian evolution was vindicated? In the 1920s, Tennessee schoolteacher Bertram Cates was put on trial for violating the Butler Act, a state law that prohibited public school teachers from teaching evolution instead of creationism. Christianity has had its day. It has a history that has proven to be wanting in the public square. History has shown that Christianity has been riven by infighting factions. We need to focus on a material universe where the star factories are the crucibles for producing life. I also need to tell you that, for me, the greatest barrier to acknowledging an all-powerful, good, and loving God is the problem of evil. Survival of the fittest explains the presence of what we call evil very well. How do you fit that into your tidy world view, Caleb?"

"I don't pretend to have all the answers, Jed, but this I do know: There is a cosmic drama going on between good and evil. Our created time-continuum in which so much pain and suffering has occurred is a tiny blip weighed against God's eternity. I totally trust that God will provide the answers when I stand in eternity." Caleb reluctantly ended with, "I don't understand Jed, that every crackpot theory, apart from the biblically revealed God, is given a serious scientific evaluation. If you will not seriously consider the obvious fact that there is a great Creator, then our world views are in collision. Surely you can understand that a Being capable of creating a vast universe from nothing is able to create adult people and a mature world fully provisioned with everything needed for life to expand and explore. Please realize, Jed, that people want to be autonomous and are rebels by nature. You may not even be aware of it, but pride causes you to hate the idea of a God because you want to be in His place. You, like many others, want to possess the mind of God. It never ceases to amaze me that puny people, who are so fragile and die so quickly, are possessed of such arrogance and pride. The golden rule of Christianity has never been applied in the public square. To love God and your neighbour as yourself is the only answer for this world, but it has been deemed to be unworkable. That's why the crowds hearing Jesus's words grew to hate Him and killed the author of life. Why? *What is it all for?* You will not find Him, Jed—but He may find you."

Caleb sorrowed over the end of his relationship with Jed, and so did Mirjam. She had fallen hard for the handsome professor, but her commitment to her God brought an end to the relationship.

The answer to "Who am I?" was slowly finding its way into Caleb's head. The process was like osmosis. Imperceptibly, over many years, life's meaning began to take shape, and it did not happen by deductive reasoning. The example shown by Jesus Christ, who modelled a life of love and service, showed Caleb the way. Sentience and instinct often struggled for control, and prayer tipped the balance to wanting to serve God and his neighbour. The enormity of his ignorance and sin also made him realize the amazing redeeming work of his Saviour. "Teach me, my God, to love and serve you forever. There is a hole in my soul that only You can fill. To have joy and pleasure in communicating with You and knowing You," formed the basis for the answer to Caleb's *raison d'etre*.

***

In the Parenting Crucible

"Leave me alone, and don't try to control my life," was the angry response to Caleb's query from his teenage son, Caleb Jonathan. "Why do you always ask me so many questions about everything? And another thing … quit telling me about all the eligible girls I could be dating, okay?"

It came so forceful, so unexpected. "Am I not allowed to ask you what you're planning to do with your present course of studies and your life?" asked an exasperated Caleb. He and Tirzah had wanted to not repeat the perceived mistakes of their own parents, who in their struggle for survival had shown little interest or available time in the development of their children. They had felt that their love should be taken for granted. Little parental interest toward education proved to be an obstacle to any future academic studies for their children.

"We will be more involved than our parents, Tirzah," encouraged Caleb with conviction. "Our prosperity will enable our children to choose any career or course of studies they want. We can see to it that they never need to incur any debt, and that they get a prosperous start in life. I want, at the very least, for all eight children to achieve a Bachelor of Arts or Science degree in the study of their choice. I'm sure they'll be eager and appreciative of what we can provide for them."

"No, Caleb!" Tirzah advised. "We should not shower our children with material things. They need to learn how to be frugal in order to develop Christian caring for others. We need to teach our children life skills that enable them to love and care for each other and others. All we can do is model and teach them the beauty of serving God. After the teenage struggle for independence is over, they will remember. Also, dear husband, try to be less strident as you give advice."

"So each generation meets the challenge of finding their way," mused Lucius to a dejected Caleb. "We have received eight bright, beautiful children who are determined to find their own path, but I so hope that they will walk with God. You, Lord, never did provide a guarantee with the birth and baptism certificates."

It was a hard lesson for Caleb to confront the *why* of being centered on giving, and not taking. "You need to realize, Father, that even when you help us and others, you may be trying to exercise control," retorted an angry and weeping daughter. "If we agree with you, you give—when we disagree with you, you withdraw."

Confused and upset, Caleb responded in the only way he knew how. "I will never be perfect, but I love you and want to do what is best for you. I want to help you—not control you. I realize that of all the legacies we leave behind, our children are the most important. We would be desolate if we should lose you on the heavenward road. The role of men in today's society is changing, but my identity has been formed in the crucible of the past. The male who was the breadwinner and family leader of yesterday is under attack by the Western secular world. Your mother depended on me to provide a safe, nurturing environment for her to be a wife and mother. It was what she wanted and loved to be. Today men are asked to be more compliant and sensitive. Women are expected to contribute to family income and assume more dominant roles. That's fine by me as long as it's in conformity with God's design. Please excuse me for noticing that I see so many unhappy, harried people around me. Very few children are being born in declining Western cultures. Children are viewed as a hindrance to career achievement and increasingly expensive to raise. When pregnancies happen but aren't convenient, then precious life is killed and removed. People are increasingly focused on their own needs and wants."

"You need to let us find our own direction," retorted Delphine. "The day of the Alpha male is done. Let go! Your advice is no longer appreciated." The verbal body slam left Caleb without words as he watched the once lovely and dependent face now so determined and resolute. The tearing of the dependent bond between parent and child can cause so much pain.

"Must it always be so?" he asked as he comforted himself with the knowledge that it was his beloved Tirzah who always gave more than she received. The love story between a man and a woman will never go out of date. Ever since time began, there is nothing stronger than *Love*. Adam needed Eve, and men and women need each other. Hopefully God would allow that they could step into eternity closely together.

"Flawed from birth, with a mixture of the profane and holy," concluded Lucius as he daydreamed. "That is who I am. And now? Where am I going?

"So alone, so terribly alone without my God. Hold me, my Saviour, and keep me from the dark," erupted from an awakening Caleb.

Tirzah's cry, "Caleb! Caleb!" brought him fully back to the waking world. "You were thrashing and crying in your sleep. It frightens me when you do that."

"Just let me hold you for a while, Tirzah," responded Caleb as he wiped away her tears. "Then it will be okay."

The poet Dylan Thomas asked the scathing question:

3-*"Shall I go gently into the dark night or shall I rage against the dying of the light?"*

3-*"Collected Poems 1934-1952 by Thomas, Dylan". www.biblio.com*

When the Rubber Hits the Road

"The glory days are done, Caleb," commiserated Caleb's former partner, Bert Paradis. "It's all downhill from here on in." He had come to visit Caleb and to lend a hand as Caleb was building the massive foundation forms for his and Tirzah's retirement home. He rested his weathered, spotted forearm on a wooden brace and reminisced. "Do you still remember the days when no project was too big, and no one pushed us around?"

"Yeah, Bert, I remember, but there was a lot of dirt mixed in with the glory," Caleb responded. "I like the place where I'm at, Bert. Age has its own rewards, and both of us are still healthy and strong." The twenty-two-ounce Estwing hammers rose and fell in unison as the form ties were nailed in place. Caleb still enjoyed the hurly burly of construction that had been a large part of his working life. What a joy it was to focus on building a worthwhile project with a team of dedicated, skilled workers.

Academia also had a great appeal for Caleb, and he often felt that he had a foot in both worlds. "This is the eighth time that we've read the Bible together from cover to cover," he told Tirzah after the last words of Revelation were read and discussed. The internet provided access to an amazing pool of knowledge that was inexhaustible. Active work and sports always competed with reading for the time that always seemed too short.

"C'mon, baby!" urged Caleb as the GMC pickup coughed but failed to start. After forty years of handyman care, there were just some things that he could not keep up with anymore. If a gas motor had fuel, spark, and compression, then Caleb would always find a way to get it going. The pickup had all three but still would not start. The many computer-aided functions on newer vehicles were beyond his ability to repair. When stumped he would go on the internet and source a plausible fix and then replace the suspect electronic module with a new one. *Eureka! It works again*, but the "*why it works*" was beyond him. If there was a machine that could make his job easier or quicker, Caleb was sure to buy it. Eventually, however, the burden of maintenance was greater than the usefulness. His garage and barn held so many tools that he needed to do a yearly inventory just to remember what he had. His grandchildren would look and stand amazed and would ask why Grandpa needed so many tools.

From a Tiny Seed a Redwood Grows

And then there was gardening! There was a deep satisfaction in holding and squeezing rich, black loam that he shared with all those Nachtegal gardeners gone before. The pleasure had in tilling, planting, cultivating, and harvesting brought Caleb/Lucius in contact with his ancestors and allowed communing with the Great Gardener. For years he fed his growing family with food that was uncontaminated and fresh. When Tirzah and Caleb retired, he downsized his garden, but he would never willingly give up the joy of eating what had been freshly picked minutes before, with the life-force still intact. When the children came over for dinner, they invariably teased him by telling their children that Grandpa's food contained "*the life-force.*"

"Tell me, Caleb," asked Nora, his neighbour, "do you ever get bored slaving away in your garden?" She often came over to ask advice or provide her own view on world affairs. Caleb was puzzled by the question, since he knew that Nora loved gardening and growing flowers. There was much about her that reminded him of his feisty mother.

Caleb squinted in the bright sunshine and laid his gardening tools, which he had inherited from his father and father-in-law, to the side. Kneeling among the plants with his hands deep in the dirt, he answered, "Bored, Nora! Just no time to get bored. My father gardened until he was eighty-eight, and I hope to beat him. We have a large property to look after, eight children to keep in touch with, and sixteen grandchildren to love and appreciate. No, Nora, I'm not bored, and I hope I never will be. What about you?"

"I just find it so hard to cope with all the sadness in this world," lamented Nora. "Killings, abused children, ruthless persecutors, you name it—it's everywhere. You're a Christian, Caleb … do you have the answers? Do you know why it has to be this way?"

"No one on this flawed planet understands or can answer all the 'why' questions, Nora," placated Caleb. "But there will be an answer, and it will be supplied by God. Come look at the beautiful trumpet flowers growing from the cuttings that you gave me."

"Will those dark crescents under your fingernails be permanent?" Tirzah asked semi-seriously as she joined in the conversation. She looked at Caleb and saw the glint in his eyes. "I'll slug you if you leave marks on my new blouse should you dare to hug me with those dirty hands."

"You're daring me to try." Caleb laughed and grinned as he got off his knees and did just what Tirzah feared. "All right, slug me all you like," he teased as he hugged his girl. "I have fifteen motors to look after and over two acres to maintain, so I just can't be washing my hands all the time. Perhaps you can just wear one of my old shirts so you don't have to worry." Nora mumbled something about "silly lovebirds" and walked away with a smile.

Tropical Trumpets Blooming for Tirzah

There's no end to the pondering of 'Why am I here' mused Caleb, *but this I know: my life has purpose, and I love living and serving my God and being with Tirzah. She taught me to do small, unnoticed deeds of kindness and take enjoyment in the little things of life that are precious.* Again, his musings turned up memories of a time when his and Tirzah's lives were threatened.

***

Growing Together and Meeting the Challenges

"I can't see, Tirzah!" twenty-six-year-old Caleb yelled as the small front-wheel-drive car ploughed through the blinding snowstorm. A Christmas visit to parents living in Alberta started out in fine, sunny weather and good road conditions. After they passed the town of Revelstoke, the snowstorm started and lasted all the way to Calgary. Caleb pulled into a roadside parking lot and waited for a large semi-trailer truck to head out onto the now deeply snow-covered road. Tirzah held her womb where their first, four-month-old baby was beginning its first tremulous movements, and she feared for their safety. Hour after hour she watched as Caleb latched onto the tail lights of the semi. The huge transport cleared away the snow and allowed enough visibility to go on. "We made it, sweetheart, thanks be to God and the semi," Caleb exulted as the lights of Calgary came into view. "No thanks to the maintenance crews who allowed such dangerous conditions on Canada's main cross-country highway."

A joyful reunion with Caleb's parents and siblings followed. The weather hit a record of -40° F, and the couple were sharply reminded that they indeed had left the "Mediterranean" of Canada.

"Let's go for a short walk in the bright sunshine," Caleb proposed. The still dry air gave no indication that it was so bitterly cold.

After one block Tirzah stopped. "Caleb, we need to go back. My legs and face are getting numb." A kind motorist noticed their plight and, with the car heater blasting at full heat, brought the couple back home. Warm blankets and hot drinks soon revived them as they recounted to their family the wonders of their seemingly distant Hawaii honeymoon.

CHAPTER X
Caleb's Portion—Found

I came with the treasure of God
I will leave with the treasure of God

WHERE ARE YOU GOING

"HEY, OLDTIMER! WHY SO FAST?"
YELLED THE YOUNG MAN AS I TRIED TO GET PAST.
SO STRANGE TO HEAR AS I PAUSED IN MY PACE,
TO MEET ONE SO YOUNG—OPTED OUT OF THE RACE.

IT SHOULD BE ME IN THE SLOW LANE,
MY LEFT HIP COMPLAINING FROM THE PAIN.
I SMILED AND INVITED HIM TO KEEP UP.
HE LAUGHED BACK AND STOOPED TO PICK BUTTERCUPS.

I WANTED TO TELL HIM THAT I AM GOING UP THERE,
WHERE THE MORNINGS ARE BRIGHT AND THE PEOPLE ALL CARE.
JESUS, MY LORD, WILL WELCOME HIS OWN.
ALL WHO LOVE HIM HE WILL NEVER DISOWN.

THE MOMENT WAS THERE BUT THEN SLIPPED AWAY.
I REGRETTED THAT I HAD NOT STOPPED FOR A TALK.
HURRY! HURRY! CAN BE SUCH A WASTE. BUT I PRAY
THAT YONDER YOUNG MAN FINDS THE DOOR AND WILL KNOCK.

Caleb

The angry outburst erupted from the rheumy-eyed old lady sitting in the back row. "I am the oldest one here, not her," she croaked, pointing to the one-hundred-year-old birthday lady whose centennial they were celebrating. Caleb had been asked to lead the group of church volunteers, who every week sought to bring the gospel message with lightness and laughter into the lives of the elderly people at the Manor. The harassed caregiver quickly told him that Emma was only ninety-two but always insisted that she was the oldest resident of Easter Manor.

When Caleb and Tirzah sat down to talk with Emma, she continued her diatribe. "When are you hallelujah shouters going to stop talking about 'pie in the sky' and face the fact that after a person dies, that's it! No one cares about me, and I don't care about anybody. Lies, all damned lies, that's all I hear. I'm not afraid to die, so just go away." She peered out at Caleb from under her bushy eyebrows to gauge his reaction, and his memory went back to a time long ago when an old lonely man named Louie pulled his car out of the snow bank. He wondered how many people come to this point in their lives—to end so bitter and forsaken with only an imagined toughness and independence to fuel their resentment against God and fellow humans.

"No! I have never had children—didn't want any," Emma responded to the question. "And before you ask, I've had three husbands—two have died and the last one is gone who knows where. If you want to help me, then just announce to all present that I, and not her, am the oldest person here."

"Do you believe that there is a God?" Tirzah asked her gently.

"If there is, He certainly doesn't care about me," retorted the old lady. "So just leave it at that. I am tired and want to go back to my room." Emma's endgame had come full circle.

***

The comforting mellow clouds in Caleb's mind left by the morphine injection slowly receded and he became aware of the new addition to his body. The defibrillator implanted in his chest wall would become the mechanical guardian to possibly prevent an untimely death from the rogue gene that could be in his body. A sharp pain jabbed his brain as he remembered his three siblings who had died so unexpectedly. He sank back into the subconscious level and asked God if the decision made was the right one. If God is in complete control, as he firmly believed, why did he try to guard against death and prolong his life? Should we be fatalistic, or are we responsible under the sovereignty of God? Nothing happens by chance, and we are not free moral agents. He wills our wills to will and make the good choice. Many more questions crowded in, but he purposed to work it out later, after a good sleep.

Who am I? That was always the first question that needed to be dealt with. Living during a time of incredible change and upheavals impacted that question. Born at the end of the Second World War, boomer Caleb had lived during the emerging nuclear threat that had the ability to annihilate mankind. There could be no naivety after Hiroshima and Nagasaki. The doomsday clock was ticking toward the inevitable end. Never before had a weapon been invented and not used. Is there a God in control, or is the emerging technical ability of humans' proof that evolutionary humanism has elevated us to be our own gods? What was the purpose of the brutal killings of millions during the great wars and revolutions of the twentieth century? Endless debates and theories have been put forward, but the prevailing opinions, for now, in the developed Western world seem to be that there are no absolutes. Many postulate that we are products of chance in a pitiless universe. We are probably alone in the universe, and it is up to us to do the best we can. What that "best" may be is an amorphous collection of ever-changing relativistic social theories. Is religion the opiate of the masses, as Karl Marx stated? Is it probable that living organisms could have spontaneously started in some primordial chemical broth or evolved in space? What is the meaning of a universe so vast that it boggles the mind? Can we truly know that there is a meaningful purpose and ending to this human existence? Can

God be found, and how do we go about it? Questions, questions, so many questions and opinions.

Searching

Narcissism rather than the opinion of the "greats" was always the first avenue of Caleb's inquiry in trying to find out the *who* of being. He had always naively thought that if it would be possible to delve deep enough into his own psyche, then perhaps answers could be found. He possessed the firmly held conceit that since he was the center of his universe, it would be logical that answers could be found there—at the center. After all, did not all the great philosophers and the giants of human history develop their genius from their inner world? But try as he might, there was nothing but chaos and black desolation when he turned inward. Without an umpire, a scorekeeper, a powerful being who really cared, nothing made sense.

If I am the pinnacle of evolutionary selection, and my DNA information strands are encoded from the ages past, then somewhere somehow there should be a recognizable memory of my origin and who I am, thought Caleb. *All that I am has come from outside of myself or entered my consciousness through my primordial genetic codes. Since I exist as an infinitely complex being, but do not know where I came from, there must be a Creator who has created me. I am; therefore, God is. I certainly have been gifted with an imagination that can speculate on many scenarios, but I cannot accept the mathematically improbable concept that in order for that first living cell to originate, thousands of biological functions had to start simultaneously. When I try to imagine it, my mind recoils because it becomes absurd. I realize that thousands of minds much greater than mine do accept this improbability, and I wonder why. Is it plain to only some that all the brilliant constructions of man are fallible and doomed? Does the second law of thermodynamics not postulate that all closed, organized systems tend to a state of entropy? If man* becomes his own god, then without a source of incoming energy, the ...

"*center cannot hold*" *and we will forever be* <u>Waiting for Godot</u>.

4- "*Estragon: We always find something, eh Didi, to give us the impression we exist?*"

Why is it so hard for intelligent people to accept that if we are possible, God is much more probable? Could it be that God has hardwired people in different ways? Can answers be found outside the plane of human experience and existence? There must be a way!

4- Bradby, David *(2001). Beckett: Waiting for Godot. Cambridge: Cambridge University Press. p. 93. ISBN 978-0-521-59429-5.*

***

Shiny black helmets and plastic shields reflected the noonday sun into the eyes of the curious bystanders who had gathered to see the arrival of world leaders attending the latest economic summit at the UBC campus in Vancouver. Scores of riot police formed a tight cordon against the screaming and taunting push of the small group of professional agitators who methodically sought out weaknesses in the blue cordon of linked authority.

"Daddy, Daddy why are they so angry and doing so much yelling?" asked Caleb's little daughter as she hugged his leg.

"Many grown-up people are just like you, sweetheart. They hate to be told what to do. Remember when I told you yesterday to stop spilling your food on the floor? You yelled and did it again on purpose."

"Oh Daddy," she remonstrated, "I didn't act as badly as those people are behaving. They're full of hate and using such bad language. You've always taught us to be respectful of authority, especially to the police officers."

"It's only a matter of degree," Caleb explained, more to himself than to the uncomprehending child as he carried her a safe distance away from the turmoil. He continued inwardly, *Humans are all innately flawed, and it's just a matter of degree. All the tribes of mankind seem to be in turmoil and revolt. All attempted solutions mired down under the weight of flawed social engineering. Me! Me! was the shriek that ascended from the dark planet and was heard.*

Thank you, my Lord Jesus Christ," broke out of Caleb's mouth as he knew with a certainty that he, a wounded broken human, could only be restored by the wonderful, undeserved grace of God. He has given us the important answers in the Bible. Read it with eyes of faith and stand amazed.

Heaven's Gate

The dream was so real, and when Caleb awoke he immediately told Tirzah all about it before it would fade. "I watched myself lying in the hospital bed and saw the futile attempts of the implanted defibrillator to restart the shuddering heart." He gasped, "I lifted and saw you all below me, and then you faded away."

"It was only a dream, Caleb," Tirzah soothed as she hugged her shaken man. "Remember how often you've had such vivid dreams in the past? Go to your computer and write down all the details so that you can meditate on it."

Caleb kissed the finely sculpted face of his wife, but could not rid himself of the thought that it was more than just a dream.

Heaven Bent

> *I have not deserved your blessings my King.*
> *Matchless grace, to you my love I bring.*
>
> *Lucius*

Caleb's Portion

Carnal and bent, Gifted faith from Heaven's sent,
Has rescued me.
You are the one, God's only natural son,
Lived, died, and rose and me you chose
To be your adopted brother, Father's son.

Caleb

There was no awkwardness in the meeting with his Saviour. "No harps and floating on clouds, my brother," said Jesus. "You've always been a builder, and a builder you will be, only now it will have a larger scope. Did you ever wonder why we created all those galaxies and empty worlds? You have arrived at and found your portion, Caleb. But before that happens, come and greet all those who have come before you, and wait and rest for those who are still coming."

"Yes, Lord, I am eager to learn how to build for you," Caleb responded. "Teach me what I need to do."

Ages passed, and when time's bubble collapsed, Caleb also met all who came after him, but eternity changed everything. Not all whom he had known, loved, and expected were there. He now knew with a certainty that they did not want to be there, and he was at peace with it.

Tirzah was there, but the unique bond was enlarged and was no longer exclusionary. Friends who had spent a previous life in wheelchairs were now clothed in immortal bodies. Surrounded by a bright halo were all those who had been martyred for the sake of the gospel.

"Where are some of those whom I once knew and loved?" Caleb asked his Lord without any intent of prying.

"They are where they want to be," Jesus answered. "All who have rejected me as Saviour and wanted to be free have their wish. They will know for all eternity what it is to exist without my sustaining power."

The New Earth was beautiful beyond description! Everything was perfectly balanced in harmony and purpose. The oceans were gone and all life drank from the Source. "This restored Earth will be the template for what I want my builders to do," spoke Jesus. "All the gifts and talents my chosen ones have received in their first iteration will now be perfected. When you realize the power and abilities given to you for all eternity, then you and millions more will eternally complete my limitless universe."

Caleb's past temporal life blurred to a small dot as he expanded. His body was material but indestructible. Intuitively, he understood how Jesus had walked through walls, instantly transported, and was superior to all forms of matter. Light was no longer emanating from energy sources but suffused the entire universe with a golden glow. Dormant galaxies, stars, quasars, and black holes presented no entrance obstacles and were now the fertile building blocks for the eternal age, where entropy no longer existed. Gravity was suspended and used as a tool when needed. An all-sustaining, upholding energy emanated from a single source and was available to the builders.

Another powerful source of delight was the spoken word. God spoke at the beginning of time, and it was there. In eternity, the spoken word was full of visible power. All the time-bound barriers to expressing love and praise were gone. There was constant communion with the Triune God, whose presence filled the entire universe. "Your voice will be the principal terraforming tool that you will use to bring clothed beauty to the barren beauty before you," spoke Jesus.

One thousand fellow master builders joined with Caleb and asked for permission to terraform Galaxy X-Perio. "Make something beautiful, my children," echoed in every brain as the eternal task was given.

Caleb and the basis builders moved throughout their galaxy at will. They viewed the inner hub, thought themselves to be there, and were. While not having the ability to create, all the material matter could be used and transformed into variations of the earth template. What was once the black hole at the centre of X-Perio was now becoming a central hub connecting all the spirals of the galaxy. It provided the source of endless material to clothe countless barren worlds. Multi-hued gas giants arrayed in spectacular bands of colour formed backdrop panoramas for the solid planets. They were overlaid with deep nutrient covers to nourish coming plants and animals. A rich array of stellar objects existed in close proximity to one another, since gravity was controlled.

Thousands of Oholiabs and Bezalels delighted in seeking the praise of the great ones by enhancing beauty out of an infinite selection and variety of materials. Work, rest, praise, and glory all fused together in an eternity of endless being.

"There was so much more, but words fail me to remember all that I saw," Caleb told Tirzah as he left his keyboard and sat down to a delicious meal. He had always loved his God but had never imagined he could so love his Tirzah.

But Here There Are Still Promises to Keep

She walked down to the beach from the rented summer cottage and watched her children and grandchildren playing in the warm August sunshine. She had never been able to express herself as she wanted to in speech, but her life was full of love and service. Strong and beautiful, all of them, and she wanted to stop time and hold the moment forever. "You brought so much grief and anguish into our lives from the families in which we grew up," Tirzah told her God. "Now you give us material wealth, eight healthy, educated children, and a new generation of grandchildren that have all come from the love that you have allowed Caleb and me to be blessed with." They were all there, and Tirzah realized that it would probably be the last time. "Why, Lord are the divisions inevitable?" she asked rhetorically. "Why can they not learn from the past and our teachings and example? Jesus showed us that when we love and serve each other, peace prevails. When we let pride and selfish interest prevail, we start to devour each other. Grant us the wisdom to balance truth with grace in equal measure."

"It is just not that simple, dear parents," opined their confident, newly married daughter. Neeleah had spent her entire life in academia and was determined to prove her independence. "There are breeders and then there are the thinkers," she emphasized with her lovely hands that had never seen a callous. "We all have to find our niche. Your world view is not necessarily mine, and you need to respect that. I'm very happy making my own choices, and we do not need unsolicited advice. We live on a crowded planet with tremendous social problems, so adding more children may not be the moral thing to do."

How foolish and prideful, thought Tirzah, hearing the indignant tone in her daughter's voice. *I won't be there to see it, but I fear for them. Oh how I love the children given to me, and how I long to convince them to be faithful to God's world view, to not break the unity we've enjoyed. Fifty years of loving my Caleb and bearing eight children has given me a voice in knowing what joy is. We need to get over our 'wants' and submit to God's blueprint for happiness. How beautiful it is to see our grandchildren, before they learn to be hurtful, enjoying each other's company.* She grabbed her Caleb's hand and intuitively they both knew that their portion was to be found in completely trusting their Saviour.

"How have those years flown by so quickly, beauty?" Caleb whispered in Tirzah's ear. "You are almost seventy and are still so beautiful and alluring." Tirzah smiled to herself as she listened with pleasure to her husband's extravagant compliments. Time could not stop the wrinkles and effects of gravity, but it was a blessing for them both to enjoy their retirement years together. The times of past conflict had been intense but short. Both of them could not endure for long the absence of being united in love and purpose. "I am sorry!" did not come easily, especially for Caleb, but the healing effect of saying those words ended the separation. "I promise to always love you, my beloved," Caleb had promised at their wedding. He had repeated it many times more over the wonderful years.

***

From Teached to Teacher

"We'd like you to consider becoming an elder again," asked the confident young elder who had been part of the hurt visited upon the Nachtegals' former pastor and family. Caleb had already made it plain that he was no longer available for service. He and Tirzah had supported the ministry of the pastor they had served with. After ten years of service, Pastor Screve had been found wanting by some, and those who disagreed with him took the opportunity to have him dismissed. The initial anger and frustration had almost convinced the Nachtegals to leave the congregation, but forty-eight years of membership was hard to break.

"If you wish me to stay and serve as an elder, then I ask that there be a public statement of remorse for the relentless persecution visited upon Pastor Screve and his family," Caleb demanded. A statement of partial confession of wrongdoing was provided to the congregation, but a core of discontent remained. Caleb had also become a spiritual brother and friend with the Asian missionary who had been called by the church he attended. It was wonderful for him and Tirzah to see the eager and giving attitudes displayed by the converts from a different culture who had become their brothers and sisters.

"Life is full of brokenness, Caleb. Let us make the best of it and stay," Tirzah counselled. "We can both use our gifts and talents to serve and heal."

Time Stops for Neither Man nor Beast

The eternity part of Caleb's brain was acutely aware that his body and brain were declining. He had lived into his middle seventies with few ailments and had enjoyed a body that was able to work and play with few limitations. He had been able to perform the intricate, as well as the macro, tasks in life. Tirzah had noticed the decline. "Caleb, why is your hand trembling?" she asked. He had shaken the liquid right off the soup spoon as he attempted to bring it to his mouth. He remembered that his father had to drink out of a Zippy cup during his last years. It was inevitable, the way of this temporal life—growth and decline. He was momentarily saddened but then was okay with it.

"The lessons of history are never learned, dear Tirzah!" Caleb exclaimed with exasperation. "Is it just because we are aging and looking back at the past through rose-coloured glasses?" For many years since they had become empty nesters, they had watched the eleven o'clock news. The changes that had occurred in Western culture since the end of the Second World War never ceased to amaze them. On the one hand, increased respect for minorities and handicapped people was in line with Christian values. Jesus taught us to accept all levels of society, but He also admonished against destructive lifestyles. Racial intolerance and anti-Semitism were being justly and soundly condemned. On the other hand, valued traditions, religious world views, music, respect for authority, and family structures were being discarded like chaff in the wind. What had taken thousands of years to form in a civilized Christian society was being discarded in a matter of years. As they saw paganism again resurging, they experienced tears and grief caused by the desire of so many to allow the killing of unborn babies. Eight times they had felt the wonderful stirrings of life in the womb as Tirzah bloomed in womanly splendour. The miracle of holding a newborn baby was supremely wonderful.

The failings of democracy were shown when government leaders bowed to the pressure of those who rioted and pushed for abortion; to supply free drugs to addicts and support those who deny that a family is based upon the marriage between a man and woman; to allow the euthanizing of elderly or disabled people, and even dispute the given gender of male and female. The rights of murderers and criminals were often emphasized in the justice system and media over the grief of innocent victims. Here and there, isolated voices were heard warning against the prevailing loud cacophony of societal destruction. They could know from the Bible that only God's righteousness exalts a nation (Proverbs 14:34).

Age has its troubles, but Caleb was grateful for the many positives. The oft-repeated questions were fading as his portion became ever clearer. He had been born and baptized with promise. He had promised to love, honour, and obey his God with heart and soul. He had promised to always love his Tirzah. He had done so while knowing that his failings would be forgiven. He hoped that they would not have to miss each other too long in this life. He had promised to love and raise his children and to nurture and keep them safe. He had done so. He had promised to remind them to be faithful to their God and was sometimes appreciated, but often ignored. He had to learn to forgive and needed to be forgiven. He knew with certainty that he would meet his Lord and receive the eternal portion.

***

We Are One Family: Love from Vietnam

The mud balls struck Quyen all over her body as the jeering school children yelled at her to leave Vietnam. The dismal, dirty Vietnamese war had been lost to the Communists in 1976, and after a short hiatus, the persecution against the ethnic Chinese

Hoa began in earnest. Sixteen-year-old Quyen showed all the promise of becoming a beautiful woman of mixed Vietnamese and Hoa descent. Her father had been killed in the brutal war, and her broken mother spent her days in a dismal hovel on the outskirts of Saigon. "Leave, my child," whispered the old lady. "There is only pain for you here. Please take your young brother along and flee to Thailand. They are welcoming Hoa refugees there. Take the money that I have hidden from the persecutors and go to the coast. Do not spend all the money for passage but leave some for paying bribes."

"How can I leave you, Mother," sobbed the distraught girl. "Soon is only ten years old, and how can I care for him?"

"I am at death's door, my daughter," entreated her mother. "Please leave. If you stay here, you will become an abused victim of the hatred against our people, and especially against Hoa Christians. Flee to Canada if it is possible. I hear that it is a welcoming country for persecuted refugees."

The tattered sail flapped listlessly as the overcrowded wooden dhow rolled in the China Sea swells. Soon was curled in a fetal position, whimpering at Quyen's feet. Another young girl, Mein, clung to her because she had shared some of her food with her. A large dark shadow loomed to starboard, and the sudden ferocious yell of the pirates jerked everyone to wakefulness. Ten snarling men leapt over the gunwale swinging large machetes and threatening everyone who dared look up. They stripped everyone of anything valuable and killed two men who resisted them. "You there," snarled a loathsome brute, "let me see your face." He jerked Quyen upright by her long hair, and it was only the yell of his captain to get back to the boat that prevented the threatened rape.

Ten more days of wallowing in the doldrums ended when a Thai Navy patrol boat sighted them and attached a tow line. No welcoming reception greeted the exhausted and hungry *Thuyền nhân Việt Nam* (boat people) at the berthing dock. They were herded into sanitation stations, deloused, and provided with small rations of Spam and rice.

The refugee camp was located on a deserted army base, and facilities for two thousand now housed ten thousand homeless people. It took a whole year of misery before the announcement was heard over the loud speakers: "All orphan girls below eighteen and boys below fifteen should report to the camp office". Two Mennonite aid workers from Canada looked at the eager, supplicating faces and outstretched arms. They had to decide from out of a hundred which ten they would sponsor. It was a terrible choice to make, but the ten chosen included Quyen, Soon, and their friend.

Caleb and Tirzah greeted and hugged the three emaciated children with their huge liquid eyes and welcomed them to Canada. They were part of the support group that had promised to care for and assist Vietnamese refugees in finding housing and work. The response of the three to their Canadian sponsors was different for each one.

At twelve years old and seventy pounds, Soon was the size of a Western eight year old. Caleb took him along to his construction site and explained, by using sign language and example, what he wanted him to do. Caleb pointed at Soon's neon orange running shoes and gestured to him to remove them. He presented Soon with a pair of steel toed boots and was amazed when the frail boy refused to put them on. After repeated "no wants," Caleb brought him back to his sister and explained why Soon had to wear the boots. Quyen explained that Soon felt that wearing boots was beneath his dignity. Soon, shortly thereafter, hooked up with a gang and disappeared into the shadowy part of the Vietnamese community.

Mein met a senior man, married, and moved away. Her large, round face radiated appreciation for all the help she had received.

Quyen was simply amazing. She worked hard at the job provided to her at a local eggplant, was as loyal as the biblical Ruth, and bloomed. From the bullied, abused girl emerged the chrysalis of a confident, beautiful, and some would say domineering woman. She possessed a keen business mind and soon profited from real estate transactions. She met a fine Christian man from Hong Kong, got married, and raised two healthy daughters. She often phoned and then would come over to commandeer Tirzah's kitchen and cook up a dinner rich in Vietnamese cuisine. In everything that had happened, she professed her love for her Saviour and praised His protection.

We Are One Family: Love from the Congo

The government of the Democratic Republic of Congo had retaken the village of Goma on the banks of Lake Kivu. The known sympathizers of the rebel faction, led by General Kabila, had been defeated and were marched to the village square and summarily executed. Joseph Attenue had, up until 2008, managed to avoid attention from any faction, but many of his immediate family had been tortured and killed. He embraced his young bride and looked with pride at his growing family. "It is a killing field all around us, my beloved Deena," he began. "It is only a matter of time before we will be hunted or caught in the crossfire. There is no future here, for us or for our children. I will go to the emigration department and apply for us to go to a new country of peace. I hear that many Christian organizations in Canada are sponsoring refugees."

***

"Get out of here immediately, you treasonous bastard!" yelled the Goma official after Joseph had made his emigration request. "You are a young, healthy man and you need to join the DRC Army to fight for your country. If you do not sign up, then I will report you to the local militia."

***

"Pack up all our most necessary belongings as soon as you can," panic-stricken Joseph instructed his wife. "We are leaving tonight after I change our savings into American dollars. My father has told me that in Namibia there are large, safe refugee camps where we can stay. I have hired a poacher to drive us to the border. No one else is willing to take the risk."

After three days of gruelling travel southward, they crossed the open border crossing of Tanzania, and in the town of Kitwe, the old three ton surplus army truck sputtered and died. "That is as far as I go my friend," declared the grizzled poacher. "Pay me what we agreed upon and I will wish you well."

"We agreed that you would bring us to Namibia," protested Joseph. "We are only halfway, so I can only pay you one half of the agreed price." The AK-47 gun barrel lazily swung toward Joseph's midriff, and the blank stare in the poacher's eyes brooked no argumentation. He horked and spit directly at Deena and then commanded Joseph to place $1,000 US on the fender of the still-smoking truck.

"Lose yourself and do not let me see you again," He remarked with a baleful glance at the children. Be glad that you are alive."

Joseph hung the crudely lettered sign on a pole in the center of Kitwe.

**Five hundred American dollars
For a ride to Osire in Namibia.**

The response was immediate as five loudly yelling transporters vied for his business. He struck a deal with the most reputable appearing truck and driver who asked for only $450. Curses and screams erupted from the driver when Joseph produced his wife and five children as part of the cargo. "You never told me you meant for me to transport your entire family!" he raged. "I will need 30 per cent more fuel to get you to your destination. Not to mention the wear on my truck."

"The children are small," Joseph placated, "and my wife will cook for you. I will give you $50 more if you will do it. Fifty per cent now and the rest when the trip is completed." Reluctantly the driver agreed, and at five o'clock the next morning they headed south to Namibia.

The crush of milling people at the refugee camp frightened and intimidated the Attenue family, but an overworked aid worker took pity on them. "Where are you from, and why are you here, so far from your home?" she asked the dust-encrusted family. "What are your skills and how can you help us?" she continued.

"My father told me that this camp is looking for Christian preachers and aid workers," answered Joseph. "I can preach, and my wife can hold health clinics to help the pregnant ladies in the camp."

"Heaven sent!" exulted the aid worker as she hugged the entire family. "How desperately we are in need of healthy people who are willing to serve and give rather than take. You will live right beside me, and after you wash, eat, and rest we will get started."

And start they did. For two years the Attenue family worked tirelessly to help the aged, the battered, and the dying HIV-infected people. Every Sunday Joseph preached the gospel to six thousand eager listeners and was declared the camp's official minister. The three oldest children ran countless errands throughout the camp, distributing food and medicines throughout the crooked rows of shanty huts. Even the initially sullen Muslim refugees responded to the tireless ministrations of the Attenue family.

Loud cries of "No! No!" responded to Joseph's announcement that they had been accepted to immigrate to Canada. Blinded by their tears and emotions at leaving so many dear friends, Joseph and Deena knew that their precious children deserved a chance at a normal life.

Joseph greeted Caleb with a hundred-watt smile that instantly created a bond. "We are happy to be here with fellow Christians who show their love by caring about us," he exulted. His wife and five healthy, strapping boys all approached and formally shook Tirzah and Caleb's hands. Initially, Caleb was wary, since many stories had circulated of sponsors who had been used and abused by criminals who pretended to be refugees. Joseph, however, proved to be solid gold. "I have two desires," he explained to Caleb. "First, I want to serve God, and secondly, I need to provide for my family. Where can I get a job and rent a place for my family?" All requests were provided for, and it was a great blessing to watch the family prosper.

"What are you trying to do, Joseph?" asked Caleb with a wide grin. "Trying to kill yourself?" Thick smoke curled from under the sundeck where Joseph was busy barbecuing chicken for his invited guests. He had seen Caleb using his barbecue when they had been visiting and had liked the taste of the beef. They had then insisted that the Nachtegals come over for dinner and fellowship.

"This machine is not working well," an exasperated Joseph complained. "I borrowed it from a friend and threw in a bag of charcoal. This chicken is going to be well-smoked, and so will I!" he laughed. Over the years as the relationship deepened, it was apparent that the bond of Christian love transcends all barriers of race and culture. On all levels, the Attenue family proved to be a blessing for Canada and proved able to integrate well into the culture.

We Are One Family: Love from China

The small, muddy hands continued to push up the heavy glasses that refused to stay perched upon the small nose. Jian had tried desperately to hide the fact from teachers and parents that he was increasingly becoming near sighted, but at the age of ten it was glaringly obvious that he needed to wear them. "Tell me, Jian Wu," his mother asked, "why did you try to hide the fact that you were unable to even see the blackboard at school?"

Tears rolled down Jian's round face as he blurted, "Now I shall never become a general in the Army. You have to be in perfect physical condition in order to go to Officers Training School. I have the top academic marks in my class, but those stupid glasses will prevent me from ever becoming an army officer". His mother gathered the stiff boy in her arms and secretly rejoiced that he would no longer be part of the parade of young strutting boys with their toy rifles slung across their shoulders.

***

The American language professor was amazed at the persistence of the second-year university student's desire to learn English. John Cairns and his wife, Helen, solid American Presbyterians, had received no children and had signed on for a five-year teaching stint at the English teaching university.

"Why, Jian?" he asked. "Why do you continue to ask me for more course material when you already have a heavy study load? You're already far ahead of your classmates, and I can see that you're bored with the class lectures. If you insist, I can give you private tutorials, but you must promise to keep it a secret. The university doesn't allow foreign teachers to teach outside of the campus.

"Would you, please? That would be wonderful!" Jian rejoiced. "I wish to become a translator in the diplomatic core. I hear that the wages are very good, and it would allow me to travel all over the world. I promise to tell no one, not even my family, and I'd like to pay you for your work. Can we start right away?"

***

"What is the Bible, who is Jesus Christ, what do Christians believe?" asked a puzzled Jian as Helen read from her English Bible. The Bible and the works of Shakespeare were the source of the twice weekly, evening English lessons. "May I have a copy of the Bible to read from?" Jian asked. "I have been taught that there is no God and that Mao Zedong is the greatest person who has ever lived. I have read his Red Book many times, and we are told to recite and praise his wisdom. I have never heard about this Jesus who you pray to. Is he real or just a myth?"

The conversion of Jian to Christianity was a miracle in the eyes of the Cairns. He voraciously read his Bible and asked countless questions, which they did their best to answer. After he had obtained his English degree and was baptized in the midst of fellow Christians on campus, he decided to become a Christian minister.

"There is no place in China that offers the required courses of study for you to become an ordained Presbyterian or Reformed Minister," John gently explained to Jian and the beautiful Christian girl he had met and married. "We'll try to find out if you can obtain a study visa to go abroad. We've heard that this government has issued study visas for Australia."

Ai wore a loose-fitting robe to hide the fourth month bump, so that Jian wouldn't know she was pregnant. "Nothing must prevent my man from fulfilling his calling," she had decided. She knew that Jian would not leave her if he found out that they were to be parents. A flood of tears streamed down her face as she kissed her Jian goodbye. *At least I'll still have my singing work at the local opera house*, she thought as she comforted herself.

"Ai!! Step into my office immediately," ordered the portly manager of the opera house. He instantly, without preamble, charged, "Is it true that you have become a Christian? I also hear that you are married to a person who is of interest to our local police. Do you realize that I can fire you for any reason?"

"Our Constitution permits freedom of religion," a courageous Ai replied. "My husband, Jian, is a respected graduate of the university and has gone abroad to study. Is my work here unsatisfactory to you? Are there others who complain about me?" she queried with a sinking heart, realizing that her support payments were hanging by a thread.

With a pointed stare at her growing midriff, the manager turned on his tape recorder. "Do you agree, Ai Lee Wu, that in order to continue working at the opera house, you will do the following: ensure that all the lavatories and rest stations will be kept spotless; provide replacement of all sanitary supplies as needed; and have your salary reduced by half? Sign the amended agreement of your terms of employment as from this day forward." With her head bowed, but unbroken, Ai signed the despicable document. She knew that her Saviour would see and help her bear the humiliation.

The Australian Interlude

It was a long way from the Perth, Australian chicken farm where Jian worked to the university where he studied English, Hebrew, Greek, and Latin. Klaas Vere had noticed the young Chinese student reading his Bible on the bus. He quickly moved to the empty seat beside him and asked if he understood what he was reading. "Come on over to my place when you can," Klaas invited. "My wife and I would love to learn how you have come to know 'The Way.'" Thereafter, he and his wife often invited Jian for many delicious suppers and long evening discussions. Every day for two years, Jian would gaze at the photograph of his wife and newborn baby, whom he had never seen. The day that Ai and baby Bao stepped from the plane into Jian's arms was one of his happiest days ever.

Klaas Vere grabbed Jian in a nearly fatal bear hug as he exclaimed, "You have been accepted, Jian and family! Canada has approved your application for immigrant status, and the theological college is awaiting you for the next semester."

***

Caleb was busy planting potatoes when the screen door opened and slammed shut. Tirzah yelled, "It's for you, Caleb! Pastor Carl Nobles is on the phone and wants to talk to you."

"How is it going, Caleb?" Pastor Carl rhetorically asked with a tone that Caleb knew well. "I hear that you have a large recreation trailer on your property that's just sitting there idle. Would you and Tirzah be interested in hosting a young Chinese theology student for a few weeks until he finds permanent accommodations?"

"Why, sure we would," responded Caleb as he winked at his frowning wife. A trail of garden dirt on Tirzah's clean floor, as well as his unilateral acceptance of hosting a strange visitor, required some explanation. Caleb knew that his wife's generous heart would welcome the new boarder, but Tirzah did not like to be taken for granted.

Though having grown up separated by geography and thousands of years of culture, Caleb and Jian bonded instantly. The Spirit of Christ made it possible. The diminutive Chinese theology student and lanky European Canadian spent many hours discussing religion, politics, business, and every discussable topic over savoury meals prepared by Tirzah. They also shared a common appreciation for fruity wines. The relationship deepened when the Nachtegals met Ai and Bao. The common, deeply held precious love for Jesus that they shared over the years formed the basis of an enduring friendship.

Caleb, looking with the eyes of faith, saw the futile attempts by secular, humanist, social engineers to bring the human family together. Pride, greed, jealousy, and tribal animosity were producing a class of human predators that was bringing mankind to the edge of the abyss. Jesus Christ stands at the center of human history with arms wide open and with the answers to heal mankind's hurt, but everything is being tried except His objective truth. All human races can live in harmony in the bond of Christian fellowship. In Christ, all the far-flung elements of the human family can learn to love each other. Both Caleb and Tirzah were privileged to experience it.

We Are One Enduring Family

"How did it all happen so fast, my sweetheart?" murmured Caleb as he held his Tirzah. He looked at his wife, who was going to celebrate her seventieth birthday, and marveled at her inner and outer beauty. It was fifty-two years ago that he had asked her to be his girl, and it seemed such a short time ago. His older sisters had warned him about the impending ennui of middle age, but it had never happened. He remained enchanted, and Tirzah delighted in her role as wife, mother, and grandmother.

"That's what happens when you're happy and in love," replied Tirzah. "Happiness makes time fly, and misery has no ending. What blessings have been given to us, my Caleb! Our sorrows have been a small part of our lives compared to the joy. All our enduring relationships with family and friends have been rooted in an unwavering commitment to our Lord and Saviour. I just wish there was some way to convince those who were so close to us and now no longer are spiritually joined with us. We need to constantly pray for them and trust that God's plan is best."

***

The Great Divide

Chester Carlton was a charming, charismatic personality. At middle age he was handsome, fit, and lived a mostly clean life. He had put his legal profession on hold and entered the arena of politics. "Support me, Caleb and Tirzah," he asked. "I'm a Christian like you and have decided that I need to join a Conservative party in order to help vote the present corrupt rascals out of office. They're ruining the economy, giving plum government jobs to their supporters, and producing immoral legislative leadership. Can I count on your support?"

The Nachtegals smiled at each other as they heard the same familiar mantra of sixteen years ago when Chester's Conservative party was the government. They had become members of the party then and had worked hard to ensure the election of the Conservative candidate. She had promised to promote Christian family values and introduce legislation to stop corruption. Caleb and Tirzah were elated that their Member of Parliament was promoted to a cabinet position in the newly formed federal government, and they eagerly scanned parliamentary reports for the promised action items. They sent a few polite, inquiring letters, but the inane, form-letter replies disappointed them, as did the absence of any promised action. After three successive terms in government, the same accusations as those presently levelled by Chester had been levelled against the Conservatives with devastating results in the next election. The polite refusal caused Chester's smile to slip a few notches before it was again firmly put into place.

Put Not Your Trust in Princes

Caleb pondered if the Greek philosopher Diogenes had ever found the honest man he had been searching for. In the book of Proverbs, Solomon relates that among a thousand he had found only one man who was righteous (Ecclesiastes 7:28). Not a result to engender confidence in the permanence of human relationships that are built on human trust!

Self-judgement is a risky business, but Caleb thought it possible to put aside his bias and look critically at himself. "How does God see me?" was the chilling impossibility that he started with. "How did my parents, siblings, teachers, wife, and children all view me? Did my bosses, employees, business, and personal associates consider me to be a fair and righteous person? Have I been generous and kind, or was I perceived as cold and distant?" He knew with a small degree of insight that he had behaved all the way from atrocious to genuinely desiring to help and serve. Put into the balance, he had been found wanting. He needed to be, and was, saved by his faithful Saviour, Jesus, who is the Christ, the Holy One of God. Somehow, Diogenes had missed this Perfect Man.

This Train Is Bound for Glory

Hey! John McCrae, I liked your poem.
You've gone away, but your words they stay.

Unite the faith and hold the torch high, you said.
But mortal eyes grow bleary; hands they grow weary.
You passed it on, so must I. Yes! They still bravely, singing fly.

The dark foe still has his beef with the truth.
He is the relentless other and seeks to vainly smother
All noble joy and light break out the darkest night.
Maybe you are looking down and see
The gathering, overwhelming victory.

Jesus the Son the battle has won.
To be sure, we continue to mop,
But soon that chore also will stop.
Tirzah and Caleb! Please hop aboard.
This train is driven by Jesus the Lord.

Caleb's Portion

Lucius

Glory Train

Epilogue

In accordance with the Lord's command to him, Joshua gave to Caleb son of Jephunneh a portion in Judah. (Joshua 15:13)

My flesh and my heart may fail, but God is the strength Of my heart and my portion forever. (Psalm 73:26)

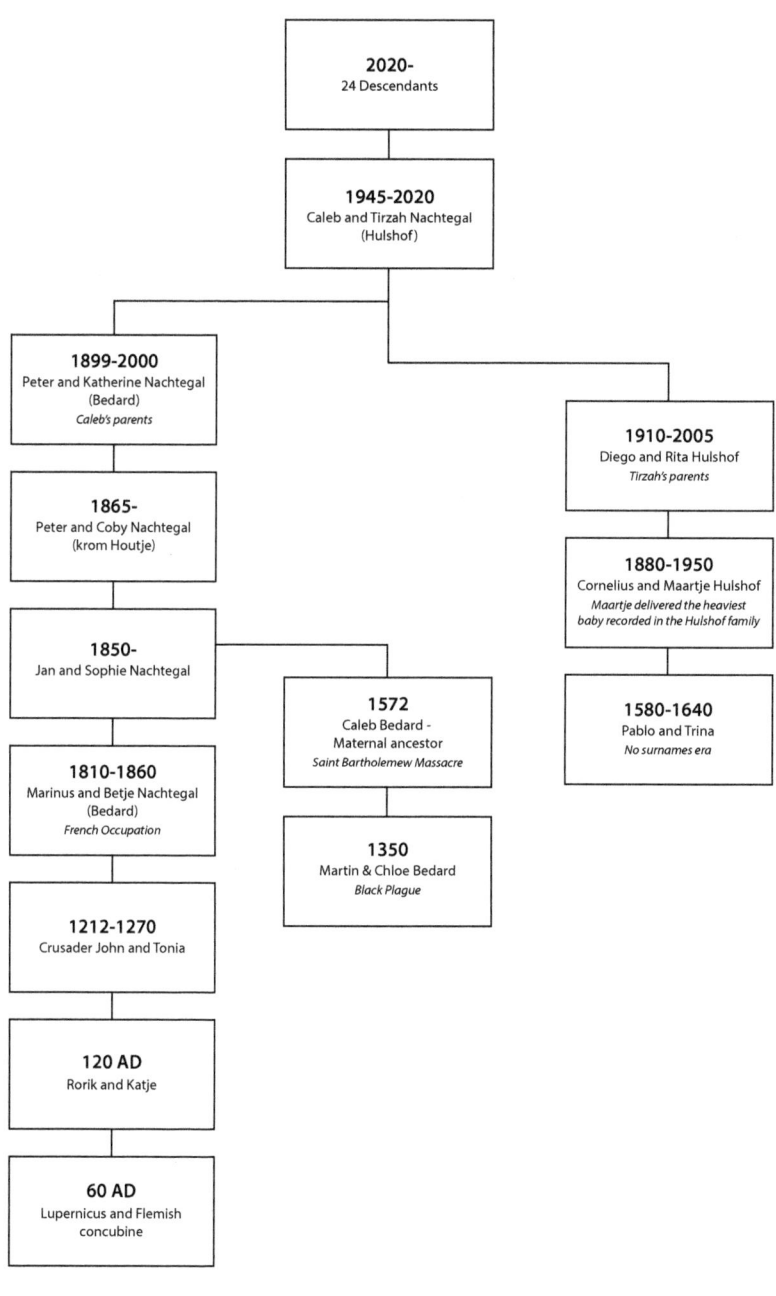

CPSIA information can be obtained
at www.ICGtesting.com
Printed in the USA
BVHW051922250921
617520BV00001B/3